In the light of the fire,

he lifted his shirt, flashing more skin as he examined a gnarled scar that ran in a short slice across the front of his right side, mirrored by another on his lower back.

A fucking stab wound, Dixon knew instantly.

I should have left. I should have let him walk home. I should have dropped him off and drove away.

Jaye pulled the shirt back down, pressing a hand against the spot and turned to face him. Then, still favoring that side, he walked slowly over.

Brow furrowed, jaw clenched, Dixon cleared his throat and tried to tell himself what was happening wasn't. He stopped looking at Jaye, with his hauntingly beautiful face, and maddeningly sexy body, hiding deeply layered pain underneath, glimpsed only through those captivating green eyes like windows to a tortured soul.

Instead, Dixon looked at the licking, twisting flames of the fire as it showed him visions of his fate. And still Jaye came closer, and closer, and closer until there were mere inches separating them. He could feel the heat coming off of Jaye's firm, tight little body, carved like marble out of muscle.

Also recommended...

You may also enjoy these other ForbiddenFiction works:

Caged Jaye by Lynn Kelling
It's Jaye Larson's nineteenth birthday, and all he wants is to spend time with his boyfriend and his mother—the people he loves most and who make life worth living. But, faced by his mother's demons, the imperfections of his relationship with boyfriend, Kris, and dangerous, homophobic strangers, one by one, all of Jaye's dreams are soon derailed. Plunging into a waking nightmare, shortly after going to bed alone, he wakes in an alley, pinned down by two men with slow, bloody rape and murder in mind. It's just the start of Jaye's fight for his life, and his sanity, as time and time again, he's forced to make impossible choices and survive, no matter what it costs.
http://forbiddenfiction.com/story/LK1-1.000251

Broken Ink by Jack L. Pyke
Carrying a tattoo on your skin no longer just comes with a risk of infection. Get the composition right, you have the latest mind-control drug on the market. It's the sex-traders' dream, or worst nightmare, depending on the concentrated dose of the ink—and just who's wearing it. For Kiyen, the ink means he's able to strip raw the minds of the best and worst of society. For Falen, the ink has ensured he's spent his early years as a willing sex slave and low-grade empath. But the ink itself has a mind of its own; when Kiyen is forced into Fal's small world, prejudice battles a pure need to touch. (M/M)
http://forbiddenfiction.com/library/story/JP2-1.000111

Arctic Absolution

Lynn Kelling

ForbiddenFiction
www.forbiddenfiction.com

an imprint of

Fantastic Fiction Publishing
www.fantasticfictionpub.com

ARCTIC ABSOLUTION
A Forbidden Fiction book

Fantastic Fiction Publishing
Hayward, California

© Lynn Kelling, 2014

CREDITS
Editors: D.M. Atkins and Rylan Hunter
Cover Design: Siolnatine
Cover art: Natalya Nesterova and Jeannie Bell
Production Editor: Erika L Firanc
Proofreading: Jae Knight and Kaye O'Malley

SKU: LK1-000188-02 FFP
ISBN: 978-1-62234-199-3

Published in the United States of America

DISCLAIMER

This book is a work of fiction which contains explicit erotic content; it is intended for mature readers. Do not read this if it's not legal for you.

All the characters, locations and events herein are fictional. While elements of existing locations or historical characters or events may be used fictitiously, any resemblance to actual people, places or events is coincidental.

This book depicts depicts fictional BDSM; it is not intended to be used as an instruction manual. It contains descriptions of erotic acts that may be immoral, illegal, or unsafe. The characters are not models for the Safe, Sane and Consensual forms embraced by most current practitioners of BDSM. The authors take license with the use of BDSM for dramatic effect. Do not take the events in this story as proof of the plausibility or safety of any particular practice.

For Terry,
who keeps me dreaming of our secluded cabin in the wild.
I love you.

Contents

Chapter 1
Robbery in Progress

It would have been the understatement of his entire thirty-two years as a citizen of Zus, Alaska to say Trooper Dixon Rowe got more than he bargained for when responding one evening to a fairly routine report of a robbery in progress. That was the start of it all, at least for him. For the other players in his life, things had already been in motion for a long time. But for poor Dixon it was like someone threw a stick of dynamite into the core of his life, cracked it open and sent the pieces flying.

It was only the second time he had ever heard of the Stop and Shop being robbed, since it was a fairly run-down, mom-and-pop type of grocery store with little money in the till and meager offerings on the shelves. Not a lot of people were out to steal six-packs of diet soda and canned food, but when you get as far out in the middle of nowhere as they were, all you were likely to find was slim pickings.

Like the dutiful Alaska State Trooper he was, Dixon was happy to have something useful and maybe even a little exciting to do before his shift was over. Driving around for hours on patrol over miles and miles of flat, frozen earth with scarcely any sign of life—human or otherwise—was tedious at the best of times.

The highway was empty. Thanks to his headlights and the soft glow of starlight, all he could see was asphalt and snow. Dixon turned on his lights, flashing blues and reds over the blank canvas of his surroundings, did a U-turn and got on his way.

Given that Alaska didn't have counties, and therefore no county police or sheriffs like the lower forty-eight, the Division of Alaska State Troopers, or AST, was unique in how it performed a much broader range of duties. They handled it all, from traffic enforcement to criminal law enforcement. All of that basically boiled down to Dixon needing to handle whatever shit went down nearby, no matter what type it was. If he could get there in time, it was his job to tackle. As the only trooper on that end of town, he was unsurprisingly the only one to respond to the call that night.

He wasn't taking any chances as he tried to assess the situation and determine what he was up against. Getting out of the vehicle, Dixon positioned himself behind the opened driver's side door of his Ford Expedition, un-holstered his Glock 22 and disengaged the safety.

There was no one waiting outside, which indicated whoever was running the store was still inside, keeping an eye on the culprit. Dixon had been only a mile away when the silent alarm was triggered, and was lucky enough to get there before the would-be thief could vanish into the wilderness. Like everything else in Zus, the Stop and Shop was isolated. For as far as the eye could see, up and down the highway, bordering both sides, were dense woods. Just a few miles down the road, the dense trees fell back, opening up to flat land and sprawling plains. Beyond those, even farther in the distance, were white-capped mountains reaching up into the sky, adding a picturesque backdrop to daily life. Nearer the store, where Dixon waited with his weapon drawn, the trees crowded in close to the highway.

Full dark had settled on them hours ago even though it wasn't that late. The cool light of the moon and countless stars, though reflecting brilliantly off of the plentiful ice, would do nothing to help Dixon find someone sheltering under the trees' dense canopy.

Before Dixon was ready for it, a dark figure of average height and slim build suddenly bolted through the glass front door of the Stop and Shop. The person didn't pause at all, though Dixon's unmistakable flashing lights were the brightest thing for miles, but veered immediately and sharply right, taking off in exactly the direction Dixon expected him to — toward the woods. In thirty more yards, the forest would have him and there would be nothing for it.

The long, boring day spent mostly behind the wheel had taken its toll on his reflexes; Dixon didn't manage to get a single word out, other than, "Shit," as he fingered the safety again, re-holstered his pistol and took off running after the suspect.

In a feeble attempt to regain control of the situation, he roared, "Drop it! Drop it right now!"

Breathing hard, Dixon sprinted as fast as he could and closed the distance between them as the suspect tripped on the slick, choppy, frozen ground, lost his grip on the stolen items and tried to regain his footing. Canned vegetables, small bags of potato chips and cardboard boxes of cereal, rice and pasta tumbled everywhere. Giving the pathetic loot a slightly puzzled glance, Dixon ran past it and tackled the suspect—a smaller man than himself—down to the brittle ice and gravel.

With a cry of pain, the culprit, belly down, stuck his hands out widely in surrender. "Okay! Okay! I'll give it back! Easy!"

Dixon twisted the man's arms behind his back and snapped on handcuffs. In a worn old black woolen coat, baggy jeans belted low enough to flash plenty of underwear, and a knit hat pulled down over his ears, at first the suspect was just a wiry bundle of clothes and not much else. Since none of the clothes fit him well, Dixon couldn't help but wonder if those were stolen, too. He was straddling the skinny fellow's legs as he fastened the cuffs. With those on, he got up and pulled the man to his feet. When he did a pat-down for any weapons, he found none.

But when he turned around, Dixon saw it wasn't a man at all.

It was just a kid.

A kid stealing food.

Dixon instantly felt like a jackass.

The Expedition's headlights shone out on them. With some resentment, the kid looked square at him. He had the palest green eyes Dixon had ever seen, the irises ringed with dark blue. The two of them mistrustfully eyed one another's faces before taking a visual scan of each other's bodies. The kid's gaze first went to the weapon worn on Dixon's hip, then his badge. Meanwhile, Dixon noted the single teardrop tattooed by the corner of the kid's left eye, and a neck tattoo that wrapped the right side of the kid's neck and disappeared under his collar.

Great, Dixon thought. *Now we've got gang members moving into town.*

Once past that superficial detail, he realized the boy had one of the prettiest faces he'd ever seen on a man outside of television, works of art, or glossy magazine covers. In a way it was unsettling. The perfection of the proportion of his features made him seem unreal. As if he beheld a strange specimen or freak of nature, Dixon found himself staring. In Dixon's experience, real guys simply weren't beautiful. They might be cute or passably attractive, but always in a rough, brutish way. He kept looking for flaws — crooked teeth, bad skin, funny ears — but the more he looked, the more he realized the tattoos were the only disguise this kid had to pass as a normal human being.

A tickle of unease formed in Dixon's belly. He started to get nervous. This boy was exquisite. It made him simultaneously hard to look at and hard to stop looking at. Long, dark eyelashes strikingly framed those strange eyes. With full, dark lips and immaculate bone structure, there was evidence enough the neck tattoo was probably an attempt to toughen up his appearance so he wouldn't get his ass handed to him every other day. Maybe the robbery was a cabin-fever-crazed kid's attempt to act like a badass, too. Hell, anything was possible.

The kid started to speak with a deep, soft, sandpapery sort of voice that acted as a light caress over Dixon's balls. Despising himself and his libido for the reaction, Dixon swore then and there to get laid and soon so he wasn't getting hard over misfit teenagers out of sheer desperation.

And I'm the one thinking of the kid as pathetic.

"Look, I'm sorry about the food. I-I'll give it back. I, uh...." Visibly swallowing his pride, the kid resigned himself, looking away, back toward the store where the owner was standing out front and staring at them. Adjusting his arms, which were cuffed behind his back in the bulky coat, cringing with what appeared to be discomfort, the kid then turned his attention back to Dixon. "I had no choice. Didn't mean any harm. I swear."

"There's always a choice, son."

"A choice to starve?" he sneered. "And don't patronize me. I'm not your motherfucking *son*. I didn't take any money and I didn't try to hurt anyone. Ask him."

Goddamn it, Dixon sighed inwardly. *This is not how I wanted to end the night, feeling like the bad guy for doing my damn job, tackling and possibly injuring some underfed man-child with a pretty face and a shitty attitude.*

Looking a little closer, he could see how thin the boy was under all those clothes. The shop keep brought a metal basket over to where the food had tumbled down, and was slowly picking it up, piece by piece.

"C'mere then," Dixon grumbled.

He took the young man by the arm and led him back to the shop keep.

"Sir, what's the story here?"

"I saw him tucking food in the coat," the wide-eyed store owner told Dixon. He was an older fellow, small but stocky, and with a head of thick, wiry, wild grey hair. "So I pushed the silent alarm. When you pulled up, he must've heard and took off. That's about it."

To the boy, Dixon asked, "You just took this food? Nothing else?"

"Yessir, trooper. That's it. I swear." To the store owner, he said, "I'm sorry, sir. If I had the money to pay, I would, but I don't. A man's gotta eat, you know."

"There are public services to assist those who can't afford food," Dixon told him.

"I don't know anything about that." It sounded defensive enough to be true.

"Exactly how old are you?"

"Twenty-one," was the reply filled with plenty of attitude. "How old are *you*?"

Dixon squinted down at him. There was about a five inch difference in height between them. The kid could easily pass for fifteen unless you looked a little closer. It was in the eyes mainly. Judging solely by those, the kid — or, man, rather — had his boyish innocence ground out of him long ago. It made Dixon feel even worse. Clearly this guy had enough problems without Dixon Rowe acting the hard-ass trooper and bulldozing him to the frozen earth, possibly busting some ribs in the process over what? A few cans of peas and bags of potato chips?

But, damn it, Dixon was in charge here, wasn't he? Making a good show of this being true, he said in a poor impression of his usually confident self, "I'll be asking the questions, if it's all the same to you."

"Yessir, Trooper Rowe."

Observant little son-of-a-bitch, isn't he? I guess I know now he can read.

The corner of Dixon's mouth twitched. The young man smiled an endearingly crooked smile up at him, all youthful sweetness on the surface, nothing but worn and wicked beneath. "I don't suppose you could help me locate those services you spoke of? In all honesty, I'm fuckin' starving. Desperation's a funny bitch."

Recognizing that he had trouble on legs handcuffed at his side, but that he couldn't fault anyone for trying to survive, Dixon turned to the store owner and asked, "Do you intend to press charges?"

"No. No, I don't think so," the man said, clutching his precious basket. "Just don't come back without some cash," he said to the boy.

"I won't," the light-eyed troublemaker promised, bristling with pride but dutifully paying respect. "Sorry about the trouble."

"No problem."

The older man shuffled back into his store while they watched. After that, Dixon had no other way to delay the inevitable. He had to figure out what to do next.

"I could still hold you for resisting arrest," he warned.

"I didn't know I was being arrested, trooper," Bright Eyes said with a show of blamelessness Dixon didn't buy for a second. "Or I would have stopped running."

Dixon rolled his eyes. He couldn't help it.

"Okay," he sighed. "Turn around and I'll take the cuffs off."

"Sure. But, you know... you can leave 'em on if you want. I kinda like 'em."

He said it with the most sinful grin Dixon had ever seen, dripping sex and hinting at endless possibilities. The blatant nature of the come-on took Dixon aback at first, making him wonder fearfully if he was easy to mark, or if he'd been looking at the kid in inappropriate ways.

Dixon tried telling himself the guy wasn't really a kid, as much as his brain insisted on thinking of him that way. He was twenty one, after all. But the size difference and his finely crafted, model-pretty features—all big, gorgeous eyes, angular cheekbones and dark, plump lips—made him seem incredibly young.

Ignoring the remark, or acting like he was, Dixon moved behind the young man and removed the handcuffs. From over his right shoulder, the distractingly good-looking fellow watched him from the corner of his eye and from under the knit hat. Judging from the look on his face, it seemed like he didn't trust Dixon not to take advantage of their positions and his authority, and was trying to ready himself for anything. The stark edginess from the younger man made Dixon instinctively want to counter it with assurances that he wasn't out to hurt anyone, and he was only trying to do his job.

"What's your name, anyway?"

"Jaye."

"Jaye what?"

"Larson."

"Hmm. Are you new around here, Jaye Larson? This town may be large geographically but it's tiny in population. I haven't seen you before, and I'm pretty sure I would remember you if I had. You've got one of those faces I wouldn't soon forget."

"I do tend to make an impression," Jaye grinned crookedly, but most of his amusement shone from his light eyes. It was unsettlingly alluring. The beauty of those eyes, with the darkness hinted by the teardrop etched in ink beside them, was captivating. Jaye Larson was defiant in a way that begged to be punished with a firm smack to the behind. "Yeah, I'm new. Maybe you can show me around."

The cuffs were off. Jaye turned to face him. Outstretching a hand, Jaye offered it for shaking. After a pause, Dixon took it and shook. Chunky silver and black rings glinted on Jaye's fingers. Dixon's eyes kept going back to the neck tattoo, wondering how far it wrapped down over Jaye's body, and if there were more tattoos hidden under all of those clothes.

"Wait here for a minute. I'll be right back."

Dixon half expected young Mr. Larson to be long gone by the time he came back out from inside the store, having purchased the stolen groceries plus a little extra of more sensible staples like bread, eggs, and milk. But, with the bags in his hand, he emerged to find Jaye leaning back against the side of the Expedition.

7

The lights were still flashing. Jaye's hands were pushed low in his jeans pockets, his thumbs hooked over the edges. He looked as effortlessly cool as a tropical sea breeze. Keenly alert and sucking on his bottom lip, he tracked Dixon who got steadily closer.

Holding out the shopping bags, Dixon said, "Here. Now I won't feel guilty about depriving a hungry man of food."

Jaye hesitated only for a minute, measuring Dixon to decipher intent first. "I appreciate that. Thank you. You know, there must be *some* way I can make it up to you...."

"Don't rob any more stores. That's how you can make it up to me."

Jaye chuckled softly, glancing away down the dark stretch of road. All around them was nothing but a flat expanse of pavement, the black, star-speckled night sky above and the glistening winter wonderland that would quickly drain the life and warmth out of you as if in revenge for daring to disturb its serene purity. Looking like he was naturally drawn to the innate cruelty of the landscape and itching to do battle with it, Jaye caught his lip between his teeth.

"You've already done so much for me. I hate to ask, but could I bother you for a ride home? I've got this trouble with my side and I fell on it the wrong way out there. Hurts like a bitch. My place is a few miles back that way and carrying these bags...."

The stark white elastic band of Jaye's underwear — trunks, from the look of it, Dixon decided, and tightly-fitting, hugging every line and curve like a second skin — caught and held Dixon's eye. That tantalizing strip of fabric around slim hips was bright in the gloom and, as hard as he tried to tell himself not to look, he did. Jaye, helpless not to notice that staring, seemed to subsequently push his hands a little farther into the pockets, inching the jeans down slightly to show a little more, shifting his stance so his shirt tugged up a bit. It exposed a tan expanse of lickable warm skin and lower abdominal muscles so chiseled Dixon's cock stood up and took instant notice. His mouth began to water. His brain provided an exceedingly unhelpful fantasy of getting on his knees, hooking a finger inside that white band to pull it down and licking right there, up through those hip dents, maybe biting or sucking a bruise to them, too.

What the holy, bleeding hell is wrong with me? Dixon marveled. *It has been a while, but I didn't think I was this far gone.*

He wrenched his eyes away, dropping his gaze to the safely boring view of his feet instead of pointing it anywhere near the temptation before him.

"Please, trooper. I'd be *very* grateful," Jaye said suggestively in that tantalizingly raspy whisper of a voice, like it was a secret, just between them. He might have looked young, but this guy knew *exactly* what he was doing.

Send him on his way. Be the ass you feel like you are. He can make it home. He deserves a walk after the stunt he pulled. It'd be a bit of penance after getting all of that free grub.

"Yeah, okay," Dixon agreed, giving up even with danger staring him in the face in the form of irresistibility.

Chapter 2

Desperation's Bitch

Dixon opened the back door and waited for Jaye to slide inside.

His fate was doubly sealed as soon as they stopped for a take-out burger on the way. Dixon pretended not to watch Jaye devour the food like his stomach hadn't seen anything more substantial than icemelt in days. In about four bites the burger was gone. Jaye humbly apologized for wolfing it down.

"Why can't you afford groceries, Mr. Larson?"

Jaye cringed subtly. "Christ, it's Jaye. *Just* Jaye. Please. I'm broke, that's why. I can't find anyone who'll hire me. I've, um... I've had some training at mechanical and electrical work. That's what I've been hoping to find but, really, I'll take anything at this point. I knew it would be more of a challenge finding opportunities out here, but I thought there'd be *something*, you know?"

"Why won't they hire you?"

Jaye caught his gaze in the rearview mirror, his expression hard but eyes brilliant as ever. "Why do you think?"

"I don't know. That's why I asked."

Chewing on his rosy lower lip, young and old at the same time, an enigma in the truest sense, Jaye stared out the side window and confessed, "I just got out."

"Of prison?"

Jaye shot him an exasperated look. Not for the first time, he scanned Dixon's strawberry blond hair and settled once more on Dixon's green-blue eyes highlighted with blond eyelashes. He was used to being stared at that way. People couldn't help themselves, really. All of that color seemed bizarrely out of place in such a desolate landscape, devoid of many hues other than brown, white, or grey. Dixon had a strong jaw and handsome features, but in a more rugged, typically masculine way than with Jaye's facial structure. His insulated coat and police uniform hung from muscular, broad shoulders. Dixon knew he made for an imposing figure, but the way his companion was looking at him made him suspect his size wasn't giving him the total advantage here.

"What were you in for?"

"Long story."

"Robbery?"

With another weary look, he answered shortly, "No."

"How long were you in?"

"Two years." *That'd put him at nineteen when he went away. Dear god.*

"Let me guess. You were innocent? Falsely accused? Victim of a warped judicial system?"

"No," Jaye shrugged, not rising to the bait as he bit off the end of a French fry. "I did it."

A few silent minutes later, they pulled up to an attractive little cabin Dixon recognized instantly. It was a very small structure with maybe two or three rooms, tops, but it was well outfitted and built lovingly by hand rather than pre-fabricated as were so many structures in town. There was a generator out back and a propane tank but it was also hooked up to the power grid. Wire trailed from the road to the corner of the roof. It had all of the amenities you could want.

"This is old man Mitchell's place. But he passed on just—"

"Last year, I know. They sent me a letter," Jaye told him in a clipped manner that said to Dixon this wasn't a conversation he was interested in having.

"He was a relative?"

"The only one I had left. Now, instead of family, I have a shitty little cabin. Lucky me."

With a smile icier than the dirt under their boots, Jaye climbed out of the back of the Expedition as Dixon held the door for him.

The cabin was dark. The generator was quiet. Dixon suspected Jaye didn't have the money to afford an electric bill or the fuel to keep a genie going. It made him feel sick to think of it. This guy was barely out of his teenage years, no family, just out of prison, no job, no money, no food, and living in a frigid, dark cabin in the middle of Alaska.

And that wasn't all.

Jaye walked up to the door of the cabin clutching his left side, limping slightly.

I did that, Dixon realized with horror. *He's in pain because of me – the big, tough trooper.*

He should have just gotten in the car and driven away, but he couldn't. Instead, he followed Jaye to the door and took the grocery bags from him so he could find his key in his coat pocket. With a wary glance, Jaye endured Dixon's presence and wore resentment for his plight like another coat to insulate him from further harm.

Once the door was unlocked, Jaye led the way inside. He picked up a book of matches and started trying to light some candles. One-by-one they began to cast a warm, amber glow about the space. They gave off enough illumination for him to manage starting a fire in the fireplace in order to heat the modest home which was as cold inside as it was out.

"Hey, you want me to do that?" Dixon offered, seeing Jaye favor his side as he crouched and got the kindling going. "You look like you're hurt."

Jaye laughed miserably at that, but quickly bit off the sound. "Yeah, I bet I do. No, I'm fine. You've been a great help. You can go. I'm sure you've got better things to do. I appreciate the charity."

Bristling, Dixon replied, "Let me get you in contact with some people who are looking to hire. I know the truck stop's been short-handed, and my sister's husband runs a sightseeing business. I can ask if they need someone. Or, you know, there are the local utility services. There are few enough of us around that there's always something that needs doing. Let me ask around. I can come back tomorrow with whatever leads I can find, ask you more about what you'd be interested in pursuing. I'd vouch for you."

The fire started crackling and growing. Dixon could feel heat coming off of it. That was good. It made him more confident he could walk away tonight and abandon Jaye here. At least he wouldn't freeze to death in his sleep.

Jaye peeled off the bulky coat, showing Dixon exactly what his hard life had done to his body—slimming it down over ropes of muscle on his small-waisted, thick-shouldered frame. He pulled off the knit hat and his hair tumbled loose around his face, reaching down to his jaw. In the light of the fire, he lifted his shirt, flashing more skin as he examined a gnarled scar that ran in a short slice across the front of his left side, mirrored by another on his lower back.

A fucking stab wound, Dixon knew instantly.

I should have left. I should have let him walk home. I should have dropped him off and drove away.

Jaye pulled the shirt back down, pressing a hand against the spot and turned to face him. Then, still favoring the left side, he walked slowly over.

Brow furrowed, jaw clenched, Dixon cleared his throat and tried to tell himself what was happening wasn't. He stopped looking at Jaye, with his hauntingly beautiful face, and maddeningly sexy body, hiding deeply layered pain underneath, glimpsed only through those captivating green eyes like windows to a tortured soul.

Instead, Dixon looked at the licking, twisting flames of the fire as it showed him visions of his fate. And still Jaye came closer, and closer, and closer until there were mere inches separating them. He could feel the heat coming off of Jaye's firm, tight little body, carved like marble out of muscle.

Jaye's breath ghosted warm over Dixon's neck and Dixon's head filled with the scent of him—sweat, skin, musk, and life—everything good and the opposite of everything barren and cold that surrounded them. Jaye absentmindedly tucked a curling tendril of chocolate brown hair over his ear. It came down in soft waves to about his chin and all Dixon wanted was to comb his fingers through it. His dick strained against his pants, achingly stiff and trying to get free. His heart pounded, his senses sharpening with alarm at how much he wanted to violate the seductively defiant miscreant before him.

Dixon told himself he was closing off the reaction, being professional, being a good cop. It was nothing more than that. He told himself Jaye didn't know exactly what he was doing to Dixon just by standing there, obscenely close, their bodies almost touching. Dixon felt his breath coming faster, his temperature rising, and not because of the fire.

Apparently without any of Dixon's inner battle, just calm and cool, knowing what he wanted and how to get it, Jaye reached up a hand and lightly touched Dixon's face, caressing over the skin of his jaw with the pad his thumb.

"No freckles," he said softly in that rough, hushed, fuck-me-hard voice. "It's funny. I've never seen a redhead without them. But maybe you've got 'em hidden somewhere else. Guess I'll have to wait and find out, won't I?"

He smiled again, but this time it was only with his lips and not his eyes at all. It was only his imagination, Dixon decided, as Jaye's eyes seemed to undress him, determining what kind of a man he was and what he might do if another cool, confident man took firm hold of his cock and tugged on it.

But, at the same time, underneath the façade of allure, Jaye's eyes were screaming. Screaming over what, exactly, Dixon couldn't say. Maybe it was because of everything that evidently had already happened, and everything still left to endure, crying out it was too much, and he couldn't do it alone. Dixon would have bet his life on it Jaye Larson was a man at the end of his rope, dangling from it and waiting for death to snap his neck, strangle him, or freeze him out. His eyes screamed for help while his lips curled in a sneering grin that was higher on one side than the other and said help would never, ever come. Not for people like him.

"You regret driving me home, don't you?" Jaye observed without inflection. It sounded too tired, too worn-out to be coming from someone barely out of their teens. It made Dixon really fucking sad. "You wish you'd never laid eyes on me. I can see it in your face. Every bit of it. It's okay. I actually get that a lot."

Dixon never knew, really, why he did it. Maybe it was guilt, or the pathetic sight of those canned peas and potato chip bags lying on muddy snow. Maybe it was the absence of youth or happiness in that awful smile. Maybe it was pheromones or loneliness. Or maybe it was the ache of his recently broken heart and the raw wound brought of being left behind to suffer, time and time again, only to finally try to break free and wind up with not much else besides fear of being pursued to keep him warm at night. Maybe it was a lot of things, or none of them at all.

Before Jaye could anticipate it, Dixon was kissing him. With a small, hungry grunt, Dixon caught those dark, luscious lips that tasted so sweet and salty, too. Jaye's mouth was warmer and softer than Dixon imagined it would be. Once he was kissing it, he didn't want to stop. He licked the taste of French fries from the silky flesh, weaving his fingers greedily through touchable long hair, liking the small, firm, lithe feel of Jaye in his arms.

Gathering Jaye up with a hand to his lower back, Dixon pressed down for more. All he knew was the hot, wet, supple willingness of Jaye's lips and tongue as he opened up without any fight at all and took Dixon right in. One moment Dixon's tongue was sliding over Jaye's sinful, suckable lips and twisting with his tongue—Jaye who, not an hour earlier, Dixon thought was a teenager and was wearing his handcuffs.

The next moment, Dixon was breaking off all contact between them as cleanly, precisely, and cold as the blade that seemed to have speared right through Jaye's side.

The rejection in the action made hurt flare up so strong and powerfully in Jaye's expression he bowed his head to hide instantly threatening tears. They shone wet on his dark eyelashes. He pushed his hands back into his pants pockets. Dixon watched him close up. Shoulders hunched, Jaye waited there like he was bracing for the sound of the door slamming, the receding crunch of footsteps, and the starting of the Expedition's engine.

Dixon didn't give him that. He didn't leave, or make it easy like he could have and should have.

"I'm sorry about that. That was... *completely* out of line."

Jaye ignored it and took a couple of limping steps sideways so he could take hold of the door's edge, ready to close it on Dixon and the biting arctic air he brought in with him. Wishing Jaye would look up, knowing pride wouldn't let him, Dixon stared helplessly at someone so seemingly abandoned by the world that it made Dixon furious.

For a long, strained moment, he stood there, letting in the chill. Jaye shivered. With resignation, Dixon turned and walked out. He was halfway down the path made of their footprints when he heard, "So, the morning? Those jobs?"

"Yeah," Dixon called, angry, but at whom or what, he couldn't have said. "I'll be here bright and early."

In the doorway, with life-giving heat at his back but dangerous possibility before him, Jaye replied, "I'm glad. See you then, trooper."

Chapter 3

No One Here

Harried, distracted, guilty, and resentful about the unfairness of life, Dixon Rowe went back to headquarters to clock out from his long, weird shift. As he walked through the locker room to get changed and get his things, he ran across the trooper taking over for him and just about to go on duty.

Her name was Sesi Ahnah and, though Dixon never asked, she seemed to be descended at least in part from the locally prevalent, native Iñupiaq people. Sesi had moved to Zus with her father and brothers as a teenager. Her father held a position of authority in local government. A few of her siblings had scattered in search of a less remote place to live, but Sesi stuck around, liking the challenge of the encroaching wild on the people and the town itself.

She gave him a curious sidelong glance as he passed behind her with a loud sigh. It was all that was needed to spur a comment.

Buttoning her uniform, she kept her back to him as he found his locker on the opposite wall and yanked it open. "You look like you've had a rough one."

With the police force based in Zus as pitifully small as it was, the few of them there were knew each other pretty well. For instance, Dixon knew about Sesi's preference for life as a single woman, compared to the exhaustion that came from trying to find a mate who didn't have a problem with a strong, independent female as their partner. Sesi, in turn, knew all about Dixon's complicated romantic history and was quite familiar with his ex, Marcus Slater. Because of this awareness of how Dixon's love life had always provided more drama than his professional one, she wouldn't have been out-of-line to suspect his foul mood might not have been because of work. But Dixon's ex had been out of the picture for a while now. Either way, his attitude told her something had happened and she was eager to find out what it was.

"Tell me about it," Dixon grumbled. He could have just gotten changed at home, but restlessness had settled into his bones. That called for either a trip to the bar or a call to a friend who was always up for helping him purge his frustrations in other ways. Stripping off the insulated jacket, he started to fumble at the tiny buttons on his shirtfront.

"You got a call?"

Her curiosity was unsurprising. Any incidents as noteworthy as attempted robbery got people talking fast.

"Yeah," he answered reluctantly. "I guess you heard. No big deal, really. Just a poor, hungry guy snatching food from the Stop and Shop. Kind of made me feel bad."

"Yeah. Jeez, that's sad. Who was it?"

"You ever hear of a guy named Larson?"

"Larson," she said, testing the name on her tongue. "Hmm. No. I don't think so. Why? What's that look for?"

She had been looking at him over her shoulder. When he tried to duck his head to hide his expression, it merely provoked more curiosity, so she turned to face him. Though his thoughts had been a whirl of emotions a few minutes ago, now they settled on one thing—his mental image of Jaye's slim body backlit by the fireplace. Its insistence produced a subtly guilty sulk, like he was a kid who Sesi had caught with his hand in the cookie jar. It was wrong to think of Jaye like that, and it was even more wrong that they had kissed.

Sesi laughed at his melancholy and walked over to him. His sulk grew. He sunk to the bench running down the middle of the aisle of lockers. When Dixon's colorful eyes turned up to Sesi's face, she smirked. He waited for her to let him have it. Clearly, she had an inkling for what was going on. Call it female intuition. Dixon had gotten himself into trouble of a specific sort. Man trouble. That was something she could probably commiserate with. It was also not the first time Dixon had been in trouble of that sort, and it certainly wouldn't be the last, which anyone who knew him would be able to tell you.

And Sesi knew him pretty well.

"Oh lord," she sighed. "What is it now? You might as well tell me, because I'll find out either way."

This was the truth. Sesi was good friends with Dixon's sister, Brekken, and Dixon famously was wont to tell his sister more than he should, even when he tried not to.

With a scrunch of his nose, he scratched his chin, scruffy with a day's worth of beard and, like he was apologizing, said, "He's damn pretty."

Sesi laughed harder than ever, sitting down beside him. "And he's the suspect? Larson?"

"Yep," he sulked, popping his lips on the P.

"Rowe," she started, talking down to him like the miserable child he was acting like. "He's not a puppy you can bring home."

"I kissed him."

He said it quickly, tossing it into the conversation like a live grenade, then pressing his lips together as he waited for the delayed explosion.

Sesi gasped with real shock. "You kissed the suspect!? You can't do that!"

"I know!"

He pushed his hand back through his red-gold hair and fumbled to say the rest before he chickened out. "He's twenty-one years old. An ex-con. He's got a gang tattoo on his face, but he was starving, and alone, and—"

"Pretty?" she provided, her laughter gone, sounding purely sorry for him now. He had gone and fallen for someone else that was no good for him, and there was nothing she could do about it.

"Yes. Pretty," he agreed. He exhaled a soft little laugh at himself and hung his head with embarrassment, hands folded in his lap.

Gently, she asked, "So, what are you gonna do?"

"Me? I'm gonna get some sleep. Do a little research, maybe make a few calls. Then I'm gonna help Larson get a job so he can afford to buy groceries and propane for his heater."

Sesi shook her head. "Maybe you need to stop being such a good guy, wearing your heart on your sleeve, trying to do more than you need to for people who only want to take advantage of you."

"That, I think, is *exactly* my problem," he agreed with a hopeless sort of half-smile. He grabbed his things and pulled on a clean, blue, long-sleeved shirt over his white undershirt. Slipping into his coat and pocketing his keys and wallet, he said in farewell, "Thanks."

"Keep it in your pants!" she called loudly after him.

"Yep!" he yelled back with a wave. "That's the plan."

It was a long night for Jaye Larson. More than ever, the cabin felt too big, like it was sprawling out around him in all directions. Full of shadowy nooks and places for someone or something to hide, he felt lost inside of it. It was only a couple hundred square feet max but, after spending two straight years in a tiny, sparse cinderblock cell where he could stretch his arms out and touch both sides of the room at the same time, he had gotten used to being comforted by cramped, mostly impenetrable areas.

In his cell, everything was under control. He knew what was in it and where everything was. He knew who could and would get in and out of it, and when. There was nowhere to hide and nowhere to go. And that was good. When you had as many enemies, real or imagined, as he did, it quickly became crucial to get a handle on all of your shit.

Lying on a few thick blankets on the wooden floor in front of the now-roaring fire, he curled up on his side and focused on the licking, writhing tongues of flame reaching up from the chunks of lumber he'd tossed into the fireplace. The golden light hypnotized him. He felt himself urging it to grow, to feed, consume and spread. Under his right hand, beneath the blankets, he traced the outline of his knife. Its nearness helped him to calm down more. The itching, scraping panic faded back a little.

He had thought coming out to the middle of nowhere to live in peace, away from everyone he ever knew, and away from the world in general, would fix what was wrong with him.

It hadn't.

Jaye wanted to be alone, but there were still people around—too many of them. As if the universe was intentionally trying to kick him in the ass, it had set Trooper Rowe in his path. Trooper Rowe who was, from first glance, obviously gay — obvious, at least, to Jaye.

Being able to read other guys had become Jaye's strong suit, his supreme talent. It was a finely honed survival skill. Before the men he encountered could act, before they could even think too clearly about their intentions, he was able sense what someone was going to do.

It was like a tickle under the skin, and it gave him just enough warning to brace himself, prepare to fight, duck, or get the fuck out of the way. He used to not try very hard at all to pay attention to things that happened around him, but getting shish-kabobbed on the end of a butcher knife did funny things to someone.

It woke Jaye right the hell up. It changed who he was and how he viewed the world. However, now he couldn't settle back down, sit back and let things play out. Now, Jaye was always on, always on guard. It was exhausting as hell.

Instead of sleeping, like he should have been doing, Jaye pulled the blankets closer around him and tried to not think of Trooper Rowe.

Rowe had appeared out of nowhere, bowled Jaye over — literally — and now seemed to be there to stay. It wasn't fair. All Jaye wanted was to be left alone. He was tired of being fucked over, figuratively and otherwise.

Suddenly, his old, inescapable, waking nightmare hit him again like a blast of arctic air. All of the muscles in his body knotted up and he cried out, curling even tighter into a ball.

Squeezing his eyes shut, exhaling all of the air out of his lungs until they burned, he fumbled for the knife, needing to have it inside his grip. He pulled the blankets back and found the handle, holding it so tightly his knuckles turned white. Then he cocked back his arm and stabbed the floorboard with the point of the blade. It dug in. The impact reverberated up his arm and he whined back in his throat.

Invisible hands moved over Jaye's body, groping at him. He couldn't cry out, couldn't say stop. He couldn't move or fight. The touching became more invasive. They were in his mouth, down his throat, up his rectum, twisting in his intestines. He drew his arm back and stabbed the floor again, digging the knife in deeper, getting it stuck there — buried in the wood.

Jaye turned his nose into the old blanket and forced himself to inhale its musty scent from being buried in his grandfather's closet for who-knew-how-long. Trembling violently, Jaye shuddered and grunted. All around him was pitch blackness stretching outward for miles, full of creeping, slithering, murderous beasts that would eat him up, pulling him apart one scrap of flesh at a time. It wasn't only the actual monsters that scared him. The imaginary ones were just as bad, if not worse. You couldn't hide from shadows, couldn't fight something without form. No matter what sort of danger crept his way, he knew he'd be facing it alone. There was no one left who cared about him, no one who would come to his aid. He was forsaken, abandoned with the beasts, a sacrifice to sate their hunger.

The solidity of the weapon in his hand was the only thing keeping him together, reminding him of the benefits of tangible things.

They're not here. They're not fuckin' here, man. Open your eyes. Open 'em!

"Do it. DO IT!"

He took a rough suck of oxygen, blew it out his lips then did it again. His eyes wrenched open. The flames were still his only company, but it hadn't passed yet. He could still feel them. With a choked sob, he clutched the knife. It took a hard, double-handed yank to free it.

Drawing the blade closer, he cradled it with care. More than anything he wished someone solid was there for him to hurt. He was tired of being the one afraid, the one expecting pain. It was only fair to give something back.

"There's no one here."

His voice sounded strange in his ears, too loud and shrill in the solitude. It scared him.

"There's no one here!"

He screamed it as loudly as he could and his voice broke under the strain, cracking apart. Dropping the knife, he rubbed both hands back over his scalp, gathering his hair in his fingers, and told himself to keep breathing.

When he had first moved into the cabin, he'd slept inside the closet with the door shut. But it was cold in there, even wrapped in furs and blankets. He was too far away from the fire and could feel the effects of the frigid climate on his body. Realizing how possible it would be for him to die that way, in his sleep, from exposure, only began to form new kinds of monsters in his imagination—creatures of the ice and wind that slowly drained the heat from your blood, feeding on it until there was nothing left of you but a brittle, cold shell and two, staring, frost-covered eyes. He knew he had to come out of his hideout and get closer to the fireplace until he was able to get the heater back on.

Only then could he go back into the snug space and get some fucking sleep.

The cabin had a bed. It was there, but useless—too soft and also too far from the flames.

I miss Cash.

"No," he murmured, shaking his head against the thought.

Cash was the last man Jaye had belonged to, as property. Jaye sold his body in exchange for sorely needed services. Fair trade.

"No."

I do. I miss him. He kept me safe. I was safe. I could sleep.

Yeah, when he wasn't raping you.

"SHUT UP!"

It wasn't rape. Jaye invited it, agreed to it. Hell, he enjoyed it most of the time when it wasn't simply tedious. The ghosts liked to insist it was rape, though, to twist it around and make it dirty, make it evil. Among other things, they also fed on Jaye's guilt and shame.

You miss that, too. Don'cha, piggy? The feel of his big ol' body climbing on top of you.

"Shut up."

Maybe if you let that piggy cop rape you, you'd feel safe again.

"FUCK."

He sat up and rubbed the heels of his palms into his eye sockets until stars exploded across the blackness behind his eyelids.

The solitude was making him crazy. He knew it. There was little to distract him from his own personal demons. When he was locked up with a wide assortment of humanity, there were always distractions. Night and day, every moment, there was something to watch out for, something to focus on, whether it was the movement of the guards, his cellmate, or other men making all sorts of noise from their own cells. Here, in the barren hell of Zus, there was nothing but the wind, and the wind talked.

It spoke in the voices of the men Jaye killed or tried to kill, and those who tried to kill him in return. The nights were the worst. Darkness lured them out—the ghosts and the silent, crawling, skittering dread. If he could turn on some lights, that would be good. That would help.

Maybe if Trooper Rowe got him a job, he could get the lights back on.

"There's no one here."

Breathing was easier now. Lying on his back, Jaye remembered the feel of the cop's lips latching onto his mouth. It was nice. It was everything warm, right, and alive. Jaye had let him do it. Jaye let the cop stick his tongue in his mouth and suck on his lips because it made him feel less alone. It grounded him to reality. It was the same reason he'd agreed to become Cash's property. Taking it up the ass, sucking cock—Jaye was willing to do all of it, whenever, however, as long as he wasn't on his own, helpless. Any reality was better than the ghosts. Things were always better when he had someone else there, holding him, kissing him, using him, anchoring him to the present.

If the cop wanted to use him, then, in trade, Jaye could get something he wanted.

Like protection. A job. A guardian.

That's how it worked. That's how it always worked.

Gonna slice open your belly, piggy. Pull your insides out. Make you watch.

In his memory, Jaye picked up the knife and stuck it in, as smooth as slicing through butter. Blood gushed over his fingers, hot and slick. In reality, he sliced only air and his hand stayed clean. The ghosts screamed anyway and melted away.

"There's no one here."

Unconsciousness caressed his weary mind. Jaye fell asleep with his fingers curled around the knife's handle. He was blessed, for once, with dreamless rest.

"What are you doing?"

Dixon stared into the mirror, waiting for an answer, realizing how crazy that was.

"What are you *doing*?"

"I'm talking to myself. That's what I'm doing."

Dixon picked up his toothbrush and ran it under the water from the tap. Once he had squeezed some toothpaste on, he started to brush his teeth. He needed a shave, to figure out what to wear....

"Dix?" There was a soft knock on the bathroom door. "You okay?"

"Yeah! Peachy."

He opened the door a few inches and saw his sister, Brekken, standing in the hall and wearing a vaguely concerned expression. She also had been blessed with their mother's coloring but regularly dyed her hair blonde to try to disguise the fact that she was really a red-head.

"You're talking to yourself again."

"I could be on the phone," he said around the toothbrush stuck in his mouth. "I was on the phone."

"I don't see a phone," she said gently, looking even more concerned and wrinkling her little nose at him.

"*Before,* I was on the phone." He spat toothpaste into the sink. The brush went back into the holder. After taking a sip of water, he spat that out, too. "What do you think I should do?"

With a shrug, Brekken suggested, "Keep it in your pants?"

He rolled his eyes. "*Besides* that, smartass. And stop talking to Sesi."

"She's my friend. We're both just worried about you."

"He needed help. My job is to help, right? I'll hook him up with a job. He won't starve or freeze to death. I won't be guilty of killing someone through neglect."

"Did Marcus leave because you were always this dramatic?"

"No, he left because he's a fisherman. And a prick."

"I thought you liked pricks."

With a smile, he stuck up his middle finger at her. She walked over and pecked a light kiss to his cheek. "Kidding. I'm kidding. I kid. You know I realize what an asshole he was. I'm glad he's out of the picture."

"But, seriously, what should I do?"

Sighing, Brekken leaned back against the bathroom vanity's counter as she thought this over. She was about a foot shorter than him and slender. Her long, dyed-blonde hair fell behind her shoulders to the middle of her back. Her blue-green eyes, similar to Dixon's, were downcast. Dixon had the same urge to protect her that he did with a lot of people. He could never leave Jaye to his own bad choices no more than he could leave her to the same fate. Everyone needed someone to bother to care at some point, no matter who they were. In Dixon's opinion, it was everyone's duty to do what they could for everyone else. Why else were they there, breathing and existing, if not to contribute in a positive way?

"I guess he doesn't have a phone, right? It might be better to talk to him that way, instead of in person."

"Nope. No phone."

Brekken glanced up at her big brother. "Ask Sesi to do it. She can go out there and talk to the kid. It doesn't have to be you."

There was no good response to that, so he said nothing. Dixon was as still as a statue, his jaw set and expression hard.

His sister groaned, "Dix...."

"I have to see if he's okay."

"No, you don't. You don't owe him anything! You're already doing a lot. Let Sesi handle the job thing. You know she'd do it. It would put some healthy space there between you and whatshisname."

"His name is Jaye."

"*Dix,*" she whined.

"I'll keep it professional. Strictly professional. I do have self-control. Now that I know there's temptation there, I'll head it off."

"Why are you doing this to yourself?" She gazed up beseechingly at him, asking him almost the same thing he had just been asking himself. "He's not, like, a new and improved version of Marcus. He's a stranger who you know nothing about. Did you even do a background check on him?"

Surprisingly, Dixon had an answer that time. "I want to give him the chance to explain for himself first. But I will. There's no warrant out for him. He's just a citizen with a past. Everyone has a past and has done things they're not dying to have everyone else know about. He's not going to hurt me, either. I'm a lot bigger than him."

"Just be careful. Please?" Brekken pursed her lips unhappily at him, giving him a stern, motherly sort of look. "You going over there now?"

"Yep," he nodded. "I'll let you know how it goes."

"Good. Just remember—he's off-limits. Completely."

"Got it. Now get the hell out of my way." Taking hold of her slim shoulders, he guided her from the room. He ducked into his bedroom and closed the door. Many things raced through his mind at once. He pushed them all aside. All that mattered was getting dressed, picking up breakfast, and getting on the road. The rest he would deal with later.

Chapter 4

Being the Bad Guy

The farther Dixon got away from the small house he shared with his sister and brother-in-law, Grant, the more things started to sort themselves out in his head. The inappropriate excitement about seeing good-looking Jaye Larson faded away. Memories of Dixon's lengthy, complicated relationship with his ex, Marcus, became starker in his mind and heart. Even if there was an attraction with Jaye, Dixon couldn't act on it, and for a whole plethora of reasons. The main one was he was still fucked up over the break-up that happened only a couple of short months ago.

It was a rocky relationship at the best of times. Marcus would be gone for many weeks when he left for a season of crabbing or fishing on the Bering Sea. He would take whatever work he could find. When he got back, he'd be in Dixon's face night and day. He'd track Dixon down when he was on duty and keep him more than busy once Dixon got home.

They lived together in Marcus's house, where Marcus set the rules, using age and ownership as leverage. He was a no-nonsense sort of man with short, prematurely grey hair, dark brown eyes and a chiseled jaw. At forty-one years old, though he was about the same height and build as Dixon, Marcus had a strength that far surpassed his size. At least, that's how it felt.

Dixon had always been afraid of Marcus, who called all of the shots and constantly made sure Dixon knew what was wanted, how it was wanted and when. In retrospect, Dixon didn't fully understand why he put up with it for so long. Sure, it was hot to have a powerful man take control sexually and practically, but their relationship never had the give and take Dixon craved in his heart. If there was something he wanted to get off his chest and Marcus had any interest at all in hearing about it, it would be pulled from him by Marcus rather than given willfully, in his own time. There was scorching intensity when they were together. Dixon would be left stranded when they were apart. He would feel like he was a boat adrift in the sea, waiting for a storm to hit, unable to relax.

It wasn't all bad, though. The sex was spectacular. Dixon was the bottom in their relationship, though his preference had always been to switch. But Marcus was a great lover. That made it more than tolerable. Another plus had been that Marcus really did love him, even if what Dixon felt for Marcus couldn't be classified as that. Marcus never failed to call Dixon on his shit, either. They understood and accepted one another, flaws and all. It was honest, it was passionate, but it couldn't have worked forever.

Marcus had cheated on Dixon. Then Dixon cheated, too. They fought, sometimes with words, other times with their fists. More often than not, it was Dixon taking the beating.

It got ugly. Dixon got out when Marcus left for the next fishing season.

He would be back soon. Dixon felt the anticipation in his bones. It seemed very probable Marcus would have a lot to say once he was back in town. Most of Dixon, when he wasn't focused on his job, was focused on making sure when the time came, he didn't slip and let Marcus get him into bed for some "just for old-time's-sake" fucking. It'd be easy, but then he'd be stuck. Once Marcus got him back in his grasp, he wouldn't let go, and Dixon knew he deserved better. He wanted to be loved by someone who could give him stability without making him afraid.

Dixon pulled up in front of the cabin Jaye Larson called home. He didn't look at it at first. His mind's eye was still fixed on the past.

Flashing back to a night from before it got really bad, Dixon remembered getting home after an unusually shitty day. Marcus was sitting on the couch, smoking a fat cigar. The smoke made the air hazy and sour.

"Dixie," Marcus said in his laid-back, arrogant way, sucking the end of the cigar. "There you are. You're finally home."

"Sorry I'm late," Dixon had apologized right away, the words coming out quickly. "An elderly couple was found dead in their home and the paperwork was—"

"Eh!" Marcus cut him off with the sound, pointing the cigar at him for emphasis. "Save it. Not your turn, is it? I've been waiting patiently all goddamned day. Every time I tried calling, you didn't bother to answer or call me back, but I didn't complain, did I? I didn't go out to find you, like I should have. Go clean yourself up and get in the bedroom."

The resentment barely had time to conjure; he was too tired to manage to be offended by the interruption and rudeness. On any other night, it would have been the start of a spectacular argument, but all Dixon could see were those body bags and that tomb-like home full of a lifetime of love and memories. Sadness squelched the hurt. "Look, I'm really not in the mood for—"

"Get in the bedroom," Marcus repeated, less tolerantly this time.

Sex before conversation. That's how he liked it. He didn't want to hear a word until he got his rocks off. The fact that he was gone for such long stretches of time made Marcus greedy and childish in his wants when he was around.

"Do we have a problem?"

Dixon shook his head, unwilling to fight about it. He didn't have the energy. The grief of the elderly couple's loved ones, the draining task of organizing the scene and getting things taken care of—it had worn him down. All he wanted was someone to comfort him, to help him relax and cope with the stress. He didn't want sex or to have to put up with a bitch-fit from Marcus, but it didn't look like he had any choice.

After he'd used the toilet, Dixon, still mostly in his uniform—he had the pants on and an undershirt, as well as his boots—douched and cleaned himself up to Marcus's standards. He wasn't quite finished yet when there was a knock at the bathroom door.

"We almost finished, sugar?" Marcus asked brusquely from the other side.

"Yeah, one second," Dixon called back. He just wanted it to be over.

Sitting in the car, outside of Jaye's cabin, Dixon remembered how he felt in that moment, how trapped he was in that bathroom, craving the sort of freedom he now enjoyed.

Sinking back into time, as much as he didn't want to, he recalled the walk from the bathroom to the bed. God, that had been awful. Squeezing his eyes shut, he could almost feel Marcus's rough hands pushing him down onto the mattress face-first. Dixon drew his legs up under him and Marcus kept Dixon's upper body angled down by pushing insistently at the back of his neck. The uniform pants were yanked down along with his underwear.

He was barely in the right position for it when two lube-slick fingers twisted meanly into his ass, wedging through his rim and pulling it open. Dixon grunted at the stretch, his body trying to accommodate the intrusion but still too tense for it to be comfortable. Marcus pushed the fingers deeper and bent them, prying Dixon open. Vocalizing a cry he tried to hold down inside his chest, Dixon buried his face in the bedding and punched the mattress as Marcus added a third finger too soon.

"Re*lax*, sugar," Marcus said, smooth and easy, totally unruffled. If anything, Dixon's show of discomfort probably turned Marcus on. "I know you like it."

Dixon tried to shift his legs apart. Marcus reached even deeper, pumping all three fingers in and out, corkscrewing them around, working him loose carelessly. Just to have something to hold on to, Dixon reached under his body and grabbed the leather belt fed through the loops in his pants. Gripping it tightly until the edges cut into his palm, he tugged on it so the pants pulled snugly against the backs of his thighs.

Marcus withdrew his fingers, getting them free. He rubbed firmly over Dixon's hole, feeling him clench, seeing him shudder and gasp for air. The fingers sheathed themselves in him once more, stroking the delicate tissues, the outer ring of muscle hugged tightly around. Ears perking at some soft sounds from behind him, Dixon heard Marcus unzipping and getting free of his jeans.

"Wait," Dixon called, trepidation putting a sharp edge to his voice, breaking it apart. "I'm not ready... *fuck*... ahh!"

Marcus entered him with a forceful push, the blunt head of his fat cock breaching Dixon's hastily prepped anus. He yelled into the bed, his voice climbing a couple of octaves. Filled up so full, so fast, Dixon couldn't breathe past the massive cock working steadily deeper into him with shallow little thrusts. He bit down on the quilt beneath his face and wrapped a hand over his head.

"Wouldn't hurt so much if you'd fuckin' relax, dumbass," Marcus scolded.

The pain subsided and the pleasure took over. That was almost worse. Ass-up on the bed, Dixon hated how good it felt to have Marcus's huge dick fucking him wide open. He hated that he was hard; he hated the moans bubbled up inside his throat. Most of all, he hated how Marcus would slow down and draw it out once Dixon started to love the feel of those thick ten inches sliding in and out of him in long, deliberate strokes. All he wanted was for it to be finished, for it to keep hurting. Then he'd have a better reason to keep being angry. He could throw it back in Marcus's face and call him out on being cruel.

Though he tried to muffle his moans in the mouthful of bedding, Marcus could still hear them. Dixon started to instinctively rock back against each press, pulling slightly forward on the withdrawal. Marcus fondled Dixon's erection, watching his body's pale skin turn pinker and pinker the more his blood got pumping.

It lasted an impossibly long time. Marcus had staying power, that was for damn sure. Soon, Dixon was wide open and Marcus was sliding easily. He'd go faster, harder, pounding Dixon's hole raw. He'd fondle his dick until Dixon's orgasm was teased torturously from him.

With a curse, Dixon came, seizing up around Marcus's cock, wringing the orgasm from him as well. Barely with his breath back, head spinning, emotions in chaos and the still-hard member lodged fully in his rectum, Dixon heard Marcus say with a grin, "So what was it you had to say?"

He had to laugh. Sometimes, that was the only thing you could do. Either that, or go crazy.

"Nothing," Dixon snapped, spitting out the wad of now-dampened cotton and rubbing his sweaty, overheated forehead into the mattress. "It was nothing."

Slowly, Marcus pulled back. The friction of the huge dick sliding out of him, leaving him empty, made Dixon bite down hard on his lower lip. The cockhead caught against his rim. Marcus kneaded a handful of Dixon's backside. "Yeah," he sighed. "Thought so."

All Dixon wanted was for Marcus to pull out and leave him alone.

"Take these fucking clothes off. I want you naked. Gonna grab something from the closet. Think I'll play with your ass for a while until I can get it up again for round two."

"I'm hungry, Marc. I had a long day."

The memory of saying that literally hurt. It was a heaviness in Dixon's chest. He said similar things closer to the end and it got him a hard, closed-fist punch to the stomach for his troubles. And Marcus would be smiling, just smiling, as Dixon coughed and wheezed, humiliated and ashamed.

"No, I don't think so. I had a *lot* of long, bad days on that boat, but I had to suck it up and face my responsibilities. Making me happy is all you've gotta worry about, Dixie. You live in my house? You sleep in my bed? You eat the food that I buy? You better follow my directions to the fuckin' letter."

"Fuck you, Marcus," Dixon said to no one, sitting alone in his car, hands wrapping the steering wheel even though he was parked. For too long, Dixon gave Marcus exactly what he wanted. It changed him. Dixon's sister barely recognized him when he showed up on her doorstep. It took a while for his ability to smile and be genuinely happy to come back. Even now that it had, the fear that he would go back to Marcus anyway kept him questioning himself, doubting himself, loathing himself.

Because, when pushed, he never did stand up to his ex. Marcus always got want he wanted. Even their break-up only really happened because of scheduling rather than due to Dixon making the choice to put his wellbeing first for once.

Unsettled by his bad behavior and poor choices, Dixon tried to gather his wits about him. Marcus was gone, at least for the moment. Dixon was in the clear. He had a way to possibly help someone in need and that was what he had to concentrate on. The rest of it could wait for another day.

Of course, the kiss with Jaye needed to get lumped in with the rest of Dixon's bad behavior and poor choices. It was time to cut the shit and be the man he had always intended to be. There was a time and a place for everything. He needed to recognize some people were not going to be good for him. Marcus wasn't good for him and Jaye Larson was definitely not good for him.

Movement caught Dixon's eye. He turned to look at the cabin. A figure was standing in the window.

Jaye.

Realizing he had been sitting in his car for a long time like a weirdo, Dixon saw it was time to leave the past where it belonged and get on with it. He pocketed his keys, pushed his sunglasses back up the bridge of his nose, grabbed the breakfast offerings he'd picked up on the way over, and got out of the car.

Chapter 5

In Pursuit

Jaye chewed on the edge of his thumbnail, watching Trooper Rowe approach the cabin. He looked good in daylight. It shone off of that red-gold, light hair, as lustrous as silk. The sunglasses were a nice touch, too. They showed off the symmetrical, attractive proportions of the man's face. His nose was nice and straight but wasn't too big. He had a cleft chin and a mouth that always seemed to be subtly smiling, even when it wasn't. It gave him a friendly sort of appearance, which Jaye figured was a good quality in someone working in law enforcement. The thick coat hid his form, but Jaye could see how nicely the cop filled out his pants. His thighs were muscular, the bulge of his crotch tantalizing. Jaye wanted nothing more than to grab hold of it and see what Rowe was really packing.

At least he was cute, Jaye told himself. That detail made it a much more appealing prospect to know he must somehow get Rowe hooked and wanting to do everything in his power for Jaye's seemingly poor, young, helpless self. Jaye had bit the bullet and seduced men much, much less attractive for his own gains.

Somewhat anxiously rubbing a hand over the blue jay tattooed hugely in black and gray ink across the side of his neck, Jaye opened the door. The cold rushed in and Rowe must have seen Jaye's wince at the bite of it, because he instantly quickened his step and hurried up to the door.

"C'min," Jaye said, gesturing into the cabin, staring right into Rowe's concealed eyes. "Morning."

The cop was holding a couple of insulated cups and a paper bag. The mouthwatering scent of coffee filled Jaye's head and he nearly moaned aloud.

"Wow, you brought breakfast. I love you." Jaye closed the door, nervousness and exhaustion making him fidgety when he would have rather appeared unfazed. He had opened the curtains to let in sunlight in a pitiful attempt to warm the space up more. The blankets he'd slept on were rolled up tightly and stowed against the wall. Though he had tried to keep things clean, he suddenly became hyperaware of how cluttered, dingy, and dirty the place must appear to someone used to nicer things. "Sorry about the shittiness of my home and everything. Thanks for coming by."

Rowe slipped off the sunglasses, folding them up and tucking them into a pocket. He set the breakfast fare down on a nearby table, small but the largest one in the cabin, with two chairs tucked up underneath of it.

"The coffee's black," the cop explained. "But I brought creamer and sugar if you want to add it. Assuming you drink coffee, of course. There's sausage and egg sandwiches. Protein and carbs. How's your side?"

Jaye breathed out a little laugh and continued to take visual measure of his guest. Tucking his hair back over his ears, feeling the ghosts tug on the ends, Jaye silently resolved to chop more of it off, and soon. The grayish blue long-sleeved thermal shirt he wore hugged his lean torso and his snug dark jeans showed off his narrow hips. Jaye slinked up to the food like a starved animal with fresh meat being waved in front of its nose.

"You don't mind if I...?" Jaye asked, indicating the paper bag. He again rubbed nervously at his neck, drawing Rowe's eye right there.

"Course not. Go ahead. Dig in. That's a pretty major tattoo, by the way."

"Thanks," Jaye replied distractedly. "I blame my eagerness on the smell of coffee. I haven't figured out how to make it in a pot over the fire yet, so I've been going through withdrawal. Sucks. You mean the bird, right? My jay?"

"Jay?" Dixon said, confused.

"Blue jay. Jaye. Kind of obvious, I know, but that's where my name came from, so it's like my talisman. It was my first one."

"First tattoo?"

"Yep." Jaye dug sugar out of the bag, ripped a couple of packets open and shook the contents into his palm. He trailed a fingertip through it and sucked the sugar from it with a satisfied groan before dumping the rest into one of the cups of steaming coffee. "Fucking love sugar. I'd eat nothing but candy if I could."

"Enjoy it while you can," Rowe said with a funny sort of faint grin.

Jaye caught it, pausing in his coffee-making to ask, "What?"

"Being able to eat whatever you want. Believe me, in a couple more years, you won't be able to gorge on candy and still look like that." The cop seemed to realize what he said and cleared his throat, ducking his head to cover for it. A smile flickered over Jaye's lips and was gone.

Leaving the coffee behind, he turned to his guest who had unzipped the coat. It was still cold enough to warrant keeping it on. Jaye saw the cop was fairly cut under all of those layers and itched to get his hands on Rowe's chest to see how hard it was. Distantly, he wondered what color his nipples were, if they were a light pink or darker. Running the tip of his tongue over the points of his teeth, he stepped closer to Rowe and asked, "You think I look good, trooper?"

"I-I shouldn't... that was... um. Inappropriate. I, uh," Rowe fumbled. He cleared his throat again and folded his arms over his broad chest. "Look, I shouldn't have done what I did yesterday. It was out of line and I'd like to ask if we could pretend it never happened."

It was more of an opening than Jaye needed. He took it immediately.

"It's not like you forced your cock down my throat," he said with a direct stare, letting his companion see his sincerity. "Which, you know, I wouldn't be completely against anyway if you asked nicely first. You kissed me. It was hot. No biggie. I have four, by the way. I know you're curious."

"F-four?"

"Tattoos." He said it slowly, his lips forming the sounds, watching Rowe zero in on the way they rounded around the end of the word. "How old are you, Trooper Rowe?"

"Thirty-two," Dixon answered distractedly, as his gaze skimmed down over Jaye's body, probably looking for a glimpse of the other two tats. A moment later, he caught himself, stopped looking and squeezed his eyes closed instead. Biting at his lips, he exhaled with audible frustration.

The cop moved away, getting around to the other side of the small table to get his own coffee, putting the piece of furniture between them. As he reached for the unclaimed cup, Jaye replied, "Nice. The last guy I belonged to was that same age. Funny."

"Belonged to? What's that supposed to mean?" Rowe seemed surprised, put off, maybe concerned for Jaye's wellbeing.

So be it, Jaye thought.

Mentally, Jaye superimposed Cash's face over Rowe's. They didn't match. Cash was a mess — bald, riddled with scars, tattoos and brands, his face slightly misshapen from badly healed breaks in his cheeks and nose. Rowe was handsome in a respectable way, a momma's boy type who always did right. The goodness shone from his pale, rosy skin, his golden hair, and his vibrant aquamarine eyes. In a funny way, though, Cash still felt safer to Jaye than Rowe. Rowe brought new types of dangers with him. Cash, Jaye knew; he was able to handle Cash, no matter what.

"Means I spread my cheeks and took his cock at a moment's notice. He repaid me by making sure I didn't get my throat slit or gang-raped to death. It was win-win, since, you know, I do love being alive and showing my appreciation by taking a cock. It's just a bonus when the cock belongs to someone as completely fuckable as you."

"You have got to be kidding me," the momma's boy cop said with amazement, his mouth actually hanging open. "Do you even hear what you're saying? It's like you have no filter. That's... wow."

The side of Jaye's bow-shaped lips lifted in a crooked smile. He had always known he was pretty, that men liked the look of his mouth, and why. It hadn't been difficult to learn to use it to his advantage.

A curl of brown hair fell over his left eye, concealing most of the open teardrop tattooed on his cheek. Jaye left it there, allowing Trooper Rowe to pretend he was innocent for a moment, in appearance at least. Eyes locked onto the cop, Jaye walked around the table, chasing after Rowe before he could think to retreat.

"Hey." Rowe started in protest, but Jaye was too fast. He reached up and wrapped a hand around the trooper's neck, pressing their bodies flush together from thigh to stomach.

Trooper Rowe was hard.

Jaye smiled. With his other hand, Jaye tugged the end of Rowe's shirt loose and pushed up under it to caress over the bare swell of his pectoral muscle. It was firmer than he thought it'd be and his fingers were buried in chest hair that was soft, plentiful and, Jaye wanted to imagine, golden red like the hair on Rowe's head.

"Kiss me," Jaye invited with a whisper, stretching up to get closer to the cop's mouth. Rowe started to lower his head to do just that, hesitating only slightly. In his impatience, Jaye decided to suck a hard kiss to the side of the cop's neck until he made up his mind. At the same time as his lips sealed tightly against the invitingly warm skin at the junction of the cop's neck and shoulder, Jaye pinched and twisted the tip of Rowe's nipple.

"Holy..." Rowe gasped. The hand wrapping the cop's neck moved, rotating and pushing down between their bodies instead. Jaye's fingers closed up tightly around the cop's dick through his pants.

With a grunt, he pushed Jaye away, disengaging from him. "What the fuck are you doing?!"

"Thanking you," Jaye replied honestly.

"Thanking me," Rowe echoed. "Jesus."

"Yeah, and I wasn't finished. It's rude to interrupt." Jaye said it seriously, taking a step back toward the cop.

"No! Holy shit, no. Stay back. God, you're a horny little monkey. Drink your fucking coffee. Eat breakfast."

"Rather taste you than the sandwich, to be honest. I mean, you're right. Protein is crucial."

Rowe held up a hand to keep Jaye at a distance. It was an admittedly feeble protest, so Jaye persevered. Despite his words, everything about Rowe's body said yes.

"Oh, come on," Jaye dared. "Tell me you hated it. Look me in the eye and tell me you think I'm disgusting. You kissed me first. You started it."

Rowe chuckled softly. "You're unbelievable. Completely."

"Thanks. See? You can't do it. Look at me. I mean it."

They locked eyes, giving Dixon an eyeful of the gorgeous creature trying to lure him in. Trouble was, in the back of Dixon's mind all of the horrifying years of heartache and pain from Marcus were still churning, sending out poison to pollute his system. For a very long time, Dixon felt like a terrible person because he was with the man he was with. If he gave in to Jaye, like he wanted to, that still made him the bad guy.

He was sick of being the bad guy.

"I *can't* do this with you, okay," Dixon said severely. It came out uneven and choked. His vision wavered and he blinked his eyes to clear them. "I'm trying to *help you*. I came here to do the *right thing*."

The force and volume in his voice, the urgency, hurt and determination, barely concealed the raw emotional scars he usually hid so well. It all combined to shock Jaye into silence.

As Dixon watched, Jaye's chest started to rise and fall more rapidly as his breathing quickened. More so than during the kiss, even, Dixon's passion was on display, unquestionable. But this time, it was passion not for sex, or for Jaye's body, but to be a good man.

Clearly, this confused Jaye at first. It was probably a foreign concept for the beautiful young man to be appreciated for the possibility in him rather than for his outward appearance. Dixon gave him time, hoping Jaye would see he wasn't going to be taken advantage of.

Time drew out, with them taking each other's measure, silent and watchful.

"You wanna help me, Trooper Rowe?" Jaye said eventually, oh-so-softly in his worn-smooth, low voice.

"Yes," Dixon agreed urgently, hoping that Jaye finally got it.

"Why? Why the fuck would you want to do that if it's not to get in my pants?"

"Because you deserve it!" he argued. "You deserve to have someone make sure you're fed and safe. My job is to protect the citizens of this town. That includes you. That's all I want. That's *all*."

"Liar," Jaye sneered viciously. He closed the gap between them again. They stood chest-to-chest with Jaye's chin tilted up, his arms hanging at his sides, his eyes captivatingly beautiful for all of their anger and determination.

Dixon almost did it. He started to chase Jaye's mouth again, wanting to feel it against his lips. Jaye's warm breath moved over Dixon's skin which each quickened, shallow exhale.

Dixon's hands moved, flexing as if to grab and hold, and god damn he was hard—it was a ceaseless throbbing that nearly overwhelmed his good intentions. Everything he wanted could be had if only he dared to take it. Jaye would let him touch, suck, or fuck him. It was all on the table. But that would only make Dixon the bad guy. That would make him Marcus.

He took a backward step and a deep breath.

"You don't want me. You want the *idea* of me. A cop who you can play for anything you need. I'm offering you help without the strings. That's the better deal, Mr. Larson. Now, do you want to hear what I have to say about a job, or should I just go?"

"My name is *Jaye*," he hissed fiercely.

"Okay. Jaye, then. What's it gonna be?"

Jaye pivoted on a heel, his arms both coming up as he grabbed his head in both hands, his fists tightening in the long, curling strands. It caused his shirt to pull up and subsequently reveal some of the bare, tantalizing skin of his lower back and the dimples right above his ass. Dixon's cock twitched at the sight, pulsing wetly in his pants. With effort, he closed his eyes to block out the sight.

Taking hold of one of the chairs, Jaye pulled it out and sat, planting his sweet ass on the wood. He drew the coffee toward him and opened the bag of food.

"Good," Dixon sighed. "Good choice."

Pale green eyes flashed dangerously at him.

Dixon grabbed his own coffee and drank. It burned its way down his throat in the best of ways.

"Okay, first off, clearly you prefer to be called by your first name. I do, too. It's Dixon."

Jaye nodded tightly, drawing his sandwich from the bag.

"Now," Dixon continued, sitting down on the opposite side of the table. "There is a position available at the truck stop—I confirmed it—but with one condition. They want to do a background check or have me get the full story from you myself and vouch for you. I decided to give you the option. I didn't run your info yet. You can tell me yourself why you were locked up, or you can tell me it's none of my business and we'll do it the other way."

Looking down at his hands holding the sandwich, Jaye sounded meeker than Dixon had yet heard him as he asked, "Can I have a minute to think about it and decide? Please?"

"Yeah. Of course. Eat. Take your time."

Jaye nodded again and took a huge bite of the sandwich, hunching down over it like he was afraid Dixon might try to take it back from him. Unable to watch the young man's desperation any longer, Dixon, sipping his coffee, looked away and watched the flames dance in the fireplace instead.

Chapter 6
Guilty

In prison, inmates boasted about their crimes. Everyone claimed innocence, but everyone also used fear as a weapon. The fact that Jaye had killed a man earned him some respect. It wasn't like he was in for tax evasion. Sure, he was fairly small and pretty, but he was also good with a knife when he had to be and would happily fight dirty in a pinch. That earned him some time in solitary, but he didn't regret it — not at all.

Outside of that insulated world of the penitentiary, life was vastly different. Jaye's crimes became shameful. They burdened and isolated him, making him an outcast. The truth may have kept him from finding a job. The *whole* truth would have certainly permanently altered the way the cop with the red-gold hair and friendly smile looked at him, and that, for Jaye, would have been much harder to bear than joblessness and destitution.

The question of whether to tell Dixon Rowe outright about what got Jaye locked up, or to send him on a fact-checking hunt of police profiles, public records and news articles was not an easy one to solve. It would have been easy for Dixon to find out Jaye's whole truth on his own, or at least most of it. There was more of a chance of the cop wanting to continue helping Jaye if the story came directly from him, with no interference. Jaye, without question, would have preferred to give Dixon free rein to use his body than to fuck with his head. Setting the whole truth free would have most definitely fucked with Jaye's head.

The ghostly touching started again, then, like it had the previous night, conjured by the subject of his thoughts.

Unseen, insubstantial fingers wrapped themselves in his hair. They prodded and poked at his body, exploring him without hesitation or fear of reprisal. It was horrible. It was nauseating. And he couldn't make it stop, because it was all in his head.

Jaye had finished his sandwich and most of his coffee. Hunching forward over the table, he tried to tell himself it wasn't real, that no one was touching him. With one hand clutched to the back of his head, tangled in his hair, he focused on his breathing.

It worked at first, but then his control slipped. He gasped once, sharply, as big, thick, clammy hands tried to pull his legs apart and fondle his genitals. After that, he held his breath for what must have been a full minute and a half before trying to inhale more normally.

"You okay?" the cop named Dixon asked with audible concern.

"I've decided that it's none of your business," Jaye told him softly after taking a deep breath and letting it out slowly, without raising his head.

"I am going to find out either way," Dixon reminded him, sounding disappointed that Jaye decided not to trust him. "Wouldn't you rather tell me in your own words?"

Piggy cop's gonna know. Piggy cop's gonna fuck you up. Piggy cop's gonna carve you into bloody pieces and fuck your corpse.

"Stop!" Jaye screamed into his hands. "Shut up!"

"Hey!"

Jaye glanced up, hands falling away from his face, startled to get a response. He'd temporarily forgotten he wasn't alone and stared, fascinated, at Dixon.

Glancing around the cabin to ground himself to reality, Jaye muttered, "Sorry, I, uh, still have some issues. My past is a touchy subject."

"I know the feeling," Dixon replied like he meant it. "Why don't you start with the charges? What were you charged with?"

"Manslaughter. Assault with a deadly weapon."

"Oh. Okay," Dixon's eyes widened slightly. "But you were only in for two years."

"Not guilty. Guilty. Respectively."

Gonna slice open your belly. Pull your insides out. Make you watch.

Involuntarily, Jaye whimpered. That wasn't the ghosts. That was memory.

His hand twitched, sliding over the tabletop in search of a knife.

"You killed someone," Dixon accused, or at least that's what it sounded like.

"They killed me first," Jaye riddled back.

"What? Who? More than one?"

"More than one," he agreed. "Two. Cut his throat, ear to ear. A smile. A better smile. Better than the one he wore while he was getting ready to rape me. They broke into my apartment, stole some shit and woke me up, knocked me out and carried me out to the alley, right next to the dumpster for easy disposal when they were finished. When I came to, I was naked and held down while they touched me—everywhere. I cut his new smile after he stuck the butcher knife through me. Right through me.

"He pulled the blade out red and set it aside. By *my* side. Blood was everywhere, gushing out of me. His friend had me pinned, but he put the knife down because he wanted his hands free to hurt me some more. He had his dick out and two fingers shoved through the slice in my side when I cut his throat. He was reaching around in there, in my guts, trying to pull something out. Stopped pretty quickly though, once he realized I'd killed him. Then I ran after his friend.

"I pushed on the gash, like they tell you to do. I was bleeding over my fingers and afraid my insides were going to start spilling out of me, but I still could run. I caught up with him and stabbed him with the knife—the other. That's why they gave me time. Because I ran. It's not self-defense if you chase them down first. He didn't die though. He should have. He earned it."

The cop's mouth was hanging open again. He managed to shut it after trying and failing a few times and said, horrified, "Oh my god."

"There is no God. I survived *that* and they sent me to prison and what do you think my life was like there, huh? Now I just want to be left alone." He shouted, "*I just want to be left alone!*"

"No," Dixon said forcefully, disgust twisting his features. "No. It's not possible. That's—"

"*Look it up!*" Jaye bellowed at him with all of the air in his lungs, getting out of the chair.

He scanned the cabin for his knife and, after a moment, realized it was in the kitchen. With effort, he stopped himself from going for it, knowing he would feel better if he had it in his hand, but he couldn't do that while the cop was there.

"Okay! Okay."

Jaye's next shuddering gasp for oxygen hitched on a small whimper of agony. The cop got up out of his chair, too. Blood pounded behind Jaye's ears and eyes. He wanted to run, to hide or fight. Something. Anything.

"Let's just calm down, okay?"

Jaye could hear the intentionally pacifying, slightly condescending tone in Dixon's voice. It was a cop voice, one used on Jaye countless times in jail by the guards and, before then, by other cops like Trooper Rowe. Hearing that tone never helped calm Jaye down, but only made him want to raise his defenses that much higher.

Sneering at the concern and reaction to his outburst, Jaye rubbed a hand over his head, trying to calm down in his own ways. He grabbed a handful of his curls — shorter than they had been when he was locked up — as it had become a self-soothing reflex. When it got bad like it was then, he needed to feel that his hair was almost twelve inches shorter than it had been. The shorter hair meant he was free. The proof of his change in physical appearance helped to settle his churning anxiety. Feeling the chopped ends of his hair cemented for Jaye that he was in the cabin, not trapped in his cell or back at his old home where fear for his safety, as well as the safety of his ex-boyfriend, ruled his life. First it was homophobes that surrounded him, threatening; then it was hardened criminals. Now it was only a cute ginger cop looking to be the good guy.

When Dixon continued speaking, it was with somewhat less of the cop voice. Sounding only rattled, he said, "I can see why you didn't want to talk about that. Clearly you were just protecting yourself, even if the jury didn't completely see it that way. You've done your time. My job is to help you to get readjusted now, so let's move on to that. Do you have a parole officer? Check in with them regularly?"

Jaye nodded without raising his gaze from the floorboards. The parole officer was the only reason he had a semi-functional cell phone, his one connection with the rest of the world. His hands still itched for the calming weight of a lethal weapon. His head assured him that'd be a very bad thing while there was a cop standing in his home.

"What can I do for you to make things better?" Dixon tried when Jaye stayed mum. "Besides the job, which is totally in the bag, by the way."

That's a lie, Jaye thought. *The cop's just saying that because it's what he thinks I want to hear.*

"The lights," Jaye murmured. "I wanna get the lights back on. I don't like the dark. It's been getting darker."

"Okay," Dixon echoed cheerfully. "Lights. Totally do-able. How about I loan you the money to get some fuel in that genie until I can contact utility services and get the electricity back on? That's a propane heater over there. It'd be better than just the fireplace. I could get some propane, too."

The prospect of maybe not having to spend another endless night alone in the cold dark with the ghosts of his attackers and worst nightmares brought sudden tears to Jaye's eyes. He turned his back on Dixon to wipe them away. Clearing his throat, Jaye grunted his assent.

Wanting the cop gone and out of the cabin so he could collect some of his shattered sense of self-worth, Jaye knew he should ignore that desire and try, instead, to express his gratitude to his new provider. That instinct was one carefully nurtured after years of simply trying just to survive each day and get to the next one.

As Jaye tried to steady himself and bury his very visible emotions, arms crossed over his chest, hands clasped to his upper arms, he felt and heard the cop approaching. Jaye's eyes closed tiredly as Dixon walked around to him, seeing Jaye's damp eyes and quivering lip. Feeling small and pathetic and powerless, Jaye forced himself to act.

With a gruff whisper, he took a step into Dixon's personal space and slipped a hand around the trooper's hip, saying, "I need to thank you."

Jaye's voice broke over the plea and it made him angry at himself. Unwanted sorrow infused every pore. His hand twitched, moving toward Dixon's fly.

Dixon caught the hand before it got there, pulling Jaye away by the wrist.

"Not like that."

"Please," Jaye said gravely, without an ounce of pride left.

"No," Dixon countered firmly, but not as the cop. He said it as a man. That's what got Jaye to lift his chin in order to look his guest and savior in the eye. When he saw a total absence of judgment and, more than that, actual understanding reflected back at him — a type that could not be faked for convenience's sake — Jaye was shaken.

He was profoundly unused to anyone knowing from their own experience what he had gone through.

"You're not currency. You're a human being and you deserve better than that. I'll be back with the fuel."

"Dixon," Jaye began, floundering for something — apology, maybe, or explanation.

"I'll be back with the fuel," Dixon repeated, walking to the door, zipping up his coat.

Because he couldn't manage a verbal thank you, he bit the inside of his cheek instead, waiting as Dixon left. The door closed heavily. Moaning with disgust at his own behavior, Jaye let his feet take him to where he was being pulled.

He lifted the knife from the kitchen drawer, hefted it, savoring its weight, then sank with it to his knees. Curling up pitifully against the cupboard, he clasped the handle and focused on making his breaths regular and even, repeating to himself over and over again, "I'm okay. There's no one here. I'm okay. I'm okay."

Chapter 7
Self-Destructive Impulses

"How did it go?" Sesi asked.

"Good. I got some answers. I'm getting fuel for him, for his heater and the genie. This is going to work out."

"Good," she said, pausing, waiting.

"I'm doing the right thing. I'm not falling into any traps. Okay?"

"You telling me or yourself?"

He traced the edge of the steering wheel with his fingertip, the phone tucked against his ear. After thinking about her question, he answered, "I don't know."

"You're going back? Dropping the propane or whatever?"

"Yeah," he nodded. "That's it. Just getting him set up. He's in a bad way, to say the least."

"Well, you go and get that done, then leave. Come over here if you want. I'll be around."

"Thanks, Sesi. We'll see how it goes. I'll call."

"No problem." There was a pause, then, "Do the right thing, Dix."

"I will. I'm trying. Bye."

An hour and a half after driving away, Dixon returned with plenty of gasoline. He'd also scheduled a propane delivery for that day, to be charged to his account. Flustered, he got out of the vehicle and went around back to start unloading the containers. He was breathing a little hard and trying to keep it together. *Get the genie started*, he told himself, *then get out. Go home. Clear your head.*

With one heavy gas can in each hand, Dixon started to walk around to the back of the cabin when he noticed, suddenly, that Jaye was outside, chopping firewood.

Dixon was surprised enough to stop in his tracks and stare for a long second. One long, chocolate brown tendril had slipped free of Jaye's knit hat, pulled down to protect his ears from the frosty air. The ax drew up, held tight in both of Jaye's hands, then fell swiftly in an arc with a *thock* as the blade split the log. Jaye tossed his head, trying to shake the curl of hair from his vision as he yanked the ax free. His jaw tensed with the effort. Green eyes slid sideways as he looked right at Dixon, then repositioned the split wood and prepared for another swing.

Dixon realized he was just standing there like an idiot, staring, and got his feet moving again.

He worked quickly, filling the bone-dry tank with gasoline before Jaye could decide to help him out rather than grow his supply of firewood. The faster Dixon moved, the more certain he became that Jaye was coming closer, or that Jaye was a few feet away, watching. So, he moved even faster.

When he turned on the generator, it kicked to life, humming loudly.

With a chuckle of relief and gladness, Dixon stood back to enjoy the sight of the fruits of his labors. Jaye would now have electricity for lights, his stove, hot water, and many things he didn't have before. That was good.

With a smile still on his face, Dixon circled back to the front of the house, bringing the empty gas cans along. He loaded them into the back of his vehicle and felt rather than heard Jaye's presence at his back. It made goose bumps race outward over Dixon's skin, over his back and arms, up his neck.

Knowing he should turn around and face Jaye, and act like this was a normal exchange between a trooper and a civilian, Dixon simply couldn't. Facing the collection of empty containers instead, he said, "I guess you don't have a phone."

"I have a crappy cell phone that needs to be charged," Jaye responded from closer than Dixon anticipated. He was only inches behind Dixon's back. Closing his eyes, waiting for a touch, certain it was coming, for Dixon it was difficult to speak through the tension.

"Good," he managed. Dazed, focused more on what he was expecting to happen rather than what he was doing, he pulled a pad of paper from his pocket and scribbled down his phone number.

Giving the scrap of paper to Jaye required turning around, so Dixon hesitated at first, his lips moving around a silent curse. Then, he bit the bullet and turned on a heel.

Jaye was right there. Dixon could smell him, feel his warmth, and fell into his light eyes.

Clearing his throat, his gaze catching on the massive tattoo wrapping Jaye's neck, Dixon held out the paper. It all dissolved into chaos as Jaye reached out to take it. Jaye's gloved hand stayed folded over Dixon's, rather than pulling away.

They both leaned in fractionally. *From the cold*, Dixon told himself.

He heard himself say, "Here ya go, J-bird. Call me if you need anything."

"You're funny," Jaye said without smiling or laughing.

His heart hammered in his chest. Dixon was paralyzed as Jaye stepped impossibly closer, withdrawing the small pad of paper from Dixon's breast pocket. Biting pensively at his lower lip, sharing body heat with Dixon, Jaye wrote down his own number with the pad laid against Dixon's chest.

The natural scent of Jaye filled Dixon's head. He was right there. That tendril, the rest of the hidden silk of Jaye's hair, it was directly below Dixon's nose, so he leaned in slightly, wanting to feel the softness of it against his skin, stopping just before making contact.

Jaye finished writing and slid the paper back into Dixon's pocket but didn't move away.

Neither of them said a word. Jaye waited for Dixon to break through his personal walls and take what was right there to be had. Dixon fought tooth and nail to keep his raging lust in check and act like the good man he always thought he was.

But then nothing had happened, and they were still unnaturally close, so Jaye moved, slowly. He laid his head against Dixon's chest and circled his arms loosely around Dixon's waist. Exhaling sharply, a little shaken, Dixon couldn't hold back from returning the hug. He clasped a hand gently to the back of Jaye's knit cap, holding him there, pressed against him.

The easiness of embracing Jaye scared Dixon.

It was *easy*.

His hands wanted to grab more tightly, move to places they shouldn't, and there would be nothing to stop him. Nothing but his conscience.

So he moved Jaye away, guiding him backward by the shoulders.

As he closed the back hatch and dug in his pocket for keys, Dixon kept his gaze trained on his feet. Jaye tracked him, standing right where Dixon put him, still waiting for Dixon to take what belonged to him, what he had earned. It upset Dixon in a profound way, that patient waiting.

He got angry, furious at the world and the evils which had broken Jaye and left him expecting to be used as collateral, believing the most valuable thing he possessed was his physical self, his skin, his beauty, his sex.

The anger grew, chased by sadness. It was an electric surge under his skin, and he needed to release some of the energy, so he bellowed, "*Fuck!*"

Jaye flinched.

Moving blindly, Dixon got into the vehicle, behind the wheel and started the engine. Jaye was in his rearview mirror as he shifted into drive and pulled away in a hurry.

A voice groggy with sleep answered, "Dix?"

"Yeah, it's me. You home?"

"I'm home. Why, you comin' over?"

"That okay?"

There was a pause. Dixon waited for Sacha to answer. He was still driving after a number of hours of waiting to be useful, wanting to do something other than patrol. All around him was flat open land. The immensity of his surroundings made him feel insignificant and lonely, but he needed a solution to the problem at hand.

Sacha was the answer. White-capped mountains edged the line

between sky and Earth. Fields colored in crisp greens, deep browns and untouched white unrolled before him as the miles slipped away under his tires.

"My roommate's coming back. You can't stay."

"It won't take long," Dixon assured him emotionlessly.

With a heavy sigh, still sounding half-asleep, Sacha complied, "Yeah. You far away?"

"Nope. Gimme a few minutes."

He hung up and pushed the gas pedal a little harder.

Sacha lived on the left side of an unimpressive but functional duplex in the more urban part of town. Dixon climbed the steps to the front door and wished it was dark out, but it was still too early. If it was dark, he'd be more able to get lost in the gloom and convince himself maybe that Sacha had chocolate brown, curling hair and tattoos.

Rapping on the door with his knuckles, Dixon glanced around but there was no one, only a huge bird swooping past overhead.

The door's lock clicked as it was turned and swung open. Sacha blinked up at him, squinting slightly at the fading sunlight, dressed only in boxers. His light brown hair stuck up in spikes, tousled from being slept on.

"Jesus. Look at you, dude. C'min," Sacha murmured, stepping aside just enough before closing the door behind Dixon and locking it again. "I just got back from work a couple hours ago. Fuckin' tired, man."

"Won't take long," Dixon repeated. He removed his duty belt and coat, then began working open the buttons of his shirt.

They walked back into Sacha's bedroom where it was as dark as night, the heavy curtains drawn. That was good. Sacha led the way with Dixon right on his heels. Once inside the bedroom, Sacha closed that door too, watching Dixon disrobe in the gloom. The shirt got tossed onto a chair. Dixon's fingers worked at his fly next.

"You lonely or somethin'?"

"Or somethin'," Dixon agreed, not smiling, all business.

"I see. Blue balls," Sacha laughed. "What're you lookin' for then, man?" It was asked hesitantly, while he rubbed his bare upper arm with a hand. "Gimme an idea or a hint. If this is gonna be like last time—"

"No. Last time was different. Get on the bed. On your knees. You're taking. Act like you love it."

Once he had gotten onto the bed, Dixon pushed the boxers down to Sacha's knees. Staring at his tight, puckered little hole, Dixon grabbed the lube from off of the nightstand. He pulled his cock free of his pants, rolled on a condom and got some lube on his fingers, smearing it along his shaft. His balls were full and heavy. His cock had been a hot, stiff line against his leg for the whole drive over here. Stroking the slick on helped a little, but mercilessly fucking Sacha's ass would help even more.

They had known one another for years, through other people. They weren't even friends, really. Dixon and Sacha could never have had a relationship or even date. They were too different for that. Dixon was a guy with shit luck in his personal life and notions of being a decent human being. Sacha got ass or pussy whenever he wanted it, but his job working nights down at the docks and his tendency to be a heartless prick usually scared people away fast. Dixon couldn't care less. Sometimes he just needed to get laid, and the options were limited on that front with living where they did. There were only so many guys that swung that way in Zus. At least Sacha would keep his mouth shut. Since Sacha knew Marcus, he also knew the shit he'd get into if anyone found out about his sexual escapades with Trooper Rowe.

He swiped lube around Sacha's hole and pushed some inside. Leaving his fingers buried for a moment, he tested Sasha's tightness.

"When's the last time you took a cock?"

"None of your business," Sacha retorted, grunting at the stretch as Dixon began to pry at him.

Dixon pulled his fingers out and stepped up close, right behind where Sacha was bent over on his hands and knees near the edge of the unmade bed, covered with tangled, dirty sheets. Guiding his dick to Sacha's hole, Dixon hooked one arm around the front of Sacha's hips, drawing him back while holding himself by the root and pushing to get inside the clenched ring.

"Fuckin' not even prepped yet, man!" Sacha complained, struggling to accept Dixon's cockhead, tensing up. Dixon slipped, his dick sliding up through Sacha's crack. Realigning, he tried again.

"I thought I told you to act like you love it," Dixon growled.

"Just go easy."

"Okay." Dixon eased up a little, letting Sacha relax into it. Sacha's hand went between his legs and he started to beat off while Dixon tried to breach him.

"Better..."

The reddened, bulbous head of Dixon's cock squeezed through Sacha's rim, past the ring of muscle. Sacha moaned. He arched and goose bumps spread over his skin. His hand picked up speed, pumping his hard-on. He shifted his knees wider as Dixon tried to go deeper.

Closing his eyes, Dixon imagined Jaye. Piecing together what he might look like naked from the glimpses Dixon had and his own fantasies, the tattoos, the lean, chiseled shape of Jaye's young, slim body, he overlaid it with what he felt. The ass he was sheathed in was Jaye. The moan he heard when he pulled the lithe body before him back onto his cock was Jaye, too.

"You know I shouldn't do this, Jaye, but you want it. Don't you?"

"I want it," Sacha sighed, pushing his ass back onto Dixon's cock, taking more of him, swallowing every inch. "God *damn*."

Dixon snapped his hips, hard, making Sacha take the rest of him, not easing up until his balls were flush to Sacha's body. Sacha clenched and Dixon moaned at the hot grip, snug around his throbbing flesh. He drew back a few inches, then pushed gently inside. Letting go of his conquest, Dixon pumped his hips, sliding wetly in and out, easier now. Sacha grunted and went with it, rocking back onto Dixon, into his thrusts. They went faster and faster, slapping against each other.

"Oh *hell*," Sacha hissed. "Fuck me so good, Dix...."

Upper lip curling in a frustrated sneer, wishing it wasn't just a fantasy, trying to make it as good as it could be to wash away temptation, Dixon tried to believe the lies he was feeding himself. He folded himself forward, over Sacha's back and took him harder, holding him still, pounding his hole.

The phone rang in Dixon's pocket.

"*Damn*," Dixon cursed, going at a brutal pace, picking up speed, just trying to finish.

"Ignore it," Sacha rasped as the phone rang again. Dixon slowed, then stopped abruptly.

Fumbling the phone from his back pocket, Dixon checked the I.D. Since he was on call, if it was an emergency, he needed to answer.

It was Jaye.

With a bitter chuckle, Dixon listened to it ring a third time, buried balls-deep in a guy who essentially meant nothing to him. It was the anger and streak of self-destruction that had always been in him, buried way down low in places only Marcus had been able to tap in to, that made Dixon answer.

"Hello?"

He held Sacha still, not letting him pull off. After a second, he found Sacha's dick and started to stroke it for him to keep him interested.

"Rowe," Jaye said in Dixon's ear. "Long time no see."

"Is something wrong?" Dixon was a little breathless as he asked. He started to move shallowly in Sacha's ass, fucking it gently. It was nice, hearing Jaye's voice tickle his ear while he worked his aching erection, getting Dixon that much closer. He wondered if he could come while he had Jaye on the phone.

"No, everything's great. Is something wrong with *you*?"

Dixon closed his lips to muffle a grunt as Sacha clenched around him, too tight, too good. Sacha moaned loudly and Dixon couldn't help but laugh.

Impatient when Jaye didn't say anything and only listened, Dixon demanded, "Why are you calling?"

"If this is a bad time—"

"Nope. Perfect time. What can I do for you?"

Sacha laughed at this and started to ride Dixon's hand, thrusting against each stroke, rocking back onto the thickened cock up his ass.

"Who are you with? Is that your partner?"

"Talk to me," Dixon urged. His voice caught as his climax chased up on him, fast.

"Okay. I guess I just wanted to know when I'd see you again, if you were going to call about the job info or if you'd stop by. My phone's kind of hit or miss, you know, so it'd probably be best if you came over. Will you come?"

Chuckling breathlessly, Dixon agreed, "Yeah, I'll come. No problem."

He was so close he could taste it. He stopped jacking Sacha and focused only on fucking him, listening to Jaye's voice.

"Rowe?"

"That's not my name. I told you to call me—"

"Dixon," Jaye said softly. "You're Dixon."

Shivering with pleasure at the gruff whisper in his ear, saying his name, Dixon pretended he didn't hear and, gasping slightly when his balls drew up tight and his cock turned to iron, asked, "What?"

"Dixon," Jaye repeated alluringly, beckoning to him.

Moaning, shuddering, twisting the phone away from his mouth, Dixon unloaded deeply into Sacha and the condom he was wrapped in.

"*Dixon... Dixon...*"

Chest heaving, catching his breath, nerves tingling throughout his body with aftershocks, Dixon managed, "I'm coming, okay?"

"Now?" Jaye asked. Dixon could hear the amusement in Jaye's voice and ignored it. "Right now?"

"Busy right now."

"Tomorrow."

"No."

Shameless, beseeching and intentionally wicked, like he knew what he was hearing and why Dixon was drawing this out, Jaye begged, "*Please*, Dixon. Please?" His voice was a seductive purr in Dixon's ear.

"Fine," Dixon relented.

There was silence for a few moments as Jaye listened to Dixon's rough breathing and Dixon let him. Sacha wrapped himself in a fist and tugged, bringing himself off in seconds.

Very quietly, so much so that he could almost believe it was only his imagination, Dixon heard, "I would've let you. You know that. Are you inside him right now? Or is he in you? How do you want it, Dix? 'Cause I'll take you any way I can."

Sacha cried out with his orgasm and Dixon hung up, ending the call.

Chapter 8

Reward

Jaye lay in the tub, soaking in gloriously hot water, bathed in light. He had turned on every single one in the cabin. The burning bulbs were a cherished luxury after so long living without. As his hands floated weightless on top of the soothing water, he let his body and mind relax, thinking about what he told Dixon about the break-in and attack.

In that moment, the attack felt like something that happened to another person, not to him. It was one hour of one day, over two years ago. Sure, it was a life-altering hour, but Jaye tried not to dwell on it.

Consciously, in his waking hours, he didn't think about how he had been identified at a local diner, where he'd had a couple of burgers with his boyfriend, then tracked home once he was on his own, the boyfriend gone for a weekend trip to see family. They'd followed Jaye because they had seen he was gay. They'd broken a window, dragged him, fighting, from bed, and punched him in the temple.

The lights went out.

When his eyes opened, his pants were off. His shirt was gathered up around his arms, which someone sat on. Fingers wriggled up inside his ass as they whispered threats, describing the ways they were going to disembowel him before they started to carry out those threats, sheathing the butcher knife in his gut while he made awful screams around the wadded up underwear stuffed in his mouth, trying somehow to voice the pain.

The attack was a nightmare come true and, usually, stayed in the dark. The daylight helped push the memories farther away. Though scars, both physical and mental, followed him ever since — not to mention the ghosts that multiplied and came out at times of extreme panic—it was more of a challenge for Jaye to get past the larger problem at hand.

He was trying not to remain the person he became in prison.

The event that landed him behind bars was a snippet of time. His time locked up was two solid years of his life. Over seven hundred days. Jaye liked to think he was already on the way to recovery from what had happened to him in that alley, and that he could recover from what prison did to him, too, given the chance, space, and a good stretch of uneventful existence.

Deep down, though, he didn't truly believe he would.

Rather than reclaiming the identity he had before the attack, or even managing to live as a shadow of his former self, he was doomed to exist as the ex-convict he most certainly was.

In prison, everything he did, day in, day out, was because of the system, the guards, or Cash. Nothing else mattered. *He* didn't matter.

Since he hadn't ever had any sort of contraband to trade, sex was his only currency. Jaye stayed alive in dangerous circumstances because he put out without a fight for someone powerful enough to protect him. As much as Dixon believed someone's body wasn't something to barter with, Jaye knew it wasn't true. It just depended on the situation.

Now, Jaye was in a very bizarre sort of situation. He was right where he had wanted to be for so long, where he dreamed of being—apart from things. He liked the wilderness, the quiet, and the space. It calmed him in a deeply needed way. Most times, even if he wanted to go looking for another human being, it took him a while and a long walk to find one. It was nice to be alone. He would have liked it to stay that way. He longed to become a recluse.

Unfortunately, he did require things like heat, electricity, and money. That meant getting a job, getting involved in the world. The idea didn't thrill him, but one thing that did interest him, very much, was Trooper Dixon Rowe.

Jaye wasn't used to paying any heed to his own desires and attractions. He was still stuck in the prison mindset where he ate, slept, pissed, shit, showered, fucked, and moved around only when it was permitted. Hunger, physical discomfort, and even terror weren't conditions he could expect deliverance from, let alone lust or loneliness. Not since he'd had a boyfriend in high school, before life turned to shit, had he let himself care about whom he was with or what he wanted. He and his boyfriend — a teenager named Kris — had lived together. They had been in love. Or, at least they said so in the heat of passion, or late at night, or when saying a temporary goodbye. But Jaye was alone during the attack, and he never saw Kris again. Kris vanished, with not even one visit or one letter in all of the time Jaye was behind bars.

Jaye's heart hardened. It wasn't heartbreak. It was a shriveling up, drying out, and deadening. Love wasn't something he wanted, nor was he capable of giving. It was only something that happened to other people, and got them in trouble.

At first, Jaye thought Dixon was just a means to an end. Hell, Dixon had already paid off. Jaye was floating in the proof of it. He had hot water and freedom from the nightmares darkness brought. That should have been enough. The fact that Dixon didn't even want to be compensated for his expense and troubles should have been the icing on the cake. It should have ended there.

But Jaye liked Dixon. He liked that Dixon tried not to look, tried not to touch, even though he wanted to. Jaye could see he wanted to. The cop was trying so hard to be the respectable, honorable guy and keep his hands off, but every so often he gave in anyway, just a little. It was so hot, Jaye had no chance of resisting the allure of that inner battle. Those glimpses of proof that Dixon could give in, if pushed, if tempted enough, made Jaye want to push, to seduce. It was a game, and fucking Dixon was the prize.

Dixon was strength, warmth, goodness, light, and promise. He was hope and possibility. Maybe life didn't have to be as bleak and bad as it had been. Maybe, it could be better.

Of course, a lot of that was just sentimental bullshit. The reality was even if Dixon came through on the job, there still might be things Jaye could discover he needed help with, or protection from. Jaye had called Dixon because he was afraid Dixon was done with him. There'd be a call about the job information, a new name, a new phone number, and that'd be it. Jaye would never hear from him again. There was a chance Dixon would stay away because of how Jaye had crossed lines in trying for more. The call had been made with the intent to show Dixon Jaye wasn't crazy, he could behave and wasn't a victim of his past mistakes and tragedies. He had just been playing by rules that weren't in effect anymore, and didn't know how to stop. Even if Jaye wanted to belong to Dixon in a sexual way, to be *his* in every sense, the way he was Cash's, it wouldn't happen if Dixon wasn't interested in being Jaye's possessor.

If Jaye was able to lure Dixon back with rationality and friendliness, and convince him to stick around by drawing the seduction game out more over time, it could pay off in a big way over the long-term. Jaye had told himself he could still work around Dixon's good guy mindset.

But then, Jaye called. Dixon answered. And...

Drawing up his legs in the bathwater, making gentle ripples, Jaye sank down and immersed himself a little more. Hot liquid enveloped him, licking at his skin. He couldn't stop thinking of what he'd heard through the phone. Wholly unused to being seduced in his own right, Jaye found himself floundering.

Dixon knew it was him calling, and even if he hadn't known, there was no good reason why he hadn't hung up once he did. Why had he stayed on the line, drawing out the call while he was doing things Jaye could only imagine?

It had been so long since he had wanted purely for the sake of wanting. Stiff and aching, needing relief, he stroked himself slowly, his hand sliding easily in the luxuriously hot water, splashing softly. Dixon was a gruff, remembered echo. Jaye replayed in his mind the sounds of Dixon fucking, Dixon gasping, Dixon saying he was coming, meaning it just the way it sounded.

That phone call changed everything.

It was game on.

Now, Jaye knew, for a fact, Dixon was playing the game, too. If Jaye played carefully, he had a real chance to have everything he never believed could be his. He would get the protection he craved from someone who cared about him as a man, and not just an easy fuck. That kind of devotion was the big prize and one Jaye would have done anything it took to get.

Moaning loudly in the stillness, head thrown back, tugging faster, he chased his release then found it, thinking of Dixon. His seed splashed over his dripping skin, over calm waters, seeping through his fingers, and Jaye gasped, laughing out loud.

Chapter 9

Dixon's Helping Hand

It had been a long day. Earlier, Dixon had accompanied an AWT Trooper in locating an illegal kill. There had been shots fired, and they hadn't known what they might be walking in to. The game was a moose, a bull with antlers only thirteen inches across. The bull was just a few years old and the penalties for shooting such an animal were severe. There would be hefty fines and jail time for the hunter. In the meantime, they'd had to take a boat out to find the animal and bring it back before bears tracked the scent right into town.

After that physically exhausting task, there were a few minor calls to check out. One was a guy passed out in his vehicle after leaving a bar. Someone could easily freeze to death that way, once the sun and the temperatures went down. Dixon brought the guy in until he sobered up and could call for a ride home.

When he was finally done, it was late. The sun had been down for hours, but he had made a promise — possibly a stupid promise, but a promise nonetheless — and needed to follow through.

The last place he wanted to be was Jaye Larson's cabin. At that point in his long day, he would even have taken an unexpected encounter with Marcus over facing Jaye. Pulling up in front of the cabin, Dixon groaned heavily and gathered his wits.

It had been another astonishingly bad decision to answer Jaye's call when he was with Sacha. Dixon knew why he did it, though, and was ashamed of himself. The irresistible lure of the forbidden had won out over common sense, yet again. His best hope was Jaye would be polite enough to pretend it was an innocent conversation and let it go.

Dixon climbed out from behind the wheel of his Expedition and followed the path to the cabin's front door. With a deep breath for courage, he raised his fist and knocked.

"Jaye? It's me! Dixon Rowe!" he called loudly.

"Yeah, Dix! It's open. Come on in," Jaye replied from within.

Steeling himself, Dixon grabbed the handle, turned and pushed inside.

It was markedly warmer in the modest home than it had been on his other visits. The place glowed with lamps and overhead lights, every single one turned on. Those improvements made Dixon smile despite his misgivings. He went inside and closed the door behind him to keep heat from escaping.

But he didn't see Jaye.

Without thinking about it first, he called, "J-bird?"

There was a chuckle from the bathroom. Dixon took a step toward it.

"In here. I need your help for a second. I promise I'm decent."

"You need my help in the bathroom?"

"Yeah, c'mere," Jaye said lightly. It was the absence of concern or worry in Jaye's voice that vanquished some of Dixon's fears. He walked over to the bathroom doorway and hesitantly peered within.

The sight of Jaye shocked Dixon silent for a long moment.

Then he blurted, "You cut your hair off."

"Duh," Jaye chuckled, smiling. Instantly, blood began to fill Dixon's cock at the sight of the sweet dimples that framed that easy, honest grin. He wanted to touch them, kiss them, and trace them with the tip of his tongue. Derailing this train of thought, a flash of green drew his gaze upward as Jaye gazed at Dixon in the mirror's reflection above the sink.

Of course, facial features weren't all Dixon noticed.

Jaye was shirtless, wearing only a pair of old jeans that hung from the perky swell of his ass. With his arms raised, he combed his fingers through what little hair was left on top of his head. Only an inch or two of length remained, with a pair of scissors still at the ready. Dark curls littered the bathroom floor.

Dixon's eyes went everywhere. The shorn curls, the dimples above Jaye's ass, the etched muscles of his back. The tattoos. The scars.

It was the anger that spoke first, before logic and libido could catch up.

"Why'd you cut your hair?" Dixon demanded with much more disappointment than was appropriate.

"C'mere," Jaye said softly, inclining his head, biting at his lower lip in concentration. "Check the back. I can't tell if it's evened out or not."

"I'm not cutting your hair," Dixon protested, for the wrong reasons.

"Who else can I ask to help? Come on. I realize it's not part of your job description."

"But," Dixon stuttered, stepping up closer to Jaye's back, taking the scissors and comb when Jaye handed them over. "I mean, have you lost your mind? Why would you...?"

Tendrils that had fallen to chin-length before now fell over Jaye's forehead, and no further. The hair was even shorter around his ears, in back and around his neck. Dixon combed through the rich brown strands, over Jaye's scalp, and trimmed the rough spots. Jaye's lips twisted in a pleased grin and he stayed still while Dixon worked.

The tattoos were distracting, as was the scar. Dixon's gaze slipped over to the mirror and away, countless times, going to Jaye's dark nipples, to the black and grey inked blue jay wing wrapping his chest, the spiderweb etched in the skin around his left elbow, and the gnarled scar on his abdomen. Then his gaze snagged on something else, a mere glimpse of the edge of the fourth tattoo, peeking out from under the waistband of Jaye's pants, below his navel, right above his cock. It looked tribal. Dixon wanted to get down on his knees and drag his tongue over the inked skin there, to open Jaye's pants and follow the tattoo's trail with his mouth downward.

"Oh, come on, Dix. I'm sure you can guess *why*," Jaye suggested in barely a whisper. It was furtive and low. A raised eyebrow told Dixon Jaye had an idea of where the cop's thoughts just were.

Dixon dragged the comb up to catch hair, snipped some off. Jaye's skin pebbled. His nipples stiffened. Dixon pretended, unsuccessfully, not to notice even as his mouth watered.

Between snips of the scissors, Jaye moved, just a little. He shifted to rest his hands on the sink's surface, bending over slightly in front of

Dixon. His back curved in a graceful, sexy arc as he stuck out his ass a little, pushing it back toward Dixon's groin. Dixon's chest rose and fell heavily as he stayed right where he was, with Jaye's ass brushing against his crotch, in the perfect position to get fucked.

There was no smile left on Jaye's face, nor on Dixon's.

Dixon got the point before Jaye said a word.

"Where would *you* grab hold? Hmm? A few months ago, my hair was to the middle of my back. I'd been growing it since I was five. So, tell me, *Dix*, where would *you* grab hold if you suspected I'd try to fight back?"

His chest felt too tight. He set down the scissors and comb before backing away, needing some space and to be out of that dominant position. Dixon squeezed his eyes shut when they started to burn and his vision blurred. He felt Jaye move again but didn't chance a look.

When Jaye next spoke, it was closer. He had turned around to face his savior and followed him away from the sink. Dixon could feel the weight of Jaye's stare.

He couldn't stop imagining it—men forcing themselves on Jaye, wrapping their fists in his long, beautiful curls, yanking his head back hard enough to strain the hair's roots. It was horrifying.

"My hair was a symbol of my submissiveness. I want to break away from that part of who I've been. I thought it'd be good enough when I cut my ponytail off with scissors, but I could still feel it—the pulling. Especially in the dark. I know it's only my imagination, but I'm trying to put all of that behind me. It was survival. You did what you had to do. A different world than this one. But I'm not in that world anymore. I'm not that guy. It's the past. I'm strong enough to do it, Dix. You need to know that. Don't get the wrong idea of me. I'm not someone who needs to be saved and I'm not going to be one of those people who gets stuck in their past. I intend to have a future. Simple as that. I'm sorry if I freaked you out with my story, but you asked.

"Look at me."

Maybe it was because of Marcus, and Dixon's lingering past, but it felt true. Despite Jaye being younger and physically smaller, he seemed to hold power over Dixon. His will was stronger. He was willing to do more than Dixon was, when push came to shove. Jaye didn't have the law and the rules of other men to live by. He was free to do as he saw fit. When Dixon tried to imagine living that way and bravely, confidently heeding his own urges without fear, he couldn't do it. That kind of existence was separated from him by a large wall built of things Dixon had always deemed his responsibility.

Holding on to anger like it could lead him to the right answers, Dixon was slightly startled to feel the pad of Jaye's finger gently brush a tear from his cheek. Jaye smelled of soap and shampoo. The aroma of his skin and newly washed hair was clean and light, contrary to everything else. Dixon managed to open his eyes but couldn't yet meet Jaye's stare. He looked at the mirror instead and combed his fingers through the clipped-short hair at the back of Jaye's head. It was decadently soft.

He's not the one that's screwed up. I am.

"Looks good," Dixon muttered.

"Liar," Jaye teased.

But it did look good. The shorter haircut enhanced the angles of Jaye's flawless bone structure and drew attention to the handsomeness of his features. His eyes seemed even bigger, more beautiful, and brighter. Knowing he should stop touching, Dixon's hand skated defiantly lower, to the hair at the nape of Jaye's neck, then over his tattoo—his blue jay. The backs of his fingers brushed lightly over the ink, the bird's body in flight. The thicker lines were slightly raised. He could trace them without looking. Then his fingertips slipped down to the wing curled protectively around Jaye's chest, the other visible in the mirror and extending across Jaye's back.

The light skin-on-skin contact made Jaye shiver slightly. The skin under Dixon's fingers tightened. Jaye's head tilted slightly, exposing more of his neck to be touched. But, too aware of how much of Jaye's skin was bare and begging to be groped, Dixon fought the urge. They were standing too close again. He could feel Jaye's breath warming his neck. Dixon's hand fell farther, the knuckles skimming down Jaye's arm, over the blue cobweb.

He turned away and walked out of the bathroom.

With both arms curled over his head, his hands holding it, Dixon took a deep breath and tried to get it together. He'd come there to tell Jaye about the job, and get out. That was all. But he could feel that Jaye had followed him and was right at Dixon's back, inches away, solid and warm, breathtaking and wanting.

Get out. Get away.

Listen to yourself for once in your goddamned life and leave before you make things worse.

In searching for a safer position, wanting to put temptation farther at bay but not brave enough to leave entirely, Dixon went to the couch. He sank down and sat back into it. Jaye just followed him down. Straddling Dixon's lap, he pressed closer and closer until his pelvis was positioned directly over Dixon's crotch. His hipbones were exposed, the jeans too loose, too low.

Tell him to stop. You can say stop, can't you? Or do you need to hide behind that fucking badge to act like a real man?

Tell him to stop.

Say it!

The protest sat right on the tip of Dixon's tongue, but then Jaye said, "Yesterday, on the phone...."

Embarrassment and guilt silenced Dixon right away. He bowed his head to hide his expression, but then Jaye wrapped a hand behind Dixon's neck and dipped his head to scratch his teeth just below Dixon's earlobe. Jaye's hips rolled forward, grinding.

Oh fuck. Oh God.

Stop. Stop him. Get up. Get out. Now.

Ignoring his conscience, not listening to anything but instinct, Dixon's left hand came up, fast, caressing. Jaye's right nipple was trapped between the side of Dixon's bent index finger and the pad of his thumb. Pinching and twisting, Dixon listened to Jaye's soft exhale. Reacting to the stimulation, his hips tilted more sharply forward. Dixon's right hand pushed down inside the back of the jeans. His middle finger stroked through Jaye's crack. Dixon grunted, pushing harder, wanting to feel it—Jaye's puckered knot. He wanted to go too far so his conscience couldn't try to yank him back. They'd be too far gone.

Self-destructive, aren't ya, Dixie? Marcus knew that. He loved to push that button, and you let him. You let him for years.

Gasping softly into Dixon's hair, Jaye tensed, hissing under his breath, "*Fuck.*"

He couldn't get his hand in far enough. The denim was pulled too tight by Jaye's pose, but Dixon couldn't or wouldn't stop. With his left hand, he roughly ripped open the fly of Jaye's jeans. He yanked them down lower. Not wasting a second, his middle finger went right back to Jaye's crack.

Jaye's brow creased with delicate frown lines. Rising up slightly on Dixon's lap, he muffled a moan in Dixon's neck as Dixon pulled Jaye's cheeks apart with both hands and traced his rim with the fingertip.

"Dix...." Jaye tried, sounding startled by the suddenness, the roughness. His voice wavered.

The finger pressed in, popping through the ring of muscle dry. Jaye let out a broken, throaty cry against Dixon's skin and came farther up off of Dixon's lap as the thick, long digit pressed inch-by-inch into him, gripped by the soft, snug heat of his sphincter.

Need obliterated rationality. Dixon sighed heavily with pleasure at getting to violate the gorgeous creature on his lap. The fingers of his free hand went back to Jaye's nipple and twisted it sharply while tugging the finger inside him slowly out.

"*Fuck.*"

Jaye's fingers clawed at Dixon's neck and back.

Dixon was gone. He started to pump the finger, in and out, finger-fucking Jaye until he was gasping, feet flexed and tensed from head to toe, just taking it. Jaye's mouth fell open, searching for air. After a little while, he began to ride Dixon's hand, pushing down against it like he wanted more.

Dixon growled and flipped them sideways. Jaye landed on his back on the couch with Dixon atop him. The jeans got yanked down farther. The finger was still pumping. Dixon buried his face in the side of Jaye's neck, sucked hard on his inked skin and wrapped Jaye's stiffened cock in a tight fist, stroking, squeezing with his index finger and thumb just underneath the head, swiping over the silky crown with his thumb.

Trapped, Jaye's legs were curled up between them, tangled in the jeans. Dixon watched Jaye's ingrained instinct to submit and not fight back kick in. Dixon tugged his captive's dripping cock, triggering nerve endings under the ridge. It went on and on. Jaye shuddered, making a shattered, pleading, wordless sound as he shot come over

Dixon's fingers and himself. Exploring, fondling, Dixon kept touching Jaye's dick as he shivered through the orgasm. Dixon's middle finger slid out of Jaye's tightly clenched ass. The hand came away. Jaye reached down to hold his legs up, waiting for Dixon to fuck him.

Gonna fuck you, piggy. Gonna fuck you up. We know you want it. You piggy whore.

Anguish twisted Jaye's expression. Amazingly, the fight instinct he thought was long gone started to kick in but Dixon wasn't moving and wouldn't be moved. Telling Dixon about the forced sex and rapes seemed to have brought out Jaye's ghostly buddies, despite the brightness of the surroundings. The abruptness of getting stripped and fingered when he'd been sure Dixon was going to bolt had tripped Jaye up. But he was naked, spread, covered in his own mess, and he'd asked for it, so it was time to follow through.

Dixon was still in uniform, though. He had a gun, handcuffs, a baton....

Where'd you hide it, Johnny? Only two places it could be. Better check both.

Jaye grunted, closed his eyes, and tensed up more. He had to block out the voices.

How's that stick feel in there, piggy? Gonna squeal? Gonna cry?

If you love how that stick feels, you better mind your manners. Say thank you. Say thank you, sir. Say fuck me harder with your baton, sir.

Jaye groaned. He breathed through it, taking deep inhales through his nose and blowing the air out through his lips.

Quivering, he forced himself to open his eyes and ask Dixon, "You gonna fuck me or what?" almost swallowing the words.

"You'd know it if I was. You believe me?"

"Yes," Jaye answered tightly, nodding once, too, since Dixon seemed to demand it. Dixon was still tracing Jaye's shaft and head with his fingertips, smearing semen. Two violently strong, opposing needs warred within him. He needed the touching to stop, but he also needed to lure Dixon in and keep him hooked. The second need was more important. "You were fucking someone yesterday."

"Yeah. I was."

"Who?"

"No one that matters. Someone that says yes when I need him to. That's all it was. He's not someone I'm interested in."

Dixon's hand pivoted at the wrist and rubbed down, firmly, over Jaye's balls. He took them in hand, circling his fingers around the base of Jaye's sac. It was gentle and foreign enough to help distance the memories. Focusing on the feel of Dixon's hand, Jaye pushed away the rest. Dixon wanted him. Dixon had him. That was all that mattered. Feeling absolutely possessed, struggling with the heady pleasure that brought, Jaye's gaze jumped up to the ceiling, fixing there.

"I'd never hurt you. You believe me?"

No.

"Sure," Jaye managed.

"I don't play games. If I'm going to fuck someone, they know it, because we have an understanding. Only then do I take what I want. Or they take what they want. That's how it works. No games."

There's always games.

Say thank you. Say fuck me harder, sir. How's that feel, piggy?

A shaky exhale slipped through Jaye's controls. He bit down on the inside of his cheek, trying to be still and relax. He thought this would be easier. He'd forgotten how there'd been a learning curve with Cash, too, before he grew to know what to expect.

"Now," Dixon continued. "You offered me a thank you. That can be thank you. I'm telling you now, sex has always been something that I take or is taken from me. That's how I work. I like it rough and I like to switch. Fair warning. I want you to think about that."

You like it rough, Johnny? You gonna let the piggy cop rape you? Piggy cop's gonna fuck you up.

Say thank you.

Jaye made a tight moan as it began to overwhelm him. Immediately, Dixon chased his mouth, catching it in a soft press of lips, greedily drinking down each of Jaye's gasps. "Breathe," Dixon urged.

"Okay," Jaye murmured. He took hold of Dixon's head in both hands and kissed him back, still waiting for more, for anything. Though his ghosts were feeding on his fear, Jaye's body was throbbing, aching in only good ways. It begged to be used, be manhandled and fucked for hours. He would go through with it if he had the chance, giving himself over to Dixon no matter what Jaye's feelings on the matter were. His feelings were inconsequential. All that mattered was surviving.

Dixon sucked on Jaye's lower lip and kept him in hand. His thumb brushed back and forth over the soft, wrinkled skin of his scrotum, making him shiver, making him want. The caresses were slow and light, warm and real. They helped him fight the ghosts and keep going.

Say thank you. Say fuck me harder, sir.

You like it rough, Johnny?

So far, Jaye had always been the pusher, the one with the control. He'd pushed Dixon for more, for sex, for intimacy. Now it was all flipped. Dixon was pushing. Most of Jaye's experiences with pushers were bad ones. Jaye felt out of his element, overpowered, and held fast.

Look at those burning lights, you dumb shit, he told himself. *Feel that warm air. You bought those. Time to pay.*

"You've been through hell," Dixon said, looking directly into Jaye's eyes, demanding more of his attention. The more Dixon made Jaye listen up, the quieter the ghosts became. "That stops now. No one and nothing hurts you anymore like they did. I don't want there to be anything you feel like you can't tell me. You need to get something out, get it out. No judging, no consequences. Okay?"

Where'd you hide it, Johnny?

"Okay," Jaye nodded.

"I'm scaring you."

"No," Jaye argued.

"Be honest."

Jaye took a filling breath, held it and let it out. "I was surprised. That's all." "You sure?" Dixon was scrutinizing Jaye's expression, his words. No one had ever paid such close attention to him before. An unfamiliar pang of self-consciousness drew him completely out of his head. Gratitude for Dixon's continued, intense focus started to turn Jaye on, increasing his bashfulness which only made Jaye want to spread for him more. It was a different sort of cycle, spiraling into desire instead of dread.

Dixon let go of Jaye's sac, rubbed a flattened hand up his shaft. It twitched into the touch, struggling to get hard again. This time, Jaye's breath caught in a different way. He thrust up against Dixon's hand for more.

"You like that?"

Unable to speak, Jaye's lips parted and his eyes slipped closed.

Dixon took his hand away, planting it with his other by Jaye's head, leaning down over him. "I'll back off until you've had time to think about what I said."

Glancing down, he saw Jaye's cock getting fuller, darker. "This is your call. With your history, I don't know if I'm the right guy for you. I can't change who I am any more than you can change who you are."

"Got it," Jaye whispered.

Dixon got up off the couch. Jaye stayed frozen where he was.

"The-the job...." Jaye started warily.

"I don't have any information yet. I'll let you know when I do. It was a busy day, so I haven't checked all of my messages."

Because Dixon was staring, groping unabashedly with his eyes, and Jaye was still shaken up, he let his feet come down flat to the cushions, knees still bent and tucked up to disguise his erection. Then his hand came down, too, to cover himself.

"Let me know when you've thought about what I said, if you're interested or not. If I don't hear from you, I'll call when I know about the job. Other than that, though, I'll leave you alone."

Dixon straightened himself up and left quietly. Jaye didn't move a muscle. He stayed passive, silent, and guarded until he heard Dixon drive away. Sighing heavily, he covered his face with a hand and waited for his heart to stop beating so fast, murmuring repeatedly, "Oh my god. Oh my god. Oh my *god*."

Chapter 10

Let's Make a Deal

Three days later, Jaye had a message on his cell from Dixon. He had watched the phone light up as Dixon called. It rang and rang and rang before voicemail picked it up. The weight of everything that message could contain was a foreboding weight in his gut. The tiny, seemingly insignificant icon telling him unquestionably that Dixon's voice was waiting to be heard, recorded and saved, had an effect like a siren, blaring in Jaye's head.

For so long, every aspect of Jaye's life was under the control of outside forces. The guards. The gang. The judicial system. Society. The terrifying, glorious freedom after his release was so foreign, it pushed Jaye hard into a place of fear and hesitancy. But now he was being moved again. Invisible hands were pushing him and he had to go where they led.

Dixon was one of the good guys, a cop who just happened to intend to fuck the hell out of Jaye, probably quite regularly, but only if given the formal, proper go-ahead first. It should have been less of an intimidating prospect than getting regularly fucked by Cash.

Somehow it wasn't.

First off, cops, guards and anyone who tried to use the law as a weapon felt threatening to Jaye. It was like the whole world had chosen sides. The cops, guards, and lawyers were on one side. Jaye, Cash, and everyone who had done right by Jaye in prison were on the other. In that game, Dixon was on the wrong side.

Also, Cash had been strangely pacified by the fact that Jaye was willing to give it up whenever it was wanted, without so much as a word of protest. He didn't love Jaye. It was carnal pleasure. It was fucking, getting off, purging some of the tension and filling some of the boredom.

Yes, it was companionship, too. Jaye's loyalty, his beauty, his sensuality all helped to give Cash more status in the eyes of his brothers and his enemies. Cash was grateful. Most of the time he wasn't rough, he was tender. He didn't make it complicated. If he pulled on Jaye's hair and held him down, it was just part of the act to show the other guys who was in charge, at all times. What the other guys in the gang couldn't know just from getting to watch, was that Cash *was* careful. He encouraged Jaye to act like it hurt, that it felt more intense than it did. Sure, Jaye was submissive. He was Cash's little bitch for two years, every day. Jaye got fucked no matter who was around, or what they said while it happened. He took it. He shut the hell up, didn't protest unless Cash wanted him to for the act, but that's what it was — an act.

Cash came through on his end of the deal. He made sure Jaye was untouched. If someone *did* touch Jaye, they paid for it, dearly. It was a simple, wonderful equation.

With Dixon, all of the emotional and physical safety Jaye felt with Cash was gone. If Jaye got involved with Dixon, all bets were off. Sure, he'd be taken care of in other ways. His survival in the most literal sense would be ensured, and that was a big deal when you were on your own in brutal, frozen wilderness. But his body, his head, and his heart were all fair play. He hadn't expected Dixon's intensity or his demons. So far, Dixon had felt like a bad combination of Cash's dangerous side mixed evenly with the guards' dangerous sides.

Missing Cash so much it astounded him, Jaye ignored the message on his phone as long as he could. He did sit-ups, pushups, pull-ups — anything to keep busy. He cleaned and organized the cabin, played absentmindedly with the shockingly short strands of his hair, cooked himself a meal and stared out at the horizon through the windows as if waiting for his fate to race over the white-tipped mountains, over the expansive miles and right up to his doorstep.

Jaw set, teeth gritted, eyes squeezed shut, Jaye played the message after hours had gone by, unable to fend off curiosity anymore, wanting to get it over with.

The deep, hushed rasp of Dixon's voice instantly stiffened Jaye's nipples, pebbled his skin and stirred his cock, though what he actually said was innocent enough. The job started in two days' time. Jaye had to fill out some paperwork and either call or come down to meet the boss lady before he started his first shift.

"Call me," Dixon said in goodbye.

"No fucking way, man," Jaye replied to the machine before decisively turning off the phone.

"You coming home tonight? I'm making lasagna, your favorite," Brekken said, dangling the words like a carrot before a horse. "Or are you doing more overtime?"

"I don't know yet. If I'm not home in time, save me some, okay?" Dixon answered. His voice seemed to carry far in the empty locker room, though the space wasn't all that big.

"Could you *try* to be there? You've been a phantom these past few days. We never see you. Stop working so hard and relax for once."

"Too much going on to relax," he murmured, glancing around for anyone who may be eavesdropping.

"At work?"

"Sometimes," he answered, thinking about Marcus, about Sacha, and, most of all, about Jaye. "Look. I appreciate the offer. I'll do my best to be on time. Deal?"

"Deal," his sister agreed, seeming content with that much.

He hung up the phone, tucked it away and headed out.

"Going out on a call?" the trooper behind the desk asked.

"Nah, gonna grab some lunch." Dixon smiled politely, too distracted for the grin to be sincere, sliding his sunglasses up the bridge of his nose. The sun was glaring with not a cloud in sight as he pushed through the building's front door. He was about to barrel down the steps to his Expedition when a sudden obstacle stopped him abruptly.

Someone was seated on the stairs, bundled in layers of clothes. Dixon knew right away, without question, who it was.

"The hell are you doing here?" he blurted before he could stop himself.

Jaye stood, turning to face Dixon. Both of his hands were shoved way down in his pockets. The hood of his sweatshirt was pulled up to conceal most of his head. "You said you had papers for me," he replied with all innocence, his expression unreadable.

"It's fucking *miles* from your cabin!" He tried to rein in the anger in his voice, but couldn't seem to. His face felt stretched too tight, burning suddenly too hot, his clothes too constricting even as the frigid air nipped at all exposed skin. As he mentally tried to track the huge distance between headquarters and where Jaye Larson lived, Dixon continued to sputter stupidly. "You *walked*?"

"I'm not an invalid," Jaye countered defensively, his voice unusually softened and lacking its usual cocky bravado. "I wanted to get some air, stretch my legs. It's still kind of novel to be able to step out my door and keep going as far as I want to."

"So next time *call me* and I'll come pick you up or walk with you! What if I wasn't here? I could easily have been up north. Hell, I was yesterday and the day before that."

"Then I would've walked back home," Jaye told him coolly but warily. His eyes darted back and forth, searching for onlookers or trouble, his shoulders hunched against the cold mid-day air. When he appeared to detect no one else nearby, he took a half-step closer and whispered with his head slightly bowed but his eyes upturned and locked on Trooper Rowe, "I think we both know what would've happened if I called you. You would have come over to drop off the paperwork. We have more to talk about than my job, don't we, trooper?"

Looking hard back into Jaye's green eyes, Dixon felt the rest of the world fall away. They were both back there again. They weren't standing outside together in the freezing light of day for everyone who cared to look, they were back in the cozy confines of the cabin. Jaye was taking Dixon's finger, riding it with little pushes, his dick dark, hard, heavy, and sliding slick with pre-come inside Dixon's hand. Dixon remembered the particular expression on Jaye's pretty face as his climax hit and with that memory, much of Dixon's control broke.

Screw the fact that they were out in public and outside of Dixon's workplace, baser needs were more important.

Jaye must have seen it happen because his expression tensed with warning. A muscle in his jaw twitched as he said severely, "*Don't.*"

Dixon realized he had taken a step toward Jaye with the intent to do something about the raw lust that had dug its claws deeply into him.

It hit Dixon then that he already felt like Jaye was *his*—to have, to protect, to safeguard with rules, to ravage and hide away for his own private pleasures. That was wrong. They hadn't agreed on anything. Dixon had no right to feel the way he felt.

He had crossed the line, like an asshole, like Marcus.

As Dixon wiped a gloved hand over his face and composed himself, Jaye hissed to him under his breath, "*That's* why I walked. I'm here about the job. I'm ready to get the hell out of that cabin and make some of my own damn money like a man instead of a kept boy."

"*You* started this," Dixon practically growled, lashing out, resenting the backpedaling, the shift in temperament. "You came on to me like I've never *seen* before. *Begging me* for it."

"I know," Jaye grimaced. "But, see, we're kind of at the crux of it, aren't we? We go any farther, there's no going back. I need to make sure I'm getting what *I* want before you get what *you* want. 'Cause, Dix, I know for fuckin' sure what it is *you* want."

Smiling coolly, Dixon marveled at it, the proof of how Jaye survived this long—the iron in his blood, the determination to survive, above all else.

They both heard the low sound of voices approaching. Jaye turned his back and started to walk away, toward Dixon's Expedition. With a tilt of his head and a sly glance, he beckoned Dixon to follow.

Unlocking the doors with a press of the button on the key fob in his hand, Dixon called, "Get in the front," when Jaye at first only lingered by the side of the vehicle. With a roll of his eyes and a furtive glance at the station's entrance, Jaye got in the passenger side while Dixon slid into the driver's seat.

Many things occurred to Dixon at once. Marcus would be coming back to town soon. The town would, likewise, be busy for the next few weeks as people did their traveling before winter truly hit. The truck stop would be bustling. All kinds of people would be passing through. And Jaye would be out there, at work, dealing with them every day. Townsfolk would notice the tattoos and the general look of him. They would talk. If attractive young Jaye was seen with Dixon, then people would *really* talk.

"I could pay you," Dixon began, not even looking at Jaye, really. He stared straight ahead when he said it, like he was talking to the trees or the frost.

"The fuck you could," Jaye replied defensively. "I'm not a whore. *This* is one of my conditions. You take me to talk to your friend about the job, right now, *before* we talk about the rest of it."

A small battle raged inside of Dixon. He really did want Jaye to just be his, and his alone, without others knowing or gossiping. The idea of Jaye as Dixon's private secret was an alluring one. It sickened him a little to realize he did want that. Because then he turned it around and asked himself what he'd think if Marcus wanted Dixon to quit his job and stay home to be ready to fuck and satisfy at a moment's notice.

"What's it gonna be, Dix?"

Gonna fuck you so hard, 'til you're raw and aching. Gonna fuck that tough edge right out of your sweet voice.

That was Marcus talking, but Dixon felt like he was getting closer to that place of taking out his own issues on someone else, and that was a terrifying prospect.

Then, softer, "What's it gonna be, huh?"

"I'm not like them. I won't treat you like shit, or like I own you."

"But you will. Own me."

Dixon's hands wrapped around the steering wheel, because it was safer. He couldn't turn his head to look at the living, breathing bribe sitting at his side.

When Jaye next spoke, all of the iron was gone. His voice was soft and rich, low and coaxing.

"What's it gonna be?"

Dixon decided. "Okay. I take you to talk to her, sign some papers. We'll get it all confirmed. Then I take you home. You'll get what you want first. Then, I get what I want."

He finally was able to turn and look Jaye in the eyes. There was so much burning there Dixon almost surged forward over the armrest to take hold of him. The need to touch and be close was that strong.

"Deal?"

A small, wicked grin twisted up one side of Jaye's lips. The look he gave Dixon was like he was naked and spreading right there in the damn Expedition.

"I think we have ourselves a deal, Trooper Rowe. Nice doing business with you."

And Dixon wondered if the whole thing was an act, a ploy to get Jaye everything he could possibly want. Suspecting he had been played, Dixon found he didn't really give a shit and promptly gunned the engine so they could get on their way.

The visit to the truck stop was nerve-wracking for Jaye. Gasoline and diesel pumps were arranged neatly outside. A massive garage adjoined a shop that offered food and supplies. Once they were there, strolling through the entrance and into the main building, he was intensely alert. He mapped the geography of the place as they proceeded inside, down the hallway that led to the restrooms as well as an employee-only area, noting the exits, the places to hide, and the places to beware of since they were full of customers—strangers capable of anything.

He took off his coat and his sweatshirt, folding them both over an arm. He had been wearing his nicest shirt underneath and glanced down to make sure he hadn't sweat through the fabric on his walk and tense confrontation with Rowe. The rest was a blur of color and noise. The unnatural harshness of the fluorescent lights, the whistling of the wind outside, prying at the windows, doors and edges of the structure, the restless chatter of conversation echoing off the walls—it was all eerily familiar.

"Okay. Okay," he murmured under his breath, grounding himself to reality, reminding himself where he wasn't.

Dixon led the way to a back room, secluded from the bustle of the shop. It had a couple of desks in it, some filing cabinets and bulletin boards. A massive map of Alaska filled one wall. The floors were covered with cheap carpet. The drop ceiling above their heads, slightly yellowed with age, helped banish the cavernous feel the rest of the building had.

He shook hands with a woman named Tammy Jean Polk and made the introductions. Tammy Jean had graying hair she wore twisted up in a messy bun behind her head. Her gaze was keen, and she bustled around them, setting a few things in order before closing the office door and gesturing to a pair of chairs. Jaye saw her look at his tattoos as she sat across from them — the teardrop first, then his jay — bearing it with a patient smile. There was nothing he could do about his inked skin, so it wasn't worth being concerned about.

The three of them talked, with Jaye saying the least, yet he made an effort to come off as confident, professional and capable. Throughout the private conversation, he could hear the muffled chatter of customers from outside of the small office. The lights buzzed. The danger from simply being out in public — where anyone could see and get to him if they wanted to — was so tangible he could smell it. Threat was a sour hint of blood and mayhem in the air. It was all distraction, added on to the ever-present nagging of his ghosts and phobias.

But, when the papers for his application were slid his way, he felt a knot of trepidation loosen in his chest. Smiling with genuine happiness, he filled out his name, his address, and the name of Dixon, his reference. Tammy Jean was smiling, too, when it was all finished and official.

Unable to remember the last time something that positive had happened to him, Jaye told her, "Thank you. Really, you don't know what this means to me. Thanks for giving me a chance."

"Hell, everyone deserves a chance," she agreed. "Welcome to the team."

"You said that guy you were fucking was just a lay. Is that true of all the guys you fuck, or has there been someone *special*?"

Piggy cop's gonna fuck you up. Gonna fuck you, Johnny. Say thank you.

Examining the object of his fascination, Jaye turned sideways in the passenger seat as they drove back to the cabin. The window's glass was cool behind his head. The hood on his sweatshirt was pulled up to hide his newly shorn hair and, to some extent, his face, too.

The thick fabric dulled the chill, just a little. While he still had all of those layers of clothing to hide under, he wanted to pick away at some of the mystery that was Dixon Rowe. He needed some ammunition, some facts to work with.

It wasn't exactly a tough question, but Rowe hesitated anyway. It was curious. He wasn't being shy. There was something else going on. That was clear enough. His jaw clenched, and his posture stiffened. Most telling of all, his lip almost curled up in a sneer of distaste. His eyes bored holes in the road before their tires crunched over it.

Where are you hiding it, Johnny?

Two long ghost fingers reached down Jaye's esophagus. He cleared his throat, rubbed a hand over his short hair and tried to close off parts of his head. It was Dixon who needed to talk, not him.

"Nah," Dixon muttered. "No one special."

"You fuckin' liar. Tell me. It's not like I'm gonna judge the hell out of you. Think who you're talkin' to right now."

There still was no answer at first, but he was working on it, Jaye saw. Shifty eyes, bitten tongue, white knuckles—Rowe answered without saying a word.

"How long were you together?"

"Too long," Dixon grunted through his teeth, gaze locked to the horizon.

"I know how that goes. Why don't you like to talk about it?"

"Complicated."

"When'd you break up?"

"Why do you care?"

"Because you're taking me home to fuck. Right? I feel like that gives me leeway to ask some damn questions, don't you? Unless you're just gonna drop me off with a wave and a smile. In that case, I'll mind my own damn business. But if you expect me to agree to function as your happy human sex toy for the foreseeable future, you need to cough up some back-story here. I already know you have a fuck buddy tied away. You're acting like our agreement is more important to you than that, but you've also got a major bitchface right now from the mere mention of your ex and that's a big, angry, red flag, so be straight with me. When did you break up?"

"Recently, okay?" It was said more defensively than anything else. Jaye analyzed leisurely, tracing patterns on the textured plastic of the dashboard's surface.

"How fuckin' recently? You seem pretty sore about it."

Dixon laughed maliciously at that and finally glanced his way, shooting a complex look at Jaye.

"Yeah. I was *sore*."

"Can you drop the act, please? I get it. We've all been through bad times."

Softening slightly, Dixon answered with less of that asshole quality in his voice. "I don't want you involved. He doesn't know I moved out. Probably. It's kind of hard to say. He's a crabber and a fisherman, so he's been at sea for months, working. I got out while he was gone."

There was a quiet pause. They turned as a bend in the road came up slowly. Dixon's hands crossed over one another as he spun the wheel. "Possessive guy."

"I know the type."

"I bet you do," Dixon agreed, glancing in Jaye's direction again. His eyes slipped down Jaye's body instead of fixing firmly on his face.

"You mostly a bottom or a top? 'Cause you said you switch, though you seem like a top, but if this dude is so possessive...."

He waited for Dixon to fill in the blanks as Dixon literally squirmed in his seat, straightening up a bit, pushing his shoulders back, scratching an itch on the side of his nose. It was like he had his own ghosts making him twist in the wind.

"I switch," he admitted. "Marcus didn't. With him I bottomed."

"Yeah. Okay. Keep going," Jaye prodded.

"He's hung," Dixon said very reluctantly. "So he'd use that to his advantage. Sometimes he wasn't as gentle as he could've been. He liked it when it hurt, if you know what I mean. And he's not what you'd call a people person." *Gonna slice open your belly, piggy. Pull your insides out. Make you watch.*

Oh, come on, Johnny. I bet it doesn't hurt that much. Look at you, crying like a bitch.

Jaye's tongue turned to lead in his mouth. Phantoms filled the vehicle, distorting everything, corrupting it. Staring hard at Dixon Rowe but also not seeing him at all, Jaye fought hard not to slip back into bad memories of people who had been rough with him.

He was right. He probably isn't good for me. He's probably either the perfect guy for me or the worst one.

The sudden silence from Jaye prompted Dixon to keep talking after a few quick, expectant glances.

"I mean, it's not like he was abusive. He's a sadist, for sure. You know, bondage, toys, that whole deal. Maybe it's because I'm a cop. He's not fond of the law. My own damn fault for staying with him."

Jaye's fight instinct had always been strong. Even when he couldn't actively fight back, he always kept tabs for later, and revenge. Now he was picturing Dixon held down, or tied down, and staying there, willingly, with no thought for revenge, only self-recrimination. The idea made Jaye furious.

Quietly, Jaye admitted, "Guess that's where I've lucked out. Not too much bondage gear or sex toys in prison. It was more about efficiency there. In and out, so to speak. And my boyfriend from before was pretty tame when it came to sex. We hardly ever fucked, it was mostly blowjobs."

Dixon seemed to study Jaye's expression, reading the anger and hunger for violence in it, most likely. Talking about all of the shit in his and Dixon's lives and comparing sexual war stories as they were, it made Jaye want to lash out.

"What?" Dixon asked, sounding self-conscious. There was an edginess of a more submissive sort to his tone now, which Jaye was mesmerized by. Jaye had pushed, Dixon resisted. Jaye pushed harder, Dixon caved, admitting truths about his sex life and became meek, fast.

It had been a long time since Jaye had come across someone whose instinct was to bend at the first sign of trouble which didn't fit neatly into the bounds of the legal system. When it was merely man to man, Dixon cowered.

That made Jaye angry in new ways. He had been intimidated by the intensity of Dixon's passion, but now here was proof Dixon's passion had gotten him in exactly the sort of trouble Jaye managed to avoid. Everyone who had ever hurt Jaye had come away dead or bleeding. The man who hurt Dixon was still walking free, unharmed and probably eager to get Dixon back under his thumb.

Jaye just stared and shook his head, resolving to handle the fisher-man sadist in his own way once he showed his face again. Someone had to, and if Dixon couldn't do it, Jaye would.

Chapter 11
Dangerously Vulnerable

There were a lot of reasons why Dixon didn't want to bring up Marcus. Their history together was so murky, all of Dixon's friends and family knew it wasn't wise to broach the topic with him. They didn't like Marcus. Never had. But it was Dixon's life, his choices to make and not theirs. For a long time, Dixon didn't talk about their relationship with those closest to him simply because he was sick of the looks and snide comments.

It's not like Dixon went around broadcasting the information he had just given Jaye. For obvious reasons, his sister was never explicitly told about the sadomasochism and bondage, nor how hard it was to take Marcus's massive cock. Their disapproval stemmed more from how being with Marcus changed Dixon's personality.

He got quiet. Reserved. He stopped confiding in people. He spent all of his free time at home, and when they did see him, he wasn't usually in the best of moods.

Putting aside how much of an asshole Marcus could be, Dixon was mainly ashamed — for years — of how much pleasure he got out of the bondage and sexual torture. He liked the rough sex. He got off on how Marcus made sure Dixon knew who his ass belonged to. Dixon was Marcus's obsession. When it came right down to it, Dixon was the main focus of Marcus's attention, always. It was nice to have someone care that fiercely about him, to devote so much time and energy to indulging in the kinkiest types of sex together and taking Dixon apart in every possible glorious way.

Dixon wasn't ever proud of the fact that he happily let Marcus fuck him until he couldn't stand or had to call out from his shift at work, just to recover. The pain from receiving, from being spanked, paddled, whipped, milked dry, or enduring one of the many weird clamps, vises, chastity devices, plugs, beads, dildos of all shapes and sizes—Dixon welcomed it. He often begged for it. Marcus opened Dixon to a world he never dreamed could exist, full of every decadently taboo sexual indulgence imaginable.

That was a hard thing to let go of. But for all of Marcus's devotion, he didn't ever love Dixon like he wanted to be loved. What they had when they were together was something Dixon learned slowly, through many trials of the heart, was not good for him.

Now, Dixon was faced with explaining all of this to Jaye and having to live with the fact that someone Dixon desired to be with in many sorts of ways would know his darkest secrets. Marcus loved to use Dixon's unspoken fondness for perverse play against him. It became a tool used to make him submit. If Jaye found out what Dixon was willing to do, then he had that tool, too.

The danger was Dixon didn't want to be submissive to Jaye. Or, rather, he didn't want *only* that. He wanted to switch, to play both roles, or at least have the option to choose what he was in the mood for. He wanted to be able to dominate Jaye carefully, tenderly, and show him the benefits of some of the things Marcus showed Dixon.

If they went down that road, Dixon didn't know where it was going to lead. He felt protective of Jaye already; in ways he had never felt about another person. What happened when you mixed love with passion? He had never experienced something like that before, so he had no idea. He couldn't even speculate. The idea terrified him.

They got to the cabin. Dixon pulled on the gearshift and parked, pausing with his hand on the key in the ignition. Jaye had been perfectly silent for about ten minutes, staring hard at Dixon the whole time. It was unnerving.

"This can just be me dropping you off if that's what you want," Dixon told the steering wheel rather than Jaye.

"Why?"

"What do you mean, why?"

"You wanna get what's coming to you, don't you?"

"What is this, a test?" He turned to meet Jaye's brutal, hard stare, which he couldn't figure out at all. "You've been different. Ever since

I... Every time I see you, you're more different. I can't tell if you're pissed off or scared or what, so I'm not coming in if you don't—"

"You like it when it hurts."

It hung there, in the air between them, like a poison dart. Dixon didn't touch it, didn't dare.

So, Jaye continued, "You said *he* likes it when it hurts, but you wouldn't have stayed if you weren't into it, unless he had you so brainwashed you learned to like it just to survive. I want you to admit it. Admit you like it."

Dixon knew his face was getting red. He felt the heat of his blush, the swelling horror.

He couldn't admit to that. There was no way.

He was about to give up, to tell Jaye to get out so Dixon could drive off and be free of the conversation when Jaye said sharply, "Look at me, Rowe. Look at my face. Come on, I know you've got the balls. That's it."

Jaye leaned forward, decreasing the amount of space between them. It was a dangerous move because it made Dixon forget that he wanted to escape, to end this. The desire to touch Jaye's body came back, even if it meant terrible things might happen if he did.

Light green eyes peered out of the hooded shadows concealing most of Jaye's pretty features. His mouth was sealed shut, his slim body wound tight, like he was ready to spring at Dixon if he needed to. That confused Dixon enough to make it a little less terrible to have his darkest secret so scrutinized.

"You honestly think I'm going to get into shit with a guy who likes it when it hurts? Seriously, man?"

"Whoa. No, that's not—I never did anything to hurt anyone," Dixon protested. "I was his submissive. You know how that works, right? I don't get off on hurting people."

Strangely, that only seemed to make Jaye angrier. His nostrils flared and the frantic energy radiated from Jaye in a way that made Dixon want to put his hands up, palm out, to show he meant no harm, to try to talk him down. Totally lost, Dixon asked, "What'd I say? I'm not gonna hurt you. You—"

"Admit it!" Jaye barked.

"Okay! Fine! I admit it! I like when it hurts."

"Admit he hurt you!"

"Yeah. Fine. He did."

"Physically?"

"Physically," Dixon agreed. "Emotionally. Psychologically. You name it."

"He scared you?"

The need to defend himself, to show Jaye he wasn't the bad guy, egged him on, made the words tumble out before he could properly scrutinize them. "Fuck yeah, he scared me. Why do you think I moved out without telling him? Why do you think I don't want to talk about it?"

Jaye's top lip curled back in a vicious sneer. He bolted from the Expedition before Dixon could say another word. Roaring, Jaye kicked one of the tires. He did it again and again. Dixon climbed out, watched Jaye growl through bared teeth, his hands balled up into fists.

"Why are you so pissed at me?"

"Get in the fucking cabin!"

"What?" Dixon blinked.

"*Get in the fucking cabin!*"

"Okay. Calm down first."

Breathing hard, Jaye shot him a warning glance, still looking for a fight. Dixon had seen it before, countless times, with countless perps.

It was a standoff for a minute or so. Jaye's rage eventually subsided. Without another word, he fished out his keys and turned, stalking up to the door. Unlocking it, he pushed inside. Just to be safe, Dixon waited another minute before he followed.

By the time he was in the cabin, the lights were on. Jaye was crouched by the fireplace, lighting some kindling. His coat and sweatshirt had been peeled off and tossed aside on a chair. Dixon closed the front door and took his coat off, too.

Once the fire was going, Jaye stood and worked diligently at the small buttons of his dress shirt. Dixon set his duty belt and holster aside with his coat and vest, waiting to see what came next. The anticipation was killing him.

When he couldn't take it anymore, he said, "Jaye...."

Head bowed, Jaye faced him, pulling the unbuttoned shirt off. He was wearing a t-shirt underneath and it clung to him. When he walked up to Dixon, the musky scent of his body and how he was still vibrating with tense energy affected Dixon. The soft, dark curls of Jaye's hair begged to be touched, but Dixon's hands hung at his sides as Jaye began to slowly work Dixon's buttons open next. Jaye removed Dixon's shirt, then his undershirt, too. Finally, he moved to open Dixon's fly.

They needed talk about this. That was blazingly clear to Dixon—a shout in his brain. Jaye glanced up at him and, holding his stare, started to walk backwards, toward the bed. He twisted his t-shirt off, leaving him bare-chested, exposing the tattoos.

"Fuck," Dixon groaned, cursing himself, knowing the talk wasn't going to happen like he wanted it to.

Impulse took over.

Dixon closed the distance between them as Jaye pushed his pants down with both hands, to the tops of his thighs. He wasn't wearing underwear.

Dixon got one glimpse of the tribal tattoo—all jagged edges and woven lines—extending down Jaye's pelvis before falling to his knees. The mark stretched downward from below his navel, stopping just above the root of his dick. Grasping Jaye's hipbones, Dixon fit his thumbs in the indentations just inside them, his fingers wrapping the sides of Jaye's ass. Steadying with a firm grip, Dixon moved his lips in a slow drag over the tattoo. Smooth skin and fine hair tickled them. Taking a lick, he tasted the salty tang of sweat.

Jaye's fingers scratched over Dixon's scalp, tugging at his short hair. Dixon heard him breathing, the struggle of it. A slight tremor worked its way through Jaye's body.

Sucking the flat of Jaye's lower abdomen, the defiantly inked skin, Dixon felt him getting hard. As Jaye's cock swelled and rose, it nudged him. After a light scrape of Dixon's teeth, Jaye hissed, "Shit."

Dixon's mouth shifted its target only slightly. Burying his face against Jaye's cock, nuzzling it as it thickened and strained, Dixon chased it with his lips, lightly brushing the tightening skin with them as Jaye struggled to fight the challenging enemies of nerves and lust.

Getting off on it, drawing it out, Dixon took his time, loving the sound of Jaye's ragged breaths and hushed curses. When he finally took the head into his mouth, sucking on it, Jaye was fully hard and clearly losing the battle to play it cool. He had been holding Dixon's head, but his hands fell away as soon as Dixon tasted clear fluid dripping from the slit. He licked it away, sucked to pull more out. He took Jaye deeper, inch-by-inch, into his throat, not stopping until his lips were wrapping the base, touching Jaye's tattoo again. Humming his pleasure at being allowed to do what he was doing, Dixon glanced upward.

Jaye had brought both hands up to his shortened hair and was holding his head. With a hard grunt, Jaye thrust once, reflexively, his body undulating, and covered his face.

Dixon steadied him by renewing his grip on Jaye's hips and started taking long pulls, working his mouth on Jaye, wanting it to feel good for him. Jaye's shaft was so hard and hot, it slid easily on Dixon's tongue. The hands masking Jaye's face fell away, and when they did, his lips were parted, his brow furrowed against the suction and stimulation.

Pulling off, Dixon squeezed twice, up and down Jaye's cock, rubbing the head, making him thrust against the tugging. As his fingers slid through saliva, Dixon suckled the bulbous, plum-shaped head. The tip of his tongue wriggled at the divot on the underside.

He watched Jaye's every reaction. Taking wide licks over his slit, he devoured the taste of his pre-come.

Easing the pants down further on Jaye's thighs, Dixon reached between Jaye's legs. He caressed up the soft hair covering his thigh, over the curve of his ass, cupping it. A moment later, his fingers sought the crack, rubbing through it, pulling the muscles of his cheeks apart. With two fingers, Dixon rubbed over the wrinkled knot of the hole, concentrating on the spot. They drew away for just a moment so Dixon could lick them wet, then returned to their place. While the tip of his tongue worked diligently at the tiny opening in the end of Jaye's cock, Dixon inserted the tips of two wet fingers into him. He felt Jaye clench, then relax a little when the fingers didn't try to go farther.

Stroking him slowly, focused intently on his companion's face, Dixon asked, "This is mine now?"

"Yeah," Jaye answered gruffly, his voice roughened. Dixon pushed his fingers fractionally deeper, spread them apart within the ring of muscle and loved that it made Jaye whimper. With his free hand, Dixon played with Jaye's cock. It slipped easily in his hand with the lube of saliva. "Thank you for the job."

"You're welcome."

Dixon's fingers burrowed deeper, pressing into Jaye's ass until they were half buried in the hot, silken vise.

"*Fuck*," Jaye hissed.

"Explain our arrangement for me. Right now."

The fingers tugged slowly back until they were out. Rubbing up through the crack of Jaye's ass, down again to stroke his rim in little circles, Dixon waited. He pushed back inside and pumped his fingers in slow, regular strokes. With his other hand, he fondled Jaye's balls. They had drawn up tight, so he pulled down on them, stretching the skin.

Jaye shuddered, grunted, and struggled for a voice. "I, uh... moth-er*fuck*. Okay. Um, I don't let anyone but you touch me. Anytime you want sex, whenever, wherever, however, it's your call. I'll be ready."

"What if you're not in the mood?" His hand closed loosely around Jaye's balls, reached up to enclose his dick, too. The fingers in Jaye's ass pushed as deep as he could reach and spread apart, coaxing the muscle loose. "You have a safe word?"

"No safe word. If I have to say no, I'll say it, but I've never had to say no before. It's my job to be ready. I'll be into it."

"Hands behind your head. Lace your fingers together. Good."

Jaye complied, making little gasps, face flushed, body thrumming. He was tight and just defiant enough to make it that much hotter. That tough guy act remained and it made Dixon want to fuck him into compliance, to stuff a cock up his pretty-boy ass and see how tough he was then. Jaye wasn't acting like this was old news, no big deal, just sex, like he made it sound. He was acting like a nervous, overwhelmed kid. That was hot, too. Maybe it was an act. *Probably*, it was an act, but Dixon didn't care. It was convincing enough to not matter.

Fingers laced behind his shorn curls, eyes averted, Jaye bore the fingers stuck way up inside his body with sharp little exhales, shivering subtly.

Dixon rubbed an opened hand up over the firm expanse of Jaye's abs, admiring how hard and heavy his cock was, how perfect his ass was.

"And if I want to handcuff you? Lay out my favorite toys to play with you for a while? Or play with this?" He wrapped his hand around Jaye's erection from above and pulled down on it, pressing it to another angle while keeping a tight grip on the head. "Is that okay?"

"Y-yes," Jaye managed, but his voice wavered on the word, lilting up. His hands were still laced behind his head, his eyes trained up to the ceiling.

"What do you want from *me*?" He freed his fingers in order to get Jaye's pants off. After sliding them down his legs, Dixon guided his feet out.

"Protect me. Make sure I don't freeze or starve."

"Turn around. That's it?"

Dixon stood, taking a minute to find a condom. After rolling it on, he spit into a hand and slicked the saliva over it. He bent Jaye over with a hand to his back, pressing lightly. His ass was stuck out, hands planted on the bed and feet shifted apart on the floor. His ribcage expanded with each gulp of air.

Staring at the sight of that tight, sweet ass, Dixon caressed up his back, soothingly. His palm brushed down Jaye's spine, over the outside of his thigh. "Just treat me good. It's not rocket science, you know."

"No," Dixon agreed, "But I want to be clear on things. Perfectly clear."

Fitting the head of his cock against Jaye's hole, Dixon savored the moment. The sight of Jaye's ass, bent over for him, burned into Dixon's brain. His cheeks squeezed around the end of Dixon's dick. When Dixon added pressure, thrusting while drawing Jaye back onto him, Jaye relaxed his knees, bending them as he exhaled with a moan. The moan sharpened and grew louder when Dixon breached him, popping through the rim. Dixon tugged gently back against Jaye's outer ring, then thrust farther into him.

With a thick groan, Dixon stopped talking just long enough to work his way into his conquest. He needed to make it final, to claim his stake before saying any more. When he was fully seated, Jaye was gasping, sweating, and cursing. Dixon could feel every quiver, every clench. They both paused to breathe, getting more comfortable. Taking his time, Dixon caressed over Jaye's chest, his stiffened nipples, then down over his abs and his pelvis, finally to Jaye's straining cock.

Dixon was motionless, balls-deep, just stroking gently along Jaye's erection, dragging open-mouthed kisses over his dark curls. All of the toughness had seemed to disappear. In that moment, Jaye felt purely vulnerable in Dixon's arms. He was so terribly young, had been so mistreated. It was up to Dixon now, to take proper care of him, no matter what that meant.

"You want me to care about you?" he asked.

"Not part of the deal," Jaye grunted. Speaking seemed to be a struggle for him.

"Isn't it better if I give a damn?"

"Just fuck me."

"Fuck you without caring?"

Holding Jaye by the hips, Dixon drew back, then pressed back in. Jaye's left arm came up to hook behind him, the hand wrapping behind Dixon's neck, scratching up through his hair as he relaxed into Dixon's pushes. The more Jaye yielded and opened up, the sweeter and more fragile he seemed. He was gorgeous with his dark curls, light eyes, and vibrant spirit. He was the wild, incarnate. Dixon moved unhurriedly, both of them breathing hard, shivering.

"This feel like I don't care to you? Huh?" Dixon undulated, out and in again, twisting Jaye's nipple, kissing the back of his ear. His lips brushed lightly over the shell, then kissed softly by his earlobe.

Straightening up, with Jaye still bent over, Dixon started to pound his ass, fast and hard, flesh slapping flesh. Driving the breath from Jaye, Dixon heard him gasp. Jaye's spine curved, his ass pushed out, knees spread, braced against the side of the mattress.

Drawing back a hand, Dixon let it fall with force. He smacked the side of Jaye's ass, hard, causing him to cry out. Dixon pounded him faster still and Jaye clenched up tight, tried to push Dixon out, but it just let Dixon slide deeper.

"Oh Jesus," Dixon moaned, folding over him, holding him with one hand as he fucked him raw. "Oh fuck. *Oh fuck.*"

Jaye was crying out roughly. Dixon came with an abrupt cry, unloading inside Jaye, into the condom, convulsing slightly with the force of it, shuddering against his back.

Panting, flushed, expression dazed, Jaye was boneless, held up only by Dixon's grip on him. When Dixon straightened them both, pulling Jaye more upright with him, he expected to need to bring him off. Then he saw that Jaye had already climaxed. Stroking through the hot, thick fluid, smearing it over the ripples of Jaye's abdominal muscles, Dixon used come-soaked fingers to twist one stiffened nipple.

Jaye's eyes were closed, his expression peaceful, sated, and exhausted.

"Maybe I'm not the only one who likes it rough, huh?" Dixon guessed.

The only reply he got was a soft, alluring little sound.

He pulled out, turned Jaye toward him.

Jaye's face was only more beautiful with its post-coital glow. Dixon leaned in and kissed him. Jaye made another soft sound, but Dixon drank it down, kissing his breath away. Their tongues touched. Jaye opened wider, letting Dixon lead, let him take as much as he wanted.

They broke apart, gasping again. Dixon's lips tingled.

"You gonna care about me, Dix?" Jaye asked. The sarcastic glaze over the question barely hid things that made Dixon's stomach swoop.

Dragging a thumb over Jaye's kiss-bitten lip, Dixon smiled.

He lowered Jaye to the bed, climbed atop him, straddling him, and said, "This feel like I don't care to you?" before kissing him again, gently. After hardly a moment, with Jaye kissing him back, Dixon heard him sob, felt his lips draw back as if in pain.

Jaye's hands clawed at Dixon's back, his breath hitching. Dixon just kissed him harder.

Chapter 12

Confessions in the Afterglow

"What are you doing?"

"Looking for freckles," Jaye murmured, examining the length of Dixon's naked body from where he was propped half-atop him, resting on an elbow. His fingers brushed the skin of Dixon's side like maybe doing so would remove makeup concealing tiny spots of color.

"I like your pubes," Jaye commented, sparing a glance back at Dixon's face, his expression serious.

"Gee, thanks, I guess."

Fingers played in the bush of blond curls around the root of his cock.

"I was wondering what color they'd be. Was betting on red. Blond's even better, though I do love a fire-crotch."

"How long have you been wondering, exactly?" The question was mostly a tease, but Dixon wanted to pull Jaye out of the funk he was in. After they'd finished and cleaned up, he'd gotten quiet, introspective.

"The whole time."

"At the Stop and Shop?"

"Well, not until I saw your hair color, so not when you tackled me, but yeah. There too."

"Sorry about that whole tackling thing."

"Eh." Jaye shrugged. He was still facing Dixon's legs. It seemed like he was addressing Dixon's penis, which was weird. "Not the worst thing that's ever happened to me. Got me here, didn't it? Sometimes one quick moment changes a whole lot."

"I guess it does," Dixon agrees. "You okay?"

96

"Sure. Why?"

"I don't know. My face is up here, by the way."

With a smartass sort of look, Jaye twisted around toward him. "I thought the whole idea was that you're here for me to pay attention to this."

Arm flexing, Jaye got tight hold of Dixon's dick. He squeezed up and down it, really going for it.

"*Fuck.* Stop. *Stop.*"

The problem wasn't that Dixon didn't want it, or that it didn't feel good. It felt spectacular.

Jaye drew his hand away, planted it on the other side of Dixon's body instead. He had a mean look on his face. Jaw clenched, lips pressed tightly together, he barely held the anger back, but he was too well-trained to fail completely.

"Later, okay? I'm not in a rush."

Maybe it was Dixon's absolute lack of hostility that worked to calm Jaye down. Or maybe that was what pissed him off in the first place. Dixon had no idea. Caressing Jaye's jaw, brushing a thumb over his silken lips, he noted the way a ray of sunlight and casted shadows brought out the angles in his face. It was like studying a painting by an Italian master.

"You're beautiful, you know that? You really are. It's kind of funny, because you're not my type at all. My ex is an old man compared to you. He isn't pretty at all."

"Where do you live?" Jaye asked out of nowhere.

Frowning a little, in confusion, Dixon hesitated. "Um, on the other side of town. A couple minutes from headquarters."

"Alone? I'm guessing not since you never seem to want to bring me there."

Dixon licked his lip, then chewed on it. "No, I live with my sister, Brekken, and her husband, Grant."

"Three's a crowd," Jaye remarked, like he knew all about that.

"Tell me about it," Dixon agreed.

"Then why? You have a job, money. Get your own place."

"I needed somewhere to crash after Marcus. It was easy. I don't know."

"Marcus, the abusive fuck." He pronounced the last word like he was spitting it out rather than saying it. Not wanting to get into it again, Dixon tried to ignore the contempt, the attempt to get a rise out of him.

It was nice to be laying in bed with Jaye, to have his slim, nude form draped luxuriously over Dixon, his cock lying against Dixon's thigh, but it also made it harder to talk about the unsavory aspects of life. You couldn't hide a thing when you were stripped bare like that. Rather than responding, Dixon sighed and leaned back farther into the pillow behind his head.

"You're scared to be alone, aren't you?"

"I can take care of myself. Trust me," he said with a dismissive tone. It didn't sound as confident as Dixon would have liked. It only sounded tired.

"Doesn't matter," Jaye argued. "Doesn't matter how tough you are, what you're packing, what you're capable of or what kind of training you've had. Not when they're in *here*." He tapped his finger against the side of his head. "You called him a *sadist*, not a Dom, or something like that. He hit you? Punch you?"

Dixon tried to make his expression blank, to will away the conversation he was stuck in. It didn't work because Jaye reacted like Dixon had nodded his head and said yes, no question about it.

"How often?" was the next question, since he'd gotten what he wanted to know from the first one.

Turning his face up to the ceiling, away from Jaye's stare, Dixon said, "I didn't say he did."

"Yeah, you did. Just now. So Brekken and the husband protect you. Make you feel safe. Good. No one should have to be afraid all the time."

"Look, I'm hungry. Can we...?"

It was a white flag. Jaye backed off, sat up, and swung his legs over the side of the bed. With his back to Dixon, he waited there as Dixon got up and went to get dressed.

Both of them stood in the tiny kitchen area. A small window over the sink was framed with ugly but oddly charming navy blue patterned curtains and let in some daylight. Dixon had his pants on, and nothing else. Wearing a pair of boxers, Jaye guarded a brewing pot of fresh coffee. The coffeemaker had been stowed in the back of Dixon's Expedition—a gift and peace offering he'd been holding onto to make up for the way they'd parted a few days ago.

Jaye stared blankly at the pot as it filled slowly up. Dixon, in turn, stared at him, his arms folded over the pale skin of his thickly muscled chest. It wasn't quite warm enough in the drafty cabin to warrant being half-naked, but at least the chill kept you awake and alert.

Dixon wasn't quite sure why he was still there. With anyone else, even Marcus, he would have been out of there without even taking the time to button his shirt, let alone to lounge around in bed, post-coitus. He wasn't a cuddler, never had been, never intended to be. And yet....

The coffee smelled good. There seemed to be an invisible tether that kept Jaye trailing him, led along behind. Dixon liked to think of the tether as curiosity or lust, but it felt like something different, something worse. But still, Dixon's feet didn't move. He didn't run for his Expedition and the freedom of the road. He stayed in that tiny kitchenette with the ugly curtains, watching Jaye think about God knew what. It was mind-boggling to think Jaye had committed murder, had done the things he'd done. It was worse to think about the other side of it, and what had been done to him, and why.

It was quiet for too long. The silence had made the air too thick to breathe. Like a swimmer kicking as frantically as he could to surface and inhale, Dixon blurted, "What happened to you makes me want to *scream*. I can't... I can't even..."

The confession was as thick as the air, heavy with sorrow and sympathetic pain, as well as fury. Jaye turned his way. Dixon bowed his head to hide his face as his expression contorted, trying to hold back the emotion.

"Hey," Jaye said sharply. "*Hey*. Me too."

For a second Dixon was unsure what was meant by that. Then Jaye stepped up close, looked into his eyes. It was all right there, laid out. Good god, Jaye was so angry. Dixon felt gutted with raw helplessness and here was pretty little J-bird with murder in his lovely green eyes. It didn't register right away that he was angry for Dixon, not himself.

"Guess we were both stuck in a bad place, huh?"

"Yeah," Dixon muttered, the words harder to speak when Jaye drew Dixon's arms down out of their defensive, folded position and caressed over his chest, up his neck to the side of his jaw. "Guess so."

They made some pasta, just noodles and tomato sauce. The bowls were brought back to the bed and Dixon resolved to pick up more food the next day, some meat and vegetables. The nagging feeling that he should go was there, but he couldn't. Something held him to the bed, his legs immobile. They sat there, cross-legged, picking at the noodles with forks. The fire popped and crackled in the fireplace, like nature's oldest music. Wind whistled eerily around the cabin's exterior.

"What was it like?" Dixon asked, curiosity triumphing at last.

"You tell me, I'll tell you," Jaye countered.

"Fair enough. You go first."

"That's not how it works."

"What is this, more negotiations? You should have been a lawyer."

"Yeah, missed my calling by a mile," he chuckled. His gaze flicked upward.

Dixon resisted with effort the urge to brush his fingers through those shortened curls, knowing how soft they were.

"I don't know, um," Jaye chewed a mouthful of food, swallowed and thought it over. "Cash was in charge. He had a bunch of guys that took his orders, carried 'em out. My part was pretty simple. He called me Johnny, so soon everyone else did, too. When he wanted me, some of the guys would stand guard, blocking people's view of the action. You know. They'd have their backs to us and I'd just get in position, show my ass, whatever. Then I'd just wait for it to be over, try to enjoy myself if I could."

"Oh come on, it couldn't have been that easy," Dixon pressed.

"No, you're right. It wasn't always like that. Sometimes it was a lot more public." Jaye paused, rolling his lower lip through his teeth, gnawing at the memories, his eyes unfocused. "That wasn't pleasant." He shrugged, drew into himself, hunching over on the bed around his food.

Dixon waited.

"There was this one time, in the yard. It was months ago. I was stabbed. Same side, same exact spot, so they knew what they were doing. Happened so fast, man, you wouldn't believe it. It was weeks before I was back on my feet. Once I was, though, Cash gave me the option. They knew who'd done it. It was a message, a warning. Cash's guys, they got the dude alone in the kitchens, back in storage. Some of them worked there. They held him down for me."

When he didn't continue, Dixon's imagination filled in the blanks.

What'd you do to him, J-bird? What do you do to a guy who's stabbed you, when you want to send a message and scare others away from trying the same?

"I don't want to know, do I?"

"No, you don't. But don't worry, he lived. After that, they gave me the spiderweb. It was my formal initiation, I guess. I already had my tear. That one's for the fuck burning in hell."

Shaking his head slightly, Dixon tried and failed to wrap his head around it all. "I don't know what to say."

Jaye glanced over at him, measuring him. "Don't kid yourself, Dix. I've done some bad shit. Can't take it back. It is what it is. But it's the bad-boy thing that gets you hard, right? So we're all good. Your turn."

"Fuck, man. I don't wanna get into that shit. *I don't,*" Dixon said adamantly. Setting the bowl down on the bed, he folded his hands, torn between the desire to get out in order to avoid questioning, and the need to stay.

"Tell you what? You tell me something real, no fucking around, and I'll make it worth it for you." He set his bowl aside too, climbed onto Dixon's lap. Pressing him back down to the bed, Jaye stayed planted there, a comfortable weight on Dixon's crotch. His hands began to massage Dixon's neck, his shoulders. It felt wonderful. The muscles relaxed a little. Dixon's hands slid up Jaye's bare arms, over ropes of muscle, down his sides to his hips, then around to palm his ass through the thin boxers.

"Something real, huh? Okay. Let's see. Marcus's cock is amazing. He's really talented in bed. Knows how to use it. Yadda yadda. You get the idea. But he was impatient as fuckall. He liked to get me right as I was coming home from a shift. I'd still be in uniform sometimes.

"One particular time, I was in uniform. As soon as I was through the door, he, like, *pounced*. Slipped a rope around my neck, used my handcuffs to lock my wrists behind my back, knocked me to the ground right in the entryway of the house after kicking the door shut. He took my pants off and fucked me right there, yanking on the rope.

"Once he'd come, he brought out one of his toys, this long silicone dildo. He stuck it up my ass, got me up on my knees with the cuffs still on and was working it in and out of me. I was, um... I was hard, which was humiliating. For the longest fucking time he kept me there, on my knees, fucking me with that toy until I begged for him to let me come, too. The rope was making it hard to breathe, my fucking knees and shins were killing me and the cuffs were too tight on my wrists. I didn't protest about that stuff, though. Marcus made sure not to pull the rope tight enough to make me pass out, and my hands fell asleep, but the cuffs weren't cutting my skin. It was controlled chaos. I got off on it."

Eyes closed, Dixon held on to Jaye, wondering what his expression was, what he thought of all of that. He was too chickenshit to look or ask. Remembering the rest, wanting to say it, to get it out of his head so he could let it go, Dixon struggled. It manifested in tension through his body, creases in his face, roughened breaths.

"Come on. What else?" Jaye coaxed. "What else, Dix? You heard my side. Think who you're talking to here. I ain't a saint."

"I, uh," Dixon laughed a little, his voice wavering with fear. "I, uh, wanted to ask Marcus to go with me to a Christmas party Brekken was having. We never went to stuff like that, as a couple. He didn't like to. It was after the incident in the entryway with the rope, after I'd showered and took a bunch of aspirin for my knees. We were in the kitchen. I asked him to go with me. He just, uh..."

Dixon's whole body was shaking, trapped in the old terror. Jaye found his hand, held it tightly, and rested his other hand on Dixon's chest, steadying him.

"He grabbed me by the back of the neck and smashed my face into the wall. It broke my nose. I was choking on all the blood. I tried to hit him back, and I think I clipped his jaw, but I'm not sure. He said something about how clumsy I was. That if I wasn't such a fuck-up, maybe we could've gone to the party."

Arms wrapped him. Jaye lay down on his chest. His lips brushed Dixon's cheek. Taking a deep breath, Dixon tried to stop shaking, to calm down.

"The next day, I got a baseball bat, came up behind Marcus. He was out back, at the house, in the yard. I hit him hard enough in the stomach to drop him, and told him not to fucking touch me again. I'm, uh... I'm not proud of that. Or that I didn't move out. Even then, I didn't."

"It's done," Jaye promised quietly, rubbing Dixon's arm, staying close. "There's no one here but me, okay? Look around. Sometimes that helps me."

The subtle convulsions were slow to fade. Dixon twitched and struggled to slow his breathing.

"You're safe. You're fine."

"I never told anyone that before."

Jaye kissed his cheek, caressed around the edge of Dixon's ear, over his scalp.

"I don't know what I'm doing," Dixon gasped. "I don't know why I'm telling you this shit, why I'm here. I—"

He was cut off with another kiss, this time to his lips. Jaye kissed his breath away, going deep. Stroking Dixon's tongue with his, Jaye rocked in smooth, fluid movements against his crotch, tenderly holding his face in his hands. It went on and on, with Dixon struggling for air through his nose, grunting and frowning when he felt Jaye push the pants down, shifting on his lap.

When the kiss broke, it was so Jaye could sit up more, lowering himself onto Dixon's cock once it was sheathed in a condom, biting at his lip in concentration, steadying Dixon with a hand.

Drawing his legs up, Dixon reached for Jaye again, bringing him closer once he'd been breached. Fingers clutching the back of Jaye's head, tangled in that short hair, Dixon thrust up into him as Jaye pressed down. The movement continued, going faster, harder as they kissed each other's necks, gasping.

"Fuck," Dixon hissed as Jaye ground down against him in tight circles.

"Relax. Just relax. I've got this," Jaye promised in his worn-smooth voice.

Dixon gave over more of the control to Jaye, let his body unclench, and stopped trying to do all of the work. Jaye moved, fucking himself down onto Dixon with little pushes, rising up and down while caressing Dixon's chest, tracing his gasping lips.

After hesitating, feeling his climax getting nearer, Dixon raised his arms above his head, crossing his wrists there, on the pillow. Jaye took the hint, held his wrists down with a hand, and kept going, wringing the orgasm from Dixon.

Growling, groaning, Dixon unloaded with a hard shudder.

Chest rising and falling, gaze averted, he hesitated again. After a moment or two of inner struggle, he guided Jaye off of him completely and turned to get on his hands and knees.

"Just do it," Dixon said impatiently, his face flushing red with shame and desire.

"Maybe you should try enjoying it instead of just trying to get it over with." A hand brushed up over the nape of Dixon's neck, over the back of his head. Fingers rubbed over his ass, through his crease. When they found his hole, the touching stayed concentrated there, drawing blood to his rim without venturing through.

"Handcuffs?" Jaye asked softly.

Dixon took a breath, blew it out and answered, "There," with a nod of his head toward where he'd left his things.

After getting off the bed to fetch them, Jaye brought them back. Already, Dixon had his arms in place, stretched behind his back. The cuffs were snapped on. Jaye kept them loose.

Two wet fingers twisted up into his ass. Dixon exhaled heavily, spreading his legs farther apart.

Jaye was taking his time with the prep, feeling him out. A couple of times, Dixon heard him spit and appreciated the makeshift lube, but was eager to get on with it. He wasn't used to getting a whole lot of prep before being fucked. The anticipation and foreplay were driving him crazy.

"Come on. I'm ready," he urged.

"Maybe *I'm* not. I'm not the one cuffed. You don't make the rules right now."

Dixon's face was turned sideways, resting against the bed, his ass up in the air. It was a favorite position of his, which was hard to disguise. Breathing labored, sweating, moaning softly, he slowly lost his cool, becoming wanton and desperate the more minutes passed.

Jaye was fucking him with three fingers, then four, kneading his buttocks. It must have been twenty minutes later when Dixon's impatience made him glance back over a shoulder.

Jaye only smiled at him, raising his eyebrows with a cocky, triumphant expression.

"Jesus," Dixon chuckled. "Are you *ever* gonna fuck me?"

"And what do you call this?" The fingers slipped completely out, rubbed hard over the engorged tissues of his rim and pressed back through, stuffing him full. "I love how pink your hole is. Maybe that goes with the whole pale ginger thing."

"Come on! Please."

"Mm, better. Didn't sound like you meant it, though."

"I meant it!" Dixon yelled gruffly.

There was movement on the bed. It shifted and the springs creaked. The next thing Dixon knew, something hot, wet, and soft was stroking over his rim.

"Oh fuck," he groaned, heart knocking against his ribs, pressing his face into the bedding. "*Jaye.*"

The licking continued as the fingers pumped deeply. Lips brushed over the sensitive area, which was over-stimulated and throbbing. Teeth scraped over his ass, over the edge of his hole.

"*Fuck.* Please. Please!"

The fingers tugged free and Jaye's lips brushed over the swollen orifice.

"Damn it. Oh god. *Please.*" He shuddered, humping air. He was so hard, his balls and cock ached with no relief in sight as long as he was cuffed and Jaye was concentrating on his ass. The buildup of pressure was maddening.

Finally, Jaye gave it up, got up on his knees and aligned his dick, Dixon made a desperate pleading sound, beyond words, just rasping into the mattress. His breath came in hot, quick, heavy exhales as Jaye thrust firmly into him, sheathing his cock in one push.

Grateful, relieved, blissful, and anguished, Dixon kept his ass pushed back as Jaye fucked it roughly, taking Dixon with almost brutal force. Dixon cried out, gasping, and shuddered hard with convulsions as he came untouched.

As his eyes rolled back in his head, he apologized weakly, "'M sorry."

Jaye yanked on the cuffs, drew Dixon upright to balance on his knees, then back to rest against Jaye's chest as he moved in shallow pushes. Lips dragging over Dixon's shoulder, over to his spine, Jaye breathed hard. He scratched Dixon's chest, leaving pink lines. He roughly fondled his come-soaked, half-hard cock, hips slapping against the curve of Dixon's ass.

Dixon clenched up around Jaye's cock, stuffed deep, and heard him bite back a cry as he came. Teeth sank into his shoulder. Pain flared at that spot. Jaye was panting, becoming still.

"That," he breathed, sounding wrecked, his low, rasp of a voice even more ground down. "That's my new favorite thing."

Dixon laughed.

Chapter 13
Danger on the Horizon

"Hey, g'morning," Brekken murmured across the kitchen counter, her voice hesitant.

Dixon glanced at the nearest curtained window. Outside, all was dark as night.

"Is it?" he asked.

"Days are getting shorter," she agreed. The house was silent around them. Neither of them moved, each of them waiting, but for different things. The longer the silence drew out, the more dread hardened Dixon's stomach. The queasy uneasiness suddenly made the omelet he was trying to prepare seem wholly unappealing. Restlessness had kept him awake most of the night as he'd kept running through his head everything he'd said and done with Jaye. Now, morning was trying to prevent any attempts to revive himself. He should have known that lingering bad feeling only pointed to one thing — past and present crashing together.

"Marcus came here, didn't he?"

Brekken sighed, eyes averted, arms folded.

"Damn it," Dixon seethed. He turned off the stove's burner and set aside the spatula he'd been using to shift the omelet around the hot pan.

"It was last night, when you were out. We didn't answer the knock. We'd already gone to bed, but we could see him through the window. Dix, maybe you should get a restraining order," she suggested, the fear crisp in her soft song of a voice.

"I should be able to handle my own business without getting everyone else involved. I didn't want to—"

"I know you didn't," Brekken agreed, cutting in, energized by the fight in Dixon's voice. Maybe she was simply glad it wasn't surrender or cowardice there instead. "But people will always talk. It's just how it works. Your safety is what matters. Not your pride, your *safety*. I don't like him coming here."

"I know you don't," he sighed. "It's not fair to drag you into this. Should I move out?"

He considered sliding the omelet onto a plate and just giving it to his sister, because his appetite was gone.

"No!" she blinked, her hand shooting out as if to block him, like he would leave that very moment. "That's not what I'm saying. I just don't like that he tracked you down like that. It's creepy."

Uncomfortable with the way she was looking at him, he began to wipe down the counter and clean up some of his mess. The cheese went back into the fridge. He set the cutting board and knife in the sink.

"I never told him I left. I just did. I cleared out. Now he's come back to a half-empty house, I mean of course he's looking for me."

"He could have *called*." Her anger was growing, taking over unused space between them, infusing the quiet with emotional noise. "I don't like this. He's not gonna stop until he finds you. What if he gets you alone? What if he's *armed*?"

He stopped puttering and looked right at her, giving her full eye contact to help reassure her of his conviction.

"Hey," Dixon said soothingly. "I can protect myself. I know to be careful around him."

"This is *Marcus* we're talking about! The only way to protect yourself is to keep him the fuck away!"

Shuffling footsteps to Dixon's left were followed by the appearance of Brekken's husband, Grant. Dixon had always liked him. He was a steady, solid guy with a good head on his shoulders and a loyal heart. Grant just quietly went about his duties and knew how to protect what was important to him without overstepping. Rubbing a hand over his tousled hair, Grant squinted at them in the dull light of the overheads. "What's goin' on?" he mumbled sleepily. Before they could answer, he answered for them. "Oh, this is about last night, isn't it?"

Taking a plate from the cupboard, Dixon transferred the freshly cooked egg pocket onto it with a tip of the pan, then set the plate in front of Brekken. "Here, have at it. I'm not hungry anymore." He walked to the closet to get his coat. "He's not gonna come looking for me at work, okay? It's not his style. I'll watch my back if I have to go out."

After pulling his arms through the sleeves, he turned around to find Brekken right behind him, chewing on her lip, brow furrowed with fret. "Please be careful," she whispered beseechingly, then hugged him.

"I will," he assured her. "Don't worry. I'm not likely to underestimate him. I know him too well for that."

That day Dixon spent what felt like hours sitting behind the wheel of his Expedition, waiting for a call. Staring at the road and the sky as the sun first rose, then glided steadily across the wide expanse of blue, he was paralyzed by doubtful thoughts. He replayed the past, and was helpless witness to the future scenes his brain conjured for him, sketched in uncertainty and pessimism.

In his mind, Marcus found him in many places, in many ways. Sometimes Marcus called; sometimes he was simply there, suddenly, as Dixon turned around, the way that Brekken had been there that morning, bearing ill tidings. The problem was the unavoidable nature of the issue at hand. A confrontation was coming, of that Dixon was certain.

All of the time spent with Jaye the day before lingered as a warm comfort in his heart, a reminder of his trajectory as he glided farther away from his ex and toward something new. But the things he'd confessed to Jaye rang in his mind, clanging sour notes, portending doom and misery. It was bad. In every scenario Dixon imagined, it went bad.

He irrationally imagined Marcus had been commiserating with the men who had tormented and tortured Jaye, and gotten some tips on how to put Dixon back in his place, to teach him a lesson so he'd never try to leave again. The idea of that made no sense, but it felt safer to consider terrible, improbable notions than to assume the worst couldn't happen, logic be damned.

The most plausible of his waking nightmares were the ones in which Marcus threatened Dixon's family. He would tell Dixon that if he didn't come back home, Dixon's sister would pay the price. It would look like an accident, maybe, but Dixon would know the truth, because Marcus would make sure he did. It wouldn't be provable. The charges wouldn't stick.

"I'm being paranoid," he told his Expedition, the radio squawking as if in response once in a while.

He wanted to see Jaye, to talk to him, something, anything to calm his nerves. There were two problems with that, though. Dixon didn't really want to include Jaye in his skittish delusions about Marcus if it could be helped. Marcus was Dixon's unfinished business. He didn't want Jaye feeling at all responsible for helping resolve it. In addition to that, though, he also didn't want Marcus finding out about Jaye. Who knew what Marcus would try if he knew someone had taken his place as Dixon's lover?

Then again, people did tend to talk, no matter how fiercely a secret was guarded, and the best way to ensure Jaye's safety was to be there to protect him.

As the day stretched out, and Dixon's daze lingered, he tried to think around it all. Every angle, each possibility was considered and analyzed. There had to be something he could do. The next day he'd be responsible for taking Jaye to work for his first shift, and picking him up sometime later. The Marcus problem couldn't be avoided forever.

Constantly checking his rearview mirrors, his phone, the horizon — everything — Dixon felt smaller and smaller, weaker and weaker. The Glock in his holster meant nothing. The badge on his chest meant *nothing*.

It'll be easier on everyone if I just go back to him, he thought. *Tell him I'm sorry, that I moved out because of loneliness, not to break up, that it was temporary, only temporary. It would be so much easier than the alternative. Brekken would be safe. Jaye would be safe.*

Marcus's ghost chuckled maliciously in his ear.

You didn't really think you could leave me, did you? You're gonna pay for that, you know.

And he did. He did know.

Though the earth spanned outward around him in every direction, endless, expansive and enormous, Dixon was trapped. Marcus had him in a cage. The bars were invisible, but they were there. Bad decisions had gotten Dixon where he was. He was determined to not make any more.

Dread was a certainty. It would go badly no matter what he did. The only way he could control the outcome would be to choose between his own freedom, his own safety, and those of the people he loved. And, really, that was no choice at all.

Dixon only wanted to do the right thing. That's all. Some of his options had shaken loose during the long day at work. When he got back to the house, Grant was sitting by the front door with a Remington 870 shotgun, ready for anything.

That was a hard reality to bear. Dixon had gotten his family there, to a place where danger was so close, only having weapons in hand made existence tolerable.

That made it worse for Dixon, as the guilt swelled bigger.

"Get inside," Grant told Dixon. "Bri made dinner. She's expecting you."

But, for a long moment, he could only stand there, staring at that shotgun. It was too real, too awful. The stony calm on Grant's face said a lot of things to Dixon at once.

I brought this down upon them. It was my mistake, and now they're the ones paying for it.

"Get inside, Dix," he repeated.

The sky was inky, the stars icy pinpricks. It was dark when he'd left for work, dark when he got home. The sun was escaping them, headed for warmer, more hopeful places to shine.

"It's good you're home," Grant told him. "We worried yesterday."

"Maybe you should put the gun away," Dixon suggested. The wind scattered his words as soon as they slipped over his lips, whisking them into the encroaching wild on the tops of gusts.

"My house. My gun. Go."

So, he went.

Even though he'd changed phone numbers since leaving Marcus, Dixon still waited for his phone to ring, for Marcus to track him down anyway. That night, he didn't sleep well or for very long. He constantly was peering out of windows to glance up and down the road. Once morning came, Grant waited until Dixon was leaving for work before doing so himself.

When they were both standing on the driveway, Dixon said to his brother-in-law, "You don't have to do all of this, you know. I can handle it."

"She told me about the bruises," Grant countered, still wearing an unruffled, resigned expression that said he knew where he was, and what he needed to do, for everyone's sake. "She would see them. Sesi saw them."

"Bullshit. Do you know what I do every day? What my job is like? How often I'm trekking through the fucking brush, or climbing rocks? I work my ass off. I bruise. Everyone does. It doesn't mean anything."

"No?" Grant answered, carrying some of Brekken's anger. Dixon recognized it for its weariness and persistence. "Okay, well, to you maybe. To me they do mean something. To Bri and Sesi they mean something, and if you're too confused to see it yourself, that just means we need to work that much harder to make sure you're safe."

"Sometimes they're consensual, you know."

"Just proving my point, man," Grant said. The few years of age he had on Dixon seemed great then, separating them, giving Grant the same kind of leverage of confidence and wisdom which Marcus wielded. "Go on. Tell me how much you wanted him to hurt you. I dare you to."

"I shouldn't be here," Dixon realized, saying it aloud as it occurred to him. "This isn't your business or your problem."

"Now it is. I made it my problem. It's personal, and I'm not letting it go. Neither should you. This is the only place you should be—somewhere people will protect you, no matter what, because they love you."

With a hand on the handle of his door, Dixon felt it all dragging him down. More choices sorted themselves out in his head. More paths became clearer.

"I'll see you later, Grant."

The drive to headquarters was a short one, not long enough at all to effectively distance Dixon from the feelings stirred in the driveway. He swung into the parking lot out front, and wasn't really surprised at all to see Marcus's truck parked there, idling.

Dixon didn't hesitate. He turned off the engine and got out.

Marcus got out too. He was wearing a knit hat, a heavy shirt, and no coat. A short, groomed beard covered his jaw.

"You shouldn't be here," Dixon said tiredly. When Marcus kept advancing on him, Dixon held out a hand, palm out. "Okay. That's far enough."

Marcus took two more steps anyway, pressing his luck, making Dixon have to take a backward step to maintain a safer distance.

"Where the fuck have you been?" Marcus demanded.

Dixon glanced at the front doors to the building, looking for movement, for a sign of onlookers. His heart began to race, beating faster and faster with a surge of adrenaline, knocking against his ribs, sending prickles of unease out through his body.

"I live somewhere else now. Excuse me."

He tried to walk around Marcus, but Marcus only stepped in his way. Dixon sighed.

"What's that supposed to mean? You been cheating on me? Huh? You whoring yourself out while I was gone, busting my ass to make a living?"

"Get out of my way, Marcus. Don't make me say it again." His hand was on the stock of his pistol, a warning.

"What, you gonna charge me, tough guy? For what? I'm only here to collect what belongs to me."

Dixon drew his weapon, but kept it pointed down.

"I said stand back. Now," Dixon said with a little more confidence.

Marcus smiled, hands raised mockingly as he backed up toward his truck.

"I guess we'll finish this later."

"No, we're done," Dixon told him.

"Oh, I don't think so," Marcus chuckled. But he got in his truck, started it up, and drove away.

Dixon exhaled heavily, drinking oxygen, trying to slow his heartbeat, holstering his gun. There was still no one else around, no witnesses. He could almost pretend to have imagined the whole thing.

All day long he thought he saw glimpses of a dark truck behind him, at a distance as he patrolled. By the time he had to pick up Jaye, Dixon's nerves were shot. He was tense, close to panic, but willing to do his best to pretend everything was fine, everything was normal. That's the only way he could keep Jaye out of it all and as far away from danger as Dixon could get him.

He pulled up to the cabin. Jaye was sitting on the steps out front, knee bouncing, breath fogging the air, layers of clothes bundled up around him.

Dixon opened his door, stood on the driver's side running board and called over the Expedition's roof, "You ready to do this?"

"Yeah, I guess so," Jaye replied, standing and heading down to him.

"Nervous?"

"Fuck yeah," Jaye smiled uneasily. "Stupid, I know. I mean, it's just a job."

"You'll be fine," Dixon told him, trying to sound confident and supportive, stifling with effort an urge to glance behind him at the road, to look for a truck emerging on the horizon line. It seemed he might be in the clear if Jaye was too rattled to detect something off with him. That hope was enough to get him through, at least.

They both got in the Expedition and buckled up. A moment later, they were on their way.

It was a quiet drive. The radio played, both of them busy with their own worries and preoccupations. When Dixon pulled up to the truck stop, he shifted into park and took a good look at Jaye after checking the mirrors one more time.

"Call if you need anything, but I'll be back to pick you up in a few hours. You'll do great. I know it."

"Yeah," Jaye said, sounding unsure. His dark hair was hidden under the hat and Dixon wished it wasn't. Part of him wanted to be back at the cabin, in bed with Jaye, hiding from the world. Another part of him wanted to take Jaye in his arms, to feel his warmth and vitality, and draw strength from the contact. Yet another part wanted to be gone, to get as far away from Jaye as he could, as fast as he could, before it all went wrong.

"Hey," Jaye added. "Can you maybe stick around after you take me home? We could blow off some steam or something."

"Sure. I'll see if I can clear my schedule, okay?"

"Yeah. Great. Thanks, Dix. I mean it."

"No problem," Dixon replied with a smile that was probably tighter than it should have been. Jaye was too distracted to notice. "Have a good day, J-bird."

"You too," Jaye told him as an afterthought as he climbed out. He smiled as he shut the door and waved once.

He walked up to the building while Dixon scanned the parking lot and tried to track each vehicle that rolled by on the street, but he couldn't catch everything and everyone, and knew it. Anyone who was determined enough could slip by. Dixon's persistent fear stemmed from the knowledge of how exceedingly determined Marcus could be.

Chapter 14

Just Another Day on the Job

It may have been the creeping darkness of the ever-expanding night, devouring a little more of the sunlight every day, that enabled Jaye to enjoy his first day at work rather than suffer through it. To be out in the world, contributing, doing something useful rather than cowering alone in the cabin, his little sanctuary of light in all of that pitch black, was good. It was a pure, good thing. Even if he was just sweeping and mopping floors to start with, and picking up litter around the lot, he was conquering a fairly huge obstacle in his life in the process.

Yes, people stared. They stared for different reasons than he was used to. It wasn't his weaknesses that they saw, it was the opposite. They stared because of the ways he was intimidating. A few children gaped and whispered about his tattoos. Adults, mostly other men, kept a wary eye on him, with his dark clothes, dark hair and the dangerous tint to the energy swirling around him. Jaye was personable enough to anyone who spoke to him, whether it was a co-worker or customer, but what wasn't said spoke louder.

Jaye wasn't a big guy. He was average height, slim and wiry. He was glad the hair was gone. With a much shorter cut, it helped add to his masculine vibe. When his hair was long and fairly lovely, it drew all the wrong sorts of attention. Women were drawn to it. Men loathed it, marking him with a glance as a pussy, a pansy, or a good-for-nothing.

Sometimes he still tried to brush it back, though it wasn't even there. His hand would come up as if to push strands over his ear, but all it pushed was air. That was a little spooky. It was like parts of him were becoming ghosts, joining the ones already haunting him. Perhaps, slowly, he was crossing over, beginning to join them.

Past warred with present in Jaye's actuality. Constantly, he reminded himself of where he was, and who the people around him were. Sometimes he murmured to himself his little assurances to keep the ghosts at bay, but he tried to only do that if no one else was around to overhear. If someone bumped into him, the reflex was to hit back, to go on the defensive, but if he lost control and hit someone, he'd be fired. He didn't doubt that for a second. Even the ever-present threat of administrative segregation hadn't kept him from hitting back when he'd been locked up. Back then, hitting back was the only way to preserve what mattered, namely his health and continued existence. Now, hitting back would only rob him of good things. So, he was on the ball, fighting instinct and on the alert for hours. On his breaks, he took some food out to a corner of the parking lot and sat on the ground there, with his back to a post, watching everyone and everything.

In memory, a guard knocked his tray, spilling his food, saying with a chuckle and a roaming gaze, *'What'cha got there, piggy?'*

His hand craved the comforting weight of a weapon and he hissed, "Fuck you. Fuck you and shut the hell up. There's no one here."

As he sat there, chewing, legs drawn up, eyes darting around, he thought back to the last job he'd held. It was at a shopping mall. He was a cashier in a trendy clothing store that reeked of the cologne they sprayed on the carpets. Back then, he'd smiled so often it almost became a joke with those who knew him. They called him the happiest person in the world. Smiling had since become a much rarer occurrence.

Eating his lunch, his expression hard, warning off others who might think to approach, Jaye watched a man in a knit cap pumping gas into his black truck and filling a few containers, too. With effort, Jaye tried to remember what it had been like to be that younger version of himself, before the attack, before everything changed on him. His biggest problem then had been finding a boyfriend in a town seemingly devoid of other gay people. It didn't make him sad to think of that innocence lost. Instead it made him hate the naïve boy he'd been, almost as much as the men who tried to rape and murder him had hated him. If he had been more conscious of how the world really worked, none of it would have ever happened. He wouldn't have been left as he was to carry everything he had endured like a lead weight strapped to his back. Knowledge was a burden, but it kept you alive, at least.

He tossed his trash and brushed off his pants. Then he crossed the lot to the employee entrance. Before he could grab the door's handle, he heard someone call to him.

"Hey, kid! You work here, right?"

"Yeah," he squinted, shielding his eyes. He was wearing a shirt with the truck stop's logo on it. "Can I help you?"

"I need some propane." The guy cocked a thumb at the locked cage full of small propane containers out front. It was the same guy who had been filling his truck and some containers with gas. He had a slightly weathered face, and looked like a fisherman if Jaye had to guess.

"Oh, I don't handle that, but I can get someone for you."

"What's your name? You don't look familiar."

Biting back a sharp retort, not liking the guy's curt, demanding tone but knowing he had to be polite to customers, he said, "Jaye. I'm new here."

The fisherman spit a gob of saliva on the asphalt, looking him up and down. "I can tell. Find someone who can get me some god-damned propane."

"No problem," Jaye said through his teeth, trying to keep a handle on his frustration and contempt.

He yanked the door open and went inside, letting the metal door close heavily and loudly behind him. Back in the office, he found his boss, Tammy Jean. She was on her way out to the front, so he followed alongside of her, saying, "There's a customer outside who needs access to the propane."

She glanced out through the front windows, standing on her toes and peering around. "Oh, that's Marcus. Probably doing one of his supply runs. I'll handle it. Thanks, Jaye."

With that, she hurried forward, digging keys out of her pocket.

"Marcus?" he echoed, quietly, as she left. His blood ran cold. "Oh fuck. Oh *fuck*."

Jaye kept a close eye on the clock for the rest of his shift, the minute hand moving more slowly around the dial than he would have thought possible. He couldn't stop worrying about Dixon and wanting to warn him. It became so distracting that he snuck away to the break room in order to attempt a call, just to ease his mind.

He dialed Dixon's cell, the only number for him Jaye had. When it rang and rang without being answered, it did nothing to calm Jaye's frazzled nerves. The phone could have been turned off, or muted, he knew, since Dixon was working. If he was in the middle of something important, he wouldn't be able to pick up. It made sense, but Jaye's pessimistic suspicions were stronger than logic.

While he cleaned and restocked some shelves, his mind provided him all sorts of horrible notions. He imagined Marcus running Dixon off the road, tying him up like a misbehaving dog, and dragging him home while Dixon screamed for help.

Hours passed. The end of Jaye's shift came at long last. He got all of his things, his coat, and sat out front, watching the road for Dixon's Expedition. At five minutes after Dixon was supposed to be there, Jaye tried Dixon's cell again.

It went right to voicemail.

At ten minutes after, he tried again to call, knowing it wouldn't be answered. It wasn't.

At twenty minutes after Dixon was due to pick him up from work, Jaye was frantic. Nervously spinning the rings on his fingers with his thumb, he racked his mind for ideas. He found Tammy Jean and asked if she had any other contact information, explaining that Dixon was running very late, and he was worried.

She gave him Dixon's home number, and Jaye tried that, but no one answered there either.

There was only one other idea he had, and it was an exceedingly distasteful one.

At forty minutes after Dixon was due to pick him up, Jaye stood on the side of the road in front of the truck stop, gazing in the direction of town, squinting at the hazy horizon. The sun was sinking. Darkness fell, slowly.

With the cell phone to his ear, a scrap of paper clutched in hand with a phone number for the local police station printed on it in hastily scribbled handwriting, Jaye listened to it ring. His heart was in his throat. Though it was cold out, his skin was covered in a light sweat borne of pure fear.

The last number he ever wanted to have to dial was the one he had just called. Waiting for it to be answered, he thought of Dixon.

"Yes, this is Zus AST Headquarters. How may I be of assistance?"

"T-trooper Rowe. I'm calling about Trooper Rowe."

"Yes? What's the problem, sir?"

"He, um. He was supposed to be here. He's a friend and he was supposed to pick me up from work. He never showed. He's not answering his phone, and I'm worried."

After a brief pause during which he held his breath, anticipating what they would say, wondering if they would laugh at him, he stared at the empty road. The clock ticked on.

"I'm sure he's just been detained and on his way—"

"Could you check?" he asked, voice growing shriller, more desperate. "You could get him on the radio, right? I mean, there's some way you could make sure he's all right, isn't there?"

"Sir, may I ask your name?"

The crunch of tires behind him made Jaye turn. An Expedition was rolling up on the side of the road, over loosened gravel, and coming to a stop. It was Dixon.

"Oh thank god. Holy shit. Scared the *hell* out of me, man," he sighed with huge relief. To the woman on the phone, he said, "Look, I'm sorry I bothered you. He just got here. I feel like an ass. Sorry to waste your time."

"No problem," she told him, sounding strangely relieved herself, at least enough to make Jaye feel less bad about calling.

"Bye. Sorry," he fumbled. Turning off the phone, he jogged around to the passenger side door.

Jaye grabbed the handle, yanked and saw Dixon sitting there in uniform.

"Fuckin' hell, Dix! I just called to fuckin' report you as missing— What happened?"

Dixon wasn't looking at him; he was staring past Jaye at the truck stop, unfocused, both hands on the wheel. Jaye knew that type of look, there in Dixon's tense blankness, like the fear had gotten so big it was a mean, snarling dog, snapping at your balls, making you piss yourself or cry for mommy. That's the same look new initiates in the gang would have the first time they saw someone try to push rapidly spilling blood back into their body with shaking, slick red hands.

That was shock, pure and simple.

"Dixon," Jaye said more sharply, getting into the passenger seat. "Look at me. Now. Say something."

"I had a close call. A bad traffic stop. No big deal." It was hollow and vacant-sounding. Dixon shifted into drive and checked his mirrors.

"Wait! Would you wait a second?!" Jaye yelled angrily. "Do you know how late you are? It's almost an hour after you said you'd be here! You weren't answering your phone, either."

"I was working."

"Dixon!" Jaye scolded, ready to snap. He saw Dixon glance at the time read-out on the dashboard with a strange expression of distaste. "I was really worried. I don't really worry about other people a lot. It's kind of novel for me. Can you be straight with me please? What the fuck happened to you?"

"I'm just a little late," Dixon said from what felt like miles away. He wouldn't look directly at Jaye, and he didn't sound engaged in the conversation at all. Dixon was somewhere else entirely. "Nothing to worry about. I'm fine. It's fine."

Jaye swallowed hard, feeling strangled with tension telling him something was off, something was *wrong*. He glanced around, but no one else was there. The place was practically deserted. The sun sank lower and, as the dark deepened, the glow from the lights inside the vehicle grew more powerful.

Gathering his will, getting a handle on his reactions, after a long moment Jaye said, "I saw Marcus. I talked to him. He was here. Getting gas and propane."

Dixon's head spun around fast, finally looking right at Jaye. Wearing a heavy frown, he scanned Jaye's body. "Did he touch you? *Did he hurt you?!*"

Taken aback by the volume and intensity of the reaction, Jaye sputtered, "What? No. He was a customer. It just made me worry about you. Did you know he was here?"

"I need to get you home," Dixon said with finality, facing forward, checking the mirrors yet again. The limp vacancy in his eyes was gone, replaced by furious protectiveness after one mention that Marcus and Jaye had interacted.

There was no surprise, just anger that Jaye had encountered Dixon's abusive ex.

"You knew. You fucker, you knew he was here," Jaye gaped. Pieces of knowledge shifted around in Jaye's head, and he wasn't sure how to fit them together in a way that made sense. Marcus was back. Dixon knew. Dixon had been in shock, but now he was worried about Jaye's safety. It was mostly the anxiousness talking as he said, "Dix, you're gonna stay with me tonight, right? I mean, I'm yours now. Fair and square. I want you to stay with me."

The car had been rolling forward, but Dixon pressed the brake after hearing Jaye's plea. He sighed in gruff frustration, avoiding eye contact.

"I can't. He might see my Expedition at the cabin. That'd be bad. I don't want him knowing who you are or where you are right now." He shot Jaye a brief sideways glance.

"Well, you're supposed to protect me. Can I stay with you? At your place? That'd be better, right? Let me stay with you."

"You shouldn't be near me at all," Dixon murmured under his breath. He peered in the mirror at himself and rubbed a hand over his mouth. The dark outside seemed to sift through the glass and into him, eating away at all the light that was usually in Dixon's face. The near-constant friendly twist to his lips, which had always made him seem approachable and kind, was nowhere to be found. Even if there was a lot on Dixon's mind, he usually did a good job of faking a good mood, for appearances' sake. Now he wasn't even bothering with that. Jaye had never seen him more miserable.

Jaye sensed Dixon's answer to safety concerns had always been to isolate the threat and get everyone he cared about out of harm's way while he dealt with things alone. That wasn't going to work anymore, not when Jaye needed Dixon's protection. If Dixon ran, that would only leave Jaye alone to fight for himself if danger came knocking.

It was time to show Dixon a different approach.

Reaching out, Jaye touched Dixon's face, brushing the pad of his thumb over his cheekbone, the backs of his knuckles pushing gently back over his ear and hair. Fingers tangling there, Jaye asked, "Take me home? I'm yours. Whatever you want, okay? Whatever you need, you can have it. You don't have to be alone."

Those mesmerizingly golden eyelashes, and vibrantly blue-green eyes, full of sadness—Dixon wasn't looking at him, but he didn't need to. Jaye was watching for the both of them.

"This isn't a good idea," Dixon whispered. "The best way to protect you is for you to be far away."

"Too late. You gonna send me out there alone? You gonna give up? Let me fend for myself?"

Dixon turned and caught his gaze. Jaye felt the torment in his stare, and would have given anything for the truth of what happened in that missing hour. But Dixon wasn't ready yet. He needed time. Luckily, time was something Jaye could give.

"Fuck," Dixon hissed, stepping on the gas. The car lurched into motion, taking off down the road.

Chapter 15

Instincts

That cold façade of the trooper rather than Jaye's lover mocked him during the drive to Dixon's home. Dixon had pulled away. After sharing the closeness they'd had, revealing secrets, confiding closely held truths—it stung. Sometimes, with Cash, Jaye would be left facing the thug rather than his careful lover, but it would only be for show, to keep up appearances. He found he preferred having to face a thug than an unemotional cop, not that there was a choice. Dixon was all Jaye had.

Jaye puzzled out Dixon's silence and Dixon watched the road slip away under the tires. The solitude of Alaska, the way the earth sprawled out around you, serving you up on a platter to the heavens for judging, it acted on Jaye in strange ways. He was used to being surrounded by humanity, and of the sort you must beware of, the sort that would kill you in literal or metaphorical ways should your guard drop for even a second. When you were constantly bracing yourself, expecting danger, it grew commonplace to be wound so tight. That was your norm. You watched your ass, because no one would do it for you.

In Zus, there were no people around. Those who might be there sought shelter in the warmth of closed, man-made spaces. They lurked inside, in their dens, leaving you out in the cold, alone. If you were judging circumstances by appearances only, Jaye appeared to be safe, and he appeared to not be alone. After all, he had Dixon. He wasn't surrounded by hardened criminals, murderers, and rapists. He was in a normal neighborhood, with lovely scenery. It was deceptive. The danger was just hiding itself better, luring you into the misconception that everything was fine. So, not knowing quite how to brace himself for a threat he couldn't anticipate as easily, Jaye was anxious. His anxiousness was driven by his relative safety as much as Dixon's mood.

They arrived at the house. It was small; a pre-fabricated, pale yellow structure that seemed as glaringly out-of-place as most of the buildings in Zus did. Only places like Jaye's cabin blended in with their surroundings, owning the nature from which they were born. Jaye knew the home belonged to Brekken, Dixon's sister. Dixon was really a nomad, like Jaye, going with each gust of fate's wind.

It wasn't Jaye's place to press for information Dixon wasn't yet ready to share. His place was to comfort, to console, and distract. It was also to make sure Dixon came through on his end of their deal, even if that meant showing him in subtle ways how to do it. Falling into step, repeating the dance that had kept him with Cash and kept him alive, Jaye stopped asking unwanted questions. His worries were inconsequential if Dixon deemed them so.

Dixon led them inside. "Living room. Kitchen's through there," he explained, gesturing to each room. "Bedrooms are down the hall. Bathroom's there, off the hall. Brekken and Grant have their own."

Jaye wondered what came next. He followed Dixon down the hall. When Dixon excused himself and went to use the bathroom, Jaye decided to wait in the bedroom. It was rather bare and seemed like a guest room ready to house anyone passing through rather than belonging to someone in particular. Whether he realized it or not, it was clear enough to Jaye that Dixon had no intention of staying in that place long.

Slipping his shoes off, leaving his coat draped over a chair, Jaye stretched out on the bed with his arm folded underneath his head. Dixon appeared after a few minutes and began to take off his gear and uniform. The duty belt was set aside. His fingers worked slowly at buttons and buckles. One bedside lamp cast meager light on the small room, barren of personal touches. There were no mementos, no photographs to help Jaye complete the picture of Dixon Rowe in his mind's eye. His strawberry blond hair shone in the light, his long, golden eyelashes beautiful in a delicate way. Jaye was unfamiliar with most delicate things. That beauty began to bring out old cravings of the sort Jaye hadn't felt in years, before stark concern for his survival closed off unhelpful aspects of his soul. His gaze scanned the room, looking for paper, maybe a pencil, too.

"You hungry?" he asked, testing the waters.

Dixon shrugged.

"You okay?"

There was no response, not even another shrug. Dixon just stood there with his hand set atop the bureau, reliving something Jaye couldn't fathom.

He wanted it to just be worry, fret about Marcus reappearing. He wanted that to be all, but he was scared it wasn't. Balanced in between the could-be's and the evidence of what was, Jaye could only follow the path he knew led to better things.

Sitting up, Jaye got up on his knees. He twisted his shirt up over his head and dropped it beside the bed, letting it fall to the floor. His fingers went to his fly, popping the button, tugging the zipper down. When he inched the fabric down over his hips, he saw Dixon's previously blank gaze gain focus. He was drawn out of his head, into the present, and Jaye was encouraged.

"Is this okay?" He pushed the pants down just far enough so that they were stretched across his pelvis. Fingers slipping inside the elastic band of his briefs, he nudged them down too, exposing the entirety of his tattoo, but nothing more than that.

Dixon's eyes were glued to the ink below Jaye's navel. His chest rose and fell with each breath. His arms and pecs flexed like he was anticipating a fight.

"We gonna be alone for a while?" Jaye asked.

"They're out for the next two hours. Brekken sent a text, told me to call Sesi so I wouldn't be here alone."

Jaye didn't know who Sesi was but didn't really care at the moment. He only cared that Dixon hadn't seemed to have called her.

Licking his lower lip wet, head bowed but eyes watchful, Jaye saw Dixon angrily yank the undershirt over his head. Strung tight, jaw clenched, he hastily pulled the workpants off, too, then came to the bed wearing only boxer briefs and a major attitude.

"Take 'em off. Slowly," Dixon ordered.

Jaye pretended to be a little nervous and took his time getting the clothing down his thighs. He was getting hard, and Dixon kept a close eye on exactly how hard Jaye was. It was hot, especially since Dixon didn't move to actually touch him yet, at all. It was purely visual scrutiny.

"You fucking look sixteen," Dixon breathed.

"That's because I am," Jaye said with a hint of a smile, playing along. "Gonna take care of me, Dix? I'm so *young* and *innocent*. But you're not innocent, are you?"

"Turn around. Lay down. On your stomach."

Doing as commanded, Jaye lie face-down, head turned to the side, hands splayed at his sides, up by his shoulders, as if waiting to be searched and cuffed. Dixon definitely had the same vibe as the prison guards had, a sense of authority that made him act like he was above Jaye and other civilians somehow, out of reach of consequences. It made Jaye tense up a little more than he'd have been, otherwise, even though he had reason to believe Dixon wasn't cruel like the prison guards. Still, better to be ready for anything than caught in a moment of vulnerability.

Dixon yanked Jaye's pants and briefs off, pulling them hard to get them clear of his legs, leaving him naked. Then he shoved Jaye's legs apart, spreading him. His big hands rubbed roughly, greedily up the backs of Jaye's legs, up his thighs to cup his ass. Spreading his cheeks, Dixon dragged a thumb over Jaye's opening.

"Get a pillow. Stick it under your hips. Now. Do it."

Jaye remembered some of the times Cash had gone all out to put on a show for other prisoners watching. He'd give Jaye orders, handle him with greedy, brazen touches.

Ready to get fucked, Johnny?

Jaye heard it like Cash was right there, at his back, cock in hand. That was a ghost he could deal with. Nothing set him at ease like having Cash at his back, ready and able to destroy anyone who tried to touch his things.

He wanted that feeling again, of feeling so secure he could drop his guard a little, and not be so scared all the time.

So far, Dixon had provided financial security, and proved he could fuck, but the emotional instability of their relationship worried Jaye. And Jaye's practical safety was clearly a huge issue with Marcus out there, doing God knows what.

Breathing harder, missing Cash, Jaye complied to Dixon's demand, lifting his hips to get the pillow in place. Dixon wasn't touching him anymore. He had gone to get something, came back to the bed with lube.

"Am I in trouble, trooper?" Jaye teased, ass-up, waiting for Dixon to touch him again, anticipating it with every throb of his stiffened cock. He hoped the role play would clue Dixon in on how he was acting, like Jaye was just another perp to tame, or a casual fuck, instead of someone to whom he owed more than that. Jaye wanted the truth. He wanted facts, reassurances, and action.

Dixon climbed onto the bed, growled by Jaye's ear, "Don't." The lube was opened. Dixon's body was a heavy weight on the bed between Jaye's spread legs. Dixon's left arm was braced by Jaye's head as Dixon leaned over him.

"You mean you're not gonna cuff me? Might be hot."

"*No.*" His lips moved against the shell of Jaye's ear, his breath warm and minty. "*No one* cuffs you, you hear me?"

A pleasurable shiver raced down Jaye's spine, hearing the note of warning in Dixon's voice. *That* was the kind of iron that really got Jaye hot. The more Dixon gave him of that don't-you-fucking-dare, confident attitude, the more readily Jaye would spread. He felt Dixon's thighs press against the insides of his, pinning him down.

"Anyone cuffs you, anyone *touches you*, I punch their fucking face in."

A single, wet finger slid into him, and Jaye's mouth opened around a gasp as his cock got even harder. Dixon's lips moved over his jaw, brushing lightly, tasting skin. The tip of Dixon's tongue teased, then his teeth, scraping with a hungry exhale. The finger pumped, smearing lube. It felt dirty and thrilling in the best ways.

"You didn't do anything wrong," Dixon told him, exuding seductive, heady authority and control. "The last two years? Never happened. You're innocent. Sweet, and gorgeous, fucking sexy... and *innocent.*"

Knowing better and exhaling a breathless chuckle, Jaye clenched reflexively as a second finger entered him. "When you say it, I almost believe it." The words broke, his voice crackling with the ache, making him sound as young as he looked. Dixon moaned, so Jaye kept playing along.

With two digits hooked inside his rectum, Jaye shuddered and whimpered, "Please." It sounded fragile, honest, and nervous. And it worked. Dixon made a gruff, soft noise, pulled his fingers out and positioned himself. The head of his cock pressed between Jaye's cheeks, fat, blunt, and wide. Dixon held him in place with a hand wrapping his waist and thrust inward.

"*Please*," Jaye cried, sounding no more than sixteen, sounding virginal and unsure. The word turned into a wrenching, broken whine that had Dixon groaning and gasping Jaye's name as he fed his cock into the tight, hot sheath of Jaye's ass.

The stretch was real enough, even if Jaye's shyness was feigned. Dixon was eager enough to get his whole dick in there that it did hurt a little. Jaye's gasping was real enough, too. Dixon pushed and pushed to get deeper, his hands groping along Jaye's nude, slim body in ways Cash had never dared to try.

As Jaye made another small cry, Dixon growled into his ear, "I know you want it."

Say thank you, the ghosts whispered. "Please," Jaye begged, wanting them gone, to lose himself in the reassurances behind every touch instead of letting the old fear in again.

Dixon drew back, the friction lighting Jaye up from the inside out. Jaye moaned, "*Dixon*."

His control snapping cleanly, Dixon lost it. He started to pound Jaye's hole, taking him rough and fast, dragging heated kisses over his skin, touching him everywhere he could reach, like it could never be enough. It was so good.

"Up. Come on," Dixon told him, pulling Jaye's hips up off the bed, getting him up on his knees, staying buried all the while. As soon as he could fit his hand under Jaye's pelvis, he sought his cock and squeezed.

"Oh my god," Jaye groaned. Dixon started to rock in shallow movements against his prostate gland. It made Jaye shout. "Oh fuck. *Oh fuck. Please.*" He cried out into the bed, letting Dixon take him apart, not even sure himself how much of it was still an act or not. Even the ghosts couldn't reach him. He was way beyond where they could go.

"Tell me you love it," Dixon dared, triggering him relentlessly, setting off fireworks all along Jaye's body, his nerve endings sizzling. He convulsed as his orgasm slammed into him, hard. Choking on it, he made desperate sounds against the bedding, his mouth pressed there. All he knew was Dixon inside him, sliding deep, so thick and long, and the hand pumping his cock so perfectly as his seed shot over the bed. His whole body tightened during climax, wringing it from him, and Dixon came too, with a curse and a kiss to the back of Jaye's head.

For what felt like a long, long time, they stayed like that. Jaye liked having Dixon inside him. It felt right. It made him feel absolutely possessed and cared for. It was everything he needed. They caught their breath. Dixon kept caressing him, down his sides, along his arms, up the back of his neck. Time drew out but neither of them moved or spoke.

Eventually, after the sweat on their bodies had dried and they were breathing normally, both of them spent, sated, and softened, Jaye said, barely loud enough for Dixon to hear, "I love it."

He'd never used that word with anyone but Kris, and he'd never said it before like he meant it as much as he did then, with Dixon. It felt dangerous, but the way Dixon had claimed him gave Jaye enough confidence to put himself out there in new ways. Maybe it would help Dixon trust him more, too.

He wished he could see Dixon, but he couldn't. Dixon was nuzzling the back of his head. His arms tightened their grip on Jaye's slimmer, smaller body, his cock still claiming its stake.

Anticipation woke Jaye up completely. He needed to know Dixon's secrets about that missing hour. Maybe the intimacy of their positions would be enough to make him brave, make him talk.

There was a strangled sob from low in Dixon's chest. Fresh fear bloomed in Jaye's heart.

"I did something bad," Dixon barely whispered. Then, louder, "I'm sorry. *I'm so sorry.*"

Realizing he was talking about that terrible missing time, heart racing faster and faster, Jaye knew he had to encourage Dixon to keep talking. Jaye said tightly, "It's okay. It's okay, I promise. You don't need to apologize to me for anything."

Dixon breathed loudly, trying to rein in the tears, to get control.

Jaye kept pushing in little ways.

"I forgive you, for whatever it was. Okay? If I'm innocent, then so are you."

"I'm trying," Dixon hissed. "I'm trying to tell you."

"I know. It's okay. It's okay, Dix. Stay here with me for a while. Please?"

And Dixon did.

Chapter 16
The Missing Hour

Being active, being busy was what drove Dixon since he picked Jaye up from the truck stop. He figured if he kept going, kept doing things, it would prevent him from remembering. If he didn't remember, it would be like it had never happened. He wouldn't have to deal with it. Not yet. It would stay pushed back behind action and the motion of living.

Luckily, it was so odd to have Jaye standing in his sister's kitchen cooking a big batch of chili it kept Dixon in the present. The recent past became less of a threat.

Leaning in the doorway, he watched Jaye stir with a long wooden spoon. Spices filled the air, tickling Dixon's nose. Jaye was wearing a plain white shirt, one he'd had on under his work shirt, and his work-pants, but his feet were bare. It was hard not to be aware of how Jaye looked, and how people viewed him. It was the same way Dixon had viewed him when they first met. The tattoos were what you saw first. Then you saw how terribly young he was. Next you saw how pretty he was, under the ink. It was a string of observations full of different sorts of danger, for Jaye and those casually judging him.

Now, Dixon saw him for his vulnerability and strength, apart from physical attributes. The sight of the tattoo wrapping Jaye's neck only made Dixon want to taste his skin, to feel the texture of his soft, curl-ing hair against his lips, to touch and feel Jaye react to every touch.

Of course, Dixon knew he would need to defend himself to oth-ers for simply being with Jaye. Dixon had never liked defending his choice of partners. It was a task he avoided if at all possible. That responsibility was a weight, pulling him down, but at least it was something else to keep him busy, keep him active, and keep him from slipping back a few hours' time and reliving what he'd endured on the side of that road.

From behind him, there was the sound of a key sliding into the lock in the front door, of the knob turning. Gaze fixed on Jaye, Dixon felt a wave of tension tighten his chest. Dread churned his stomach. *She can't tell you who to be with. Even if she doesn't approve, she can't keep you from being with him. It'll be fine.*

Even as he thought it, he knew it was ridiculous. His whole life was ridiculous.

Dixon turned and went to the door as Brekken was still getting it opened and her keys free. Grant was watching the road as though devils with pitchforks in hand might come racing up it at any moment.

The stark concern on Grant's face, more than anything else, was what brought the sense memories back. Suddenly, Dixon wasn't there, in the entryway of his home, ready to defend Jaye's presence to his sister, he was kneeling in the dirt, choking, retching, crying, and pleading with guttural sounds.

He couldn't breathe. His vision blurred and a low moan of horror was stifled with much effort.

Through a dense fog of shame, he heard, "Why's there a kid in the kitchen? Dix?"

"He's older than he looks," he answered defensively, coming back to himself as Brekken and Grant stepped inside. Dixon locked the door behind them. Disapproval oozed from the hard stare he got from Grant, but Dixon didn't blink or back down. "It's not safe for him to be out there alone right now."

"Why?" Brekken demanded, frowning, crossing her arms. She kept glancing to the kitchen, where Jaye was pretending he hadn't heard them come in.

"Because we're together."

"And because Marcus is a psycho," she added. "What does that mean, you're together? I thought you agreed it wasn't a good idea for you to get into this."

"It doesn't matter," Dixon sighed. "Jaye's not going anywhere. He goes where I go."

"How fucking old is he?" she hissed quietly. "Christ, Dix."

"He's legal. And *he's* not a psycho. Get over it. And be nice, please." Tiredly, he led them to the kitchen.

Jaye cleared his throat, set down the spoon and dropped the act. He turned to face them and slid his hands into his pants pockets. "Hey," he said, nodding in greeting. "Nice to meet you."

"Jaye, Brekken, Grant," Dixon said in introduction.

"I can see the resemblance," Jaye smiled. He stepped forward to shake their hands. Dixon could feel them scrutinizing Jaye. It made Dixon wildly uncomfortable. "Dinner's almost ready. Chili's one of the few things I know how to make, so I promise it won't suck."

Brekken had been staring at Jaye, but she shot Dixon a quick, sharp look he could only pretend to understand. It was hard to breathe again, and it felt like if he didn't hold his breath, his control would snap and he'd be a wreck in seconds. Shaky and overwhelmed, he muttered, "Excuse me," and hurried to the bedroom.

He slammed the door shut once he was inside and sunk to the floor, backing himself up to the wall. Head in his hands, Dixon tried to draw oxygen into his lungs, but the frightened, whimpering sounds coming out of him were only feeding his panic, so he muffled them against his arm.

"Dixon? Hey! Dixon! Look at me. You're okay. I need you to look at me."

Slowly, he began to hear. The screaming in his head had been drowning out the words. He realized he wasn't alone. Jaye was kneeling in front of him. Brekken was lingering in the hall, watching through the opened door.

"Don't touch me. Don't. Just... I can't... I can't breathe." Dixon whined, then immediately clapped a hand over his mouth as if he could catch the sound.

"Look at me," Jaye whispered. His voice was hard as iron, even as quiet and rough as it was, and it helped Dixon find something to anchor to. "Good," Jaye murmured when Dixon's watery gaze drifted to Jaye's light, pretty eyes.

A heavy exhale carried a hurt noise with it. Jaye, perfectly calm and collected, held up his opened hands to show he meant no harm, and inched closer. Dixon didn't flinch away as Jaye's hands were laid upon his arms. The contact felt nice. Dixon took hold of one of Jaye's hands.

"What'd he do to you?" Jaye asked quietly. "It didn't," he wheezed. "It didn't happen. Nothing happened."

"It did, and I need you to tell me, now, what it was. Come on. It was Marcus? He found you?"

"F-followed me."

They were both staring at him, and his tears. He turned his face away, hating it.

A box nudged his arm. It was tissues. He took it, knew Brekken had passed it to Jaye. One quick glance showed him she had a glass of water for him, too.

He pulled out a few tissues, wiped his face. "Gimme a couple minutes," he asked. "I need a couple minutes."

"Okay. Take your time," Jaye answered.

They left him there. He kept trying to catch his breath and slow the pounding of his heart.

Someone had overloaded the back of their pickup. Pieces of lumber were sticking out dangerously and it was because of this hazard that Dixon had pulled them over. The motorist got a ticket, and for a good twenty minutes set to work on rearranging the wood so they could safely continue on their way. Guitar-heavy rock music blared from the cab. Dixon didn't have anywhere else to go so he helped out when he could and supervised the progress.

Finally, the Ford in question rolled away, merging from the shoulder to the road with a honk and a wave of thanks. Dixon turned to head back to his Expedition.

That's when he saw the other pickup. It had just pulled off of the road, behind where Dixon was parked with his lights flashing. Dixon was too far away to get behind the wheel and take off. When the driver hopped down from their vehicle, motor running, door ajar, Dixon froze.

He could've drawn, but didn't. He could have shouted for them to stay back and maintain their distance.

He didn't do that either.

The best way he could explain why he didn't do those things was by claiming he temporarily forgot he was a cop, and he had the means, training, and instincts to defend his own safety. The long hours of anticipation had weakened his ability to access defensive instincts. The awful solitude of where they were, without another human being or sign of civilization in sight, broke down the rest of Dixon's confidence, leaving nothing useful behind.

Marcus strolled up to him, hands in the air, and Dixon was only a guy who'd run out without a word of explanation. The Glock strapped to him didn't exist, and it never even slightly occurred to him to reach for it, because it wasn't there. He wasn't wearing a holster, or a radio to call for assistance—he was naked and afraid. All he wanted was for Marcus to not be mad at him. That was the only way everything would be okay. He had to please Marcus.

"I'd like to talk to ya, Dixie, if that's okay with you. Not so much to ask, is it? I've shared my home with you for how long, now? That gives me some privileges. I think I've earned that. You're going to be coming home. We'll make the arrangements right now. I know you've been waiting out the time until I was back. Now I am back, so you're coming back, too."

I'm not coming back. I'm never coming back.

The words were there, in his mind. They never made it to his lips. His lips were glued together, his tongue thick and numb in his mouth.

Dixon grunted, intending dissent. It came out sounding more like agreement. Instinct told him to agree, to pacify Marcus so he didn't lose his temper. That was more crucial than standing up for his decision to move out.

No one was around, not for miles. The road was empty. Not a house or man-made structure of any sort was in sight. Dixon could hear the radio, faintly, in his Expedition. It was white noise, a background to their discussion. That was familiar. Marcus tended to leave the television playing or stereo on when he was moved to make something clear to Dixon. Their discussions were a temporary distraction for Marcus. Once they were done, he could go right back to what he had been doing. Same old, same old.

Dixon liked to get lost in the distant sounds. His mind would float away to other worlds while his body was busy. When it was safe to return, he would.

The news station was reporting that there had been a suicide bombing overseas. A dozen people had been killed in the explosion. Dixon tried to imagine just going about your business, buying food or trying to catch the bus, and being taken out in a fraction of a second by a huge, hot blast.

He didn't move a muscle as Marcus un-holstered Dixon's service weapon, undoing the strap, sliding it free. He didn't even blink as the Glock was raised to his lips. The edge of the cool metal pried them apart, slipped between them and past his teeth, his lower jaw falling to accommodate the barrel. When he made a sickly groan, he barely heard it. He wasn't in Zus, Alaska, at all. He was waiting by a bus in Syria or Israel, feeling the heat of the explosion, no time to be scared or react. It was out of his hands. He was taken, whisked away by fate. It was kind of peaceful, actually.

Somewhere less real, on the side of a road on the outskirts of a small town in the lower portion of Alaska, USA, Marcus said sweetly, "Down on your knees, Dixie. You're gonna learn not to raise weapons at me. That was a bad thing to do. That's something we're going to deal with, just the two of us, right now. You've got some penance to take. Huh? Don't ya? Sure you do. That's it, open wide. How's that taste? You wanna suck on that, or you want something better?"

The metal pressed against his tongue. It began to push farther back, so he had to relax his throat to make room. He didn't think about how at any moment, the back of his head could disintegrate with the slightest twitch of Marcus's finger, and flesh, bone, and blood would spray over asphalt. He was too distracted by the feel of desert heat on his face, the taste of dust in the air. If he concentrated hard enough, he realized he could make out the face of the person holding open a long coat. Things were taped down under there, to the person's chest. It was a woman. She was quite beautiful, but she was crying. Even through the noise of the street, the bustle of people, he could hear the crying.

"Open nice and wide for me. I feel any teeth, it'll be bad. You don't wanna make me smash out your teeth with a hammer, do ya,

Dixie? I've got one in my truck. I'd have to do it, you know, for my own safety. I'd break every one of these teeth and then we'd have to start again, and I don't have that kind of time to waste."

The barrel was removed from his mouth and instantly replaced by something else, something bigger, thicker, more yielding and longer. It was jammed all the way back, through his mouth, into his throat. Choking on it, retching violently, a hand clawed at the back of his head, forcing him to take it, preventing him from pulling back. A small, hard circle of metal dug into his temple, grinding there. He didn't think about what that was, or what it could do if Marcus's finger tightened slightly. Throat convulsing, he grabbed Marcus's legs, the desert giving way to flat, frozen, desolate earth. The thick, steady pressure from inside his esophagus, entirely blocking his airway, was unbearable. With all of his strength, survival instincts kicked in as he fought to get free and draw air. His lungs burned, tears flowed copiously from his eyes and nose. Saliva spilled over his lips, ran down his chin.

It went on and on. The world got darker. The pain grew exponentially.

He was woozy when he realized he was inhaling desperately through his nose. Marcus was ramming the back of Dixon's throat with his cock. It must have felt good to him, to have Dixon fighting like he was, because of how fast Marcus's thrusts came. Only once did Dixon begin to pull back. To punish him for the move, Marcus simply shoved his flesh back into Dixon's airway for another minute or so. Dixon beat on his leg, strangling, gagging, mouth open as wide as it would go, but to no use. He couldn't dislodge the obstruction. In fact, when Dixon gagged, Marcus just pushed deeper, and pulled him in closer.

Breathing was all he cared about for the rest of it. He didn't fight or push or open his eyes. Marcus used Dixon's mouth in a rough, messy way, and Dixon let him. The gun stayed pointed to Dixon's temple. When Marcus came down his throat, he thrust all the way in again, bottoming out, holding the back of Dixon's head as Dixon retched so hard it felt like his entire stomach was trying to chase up his gullet. The trickle of semen kept triggering the reaction. He couldn't stop. He was making a shrill noise of formless terror when Marcus freed himself.

Dixon doubled over, puking on the asphalt.

Something hit him across the back of the head. It dazed him, and he tried to crawl away, leaving the steaming vomit behind. But then he felt that metal circle again, leveled right at the center of his forehead this time.

"You're gonna crawl to your vehicle and do exactly what I say, aren'tcha?"

Dixon grunted, nodding slowly, too scared to speak.

Advancing on his hands and knees, not caring about the rocks in the dirt, digging painfully into his skin, he moved in a straight line.

"Stop right there."

He was next to the Expedition, on the driver's side. He felt his holster get slid down one arm and let Marcus remove it from him. Next, his duty belt was unbuckled and set aside on the road.

"Stand up. Slowly."

Shaking, panting, not knowing where to look or what to expect, he got his feet under him and straightened.

"Unbuckle those pants. Take 'em down to your knees. Undies, too."

It got harder to hold in the terrified moans and grunts, just raw sounds of primal fear.

He pulled his pants down, taking his boxers with them, then straightened again as his genitals began to freeze.

"Get in the vehicle. Sit down right there."

Marcus had opened the driver's side door and was gesturing to it. Dixon did as he was told. Then, Marcus reclined the seat.

"Raise those hands in the air. You don't move 'em and I won't bury this barrel in your balls and pull the trigger. Got it?"

"G-got it," Dixon managed, raising his hands.

Marcus walked around the Expedition and got in the passenger's side, still holding the gun.

Dixon closed his eyes, breathing in jagged tears, gasps, and shallow inhales.

"You can put your hands down now. That's it."

Marcus started touching him, rubbing over Dixon's bare thigh to clasp his flaccid cock. The gruff sound of Marcus's voice filled Dixon's awareness. His tone was soothing, and it anchored Dixon to familiar reactions and emotions. He knew what to do to shift things to a place where there was less mortal danger.

"I wouldn't have had to do that if you hadn't run off and raised your gun at me," Marcus was saying. "Now you know how it feels to have a gun pointed at you. It's not pleasant, is it? And the rape fantasy was your goddamned idea. You remember that, right? You asked me to cuff you, whip you with your belt. Of course, feeding your ass the end of that gun was my contribution, but you got off all the same. Didn't ya? Compared to that, I think I went easy on you today. Don't you think? You know I don't wanna hurt you, Dixie. If you'd stop screwing things up, it wouldn't have to be this way. But you know what? It's over now. We're even, fair and square."

The Expedition's doors were both shut and the heat was on full-blast. With an extra shirt from the footwell on the passenger's side, Marcus wiped off Dixon's chin and face.

Still trying to stroke Dixon stiff with his right hand, with his left, Marcus gently brushed the hair back from Dixon's forehead.

"Time to come back home. I'll let you get your things, move 'em back to the house, where you belong. I know it must be hard to have me gone so much, but now I'm here and we can be together, like we should be. Missed you, babe."

The Glock had been set on the dashboard, in front of the passenger seat where Marcus sat. Though his head was swimming, instincts continued to drive Dixon.

He was still. He didn't fight, or talk back. A sickened groan wanted to burst from his lips and he held it in with what little strength he had left.

"I can make it so good for you," Marcus promised. "You know I can."

After some time, Dixon's body betrayed him, stiffening at the stimulation. Marcus asked, "You want me to stop?"

Dixon grunted. Marcus caressed Dixon's balls, fondling the soft skin of his sac. He closed Dixon's balls up in his palm and squeezed lightly, making Dixon grunt again, for a different reason.

"Feel's nice, doesn't it?" Marcus grinned.

"Yeah," Dixon murmured, trembling and disoriented. He knew his life was in danger and he was choosing to get lost in the sensations instead of facing that. Because it did feel good.

"Know what feels even better?"

His head lowered onto Dixon's lap. With one hand, Marcus steadied Dixon's member. With the other, he kept fondling, tugging on and squeezing Dixon's testicles.

Marcus deep-throated him right away, completely engulfing Dixon in wet, soft, tight heat. Mouth falling open, face contorting with equal parts disgust and pleasure, Dixon had never hated himself more. Marcus was right, he did deserve this. He'd brought it on himself. If he really hadn't wanted it, he could have said no. He could've fought back.

He didn't fight back. He lay there, gasping roughly, not really moving at all as Marcus sucked him off. It was something Marcus was good at doing. He knew all of Dixon's trigger spots, how he liked it deep and slow, that he liked to have his balls played with. Sometimes Dixon couldn't get off if it didn't hurt a little, and Marcus knew that too.

Dixon bit hard on his lip as he came, swallowing as much of his cry as he could. Before Marcus could pull off, Dixon was quick to wipe the tears dry on his face. He was still shaking as Marcus sat up, not bothering to cover Dixon, leaving his cock lying wet and spent against his thigh.

"You're coming home to me, right Dix?"

"Mm-hmm," Dixon hummed, wanting to pull his underwear up, but afraid to.

"Good. That's real good."

Marcus got out of the Expedition, taking the pistol with him. He took the time to unload it before setting it on the dirt and giving Dixon one last wave. Then he was walking back to his truck, a pleased grin on his face.

Frantically, Dixon yanked his pants back up, the urge to vomit strong again, the sour taste in his mouth reminding him of what had just happened. He righted his seat and watched the rearview like his life depended on it.

Marcus turned around and drove away.

Dixon wasn't sure how long he sat there, staring at the barren roadway — clear in both directions. It felt like a long, long time.

Chapter 17
Disarmed

All Dixon cared about was breathing. After a little while, he decided breathing might be easier outside. He bundled up in his coat, gloves, hat, and scarf, and walked out to the living area. They all stared at him. Jaye took the hint and got his outerwear on too.

"Where are you going?" Brekken asked, clearly worried.

"Back stoop," Dixon explained, nodding at the back door.

"Oh. Okay. Okay, good. We'll finish dinner. Open some wine. Okay?"

Dixon nodded.

A moment later, they were out in the frigid air. It was pitch black, starlight and moonlight reflecting off the crisp ground. Dixon sat on the back steps, huddling for warmth. Jaye sat beside him.

"You told me you had a bad traffic stop," Jaye said in his strangely rough, low voice. "Marcus was there, wasn't he?"

There was no response from Dixon. He was trying to focus on the shapes of things in the dark.

"Well, nod or somethin' man. Come on," Jaye urged.

It happened suddenly, before Dixon could hold it in or take it back. The nauseous moan he'd held in hours earlier—pure self-recrimination and horror—bubbled up, loud in the night. He clapped his hands over his mouth and curled up into an even tighter ball, because the moan led to broken whines he hated even more.

He wished Jaye would leave. Tears streamed from his face and he held his head, wrapping his arms behind it, pressing it to his knees. His breaths began to hitch with the force of his sobs and he tried to fight it down. He really did.

After some minutes passed, Dixon collected himself a little. He was able to raise his head, blinking his eyes clear, wiping his face dry. The stony look on Jaye's face was hard to bear, so he stared straight ahead instead.

Softly, sounding like a man who would and had done absolutely anything to survive, without apology, Jaye told him, "You know what I think? I think you wouldn't be this upset about getting hit. You'd be angry, sure. Someone hits you, makes you wanna hit back. I don't see nothing in you that wants to hit back. He did something worse than hitting. 'Cause that look on your face? *That* look? I've felt that way, too."

Jaye gave it a moment to sink in, as Dixon hid his mouth behind folded hands. The longer it drew out, the more he could imagine it, even before Jaye said it.

"I'm talkin' about like after I was abducted and taken to that alley, where they stripped me, molested and tortured me. But, you know, the physical trauma isn't what has stayed with me. It's what they *said* while they were sticking that knife through me and fiddling around between my legs with their clammy, thick fingers. They wanted me scared. They wanted me *really* fucking scared. It was fun for them to tell me how they were going to pull out my guts while I was still awake, so I could *watch*. That was some hard shit to endure, Dixon. Took me a while to begin to get over it, after." He jabbed a gloved finger at his own head, pointing to the memories that wouldn't shake loose.

"I been *through* shit." His eyes were dark, beautiful, and vicious in the black of that Alaskan night. Dixon never forgot it, how young Jaye Larson looked, whispering his horrors as the breath fogged from his soft lips. "You look at me and tell me otherwise. If anyone understands, it's me."

Dixon held Jaye's stare, enduring it, his mouth sealed tight, the words not there at all. He could tell Jaye what happened no more than he could chew off his right hand. It was unthinkable.

"You can't tell me, can you?" Jaye realized, understanding the silence. "Can you show me?"

Dixon didn't think he could, but then he saw that he was pulling off one of his gloves. His first two fingers stuck out, the rest folded in, thumb lying flat. For a second he just looked at it, the hand feeling heavier than it should, not a part of him at all. He lifted it and stuck the two straightened fingers between his lips, sliding them back between his jaws and closed his eyes.

He could feel the heat radiating from Jaye, could hear his breath quicken as Dixon drew the fingers out, but left his mouth open, wide and ready, sticking the fingertips against the side of his head instead. Tears slipped down Dixon's cheeks silently.

"Stop," Jaye rasped, quickly pulling Dixon's hand away from his head, like they could do him harm. "Fuck him. *Fuck him!* Are you telling me he put a gun to your head? And you didn't call for backup, or send people after his ass right away? What's to stop this guy from coming over here right now and putting a gun to Brekken's head because you're not back home with him already?"

"No, I did what he wanted," Dixon argued. "He wouldn't do that. I wouldn't let him!"

"You wouldn't let him put a gun to your sister's head, but you'll let him put a gun to *your* head? Fucking seriously, Dixon?"

"It's not like that! It's... it's complicated, okay? *I'm* the one that fucked things up here."

"What are you talking about?" Jaye snapped.

"He was outside headquarters this morning. I raised my gun at him for no reason. I made him angry. *I* started it."

"Are you fucking kidding me? You don't make excuses for that piece of shit!"

"It wouldn't have happened if I didn't—"

"Stop," Jaye growled, grabbing Dixon's chin, holding it as he tried to sear the logic through Dixon's thick skull with the force of his stare alone.

"I'm a bad cop. I'm an idiot. I did all the wrong things! I should have told him to stay back. I let him get close enough to take my weapon. These things only happen because I *let them* happen!"

"That's not true. That's what he wants you to think. He's fucking got you brainwashed into thinking you brought this on yourself, doesn't he? He touched you? Forced himself on you? While he put the gun to your head? What a fucking nice guy."

Jaw clenched, Dixon said nothing. He knew Jaye was only trying to help, but he had it all wrong. He didn't know how many chances Dixon had to make things go another way. He let Marcus take the Glock from him, froze up. It was Dixon's fault what had happened. He had it coming for being such an idiot. In the Expedition was even worse because Dixon agreed to it. He'd had the chance to say no, to stand up for himself, to prevent Marcus from pleasuring him, but part of Dixon had wanted it. There was no gun to his head that time, no restraints. It was just Marcus, touching him, sucking him as good as he ever had.

Then the mention of the rape fantasy... That had happened a year ago. Marcus got the drop on him one night when Dixon thought he was home alone, got him down on his knees with an unloaded gun pointed at him. Dixon was told to strip and handcuffed to a pipe in the kitchen. Marcus whipped him with Dixon's belt until his back bled, then stuck the end of the gun up his ass while jerking him off, whispering things in his ear all the while, just as twisted as the shit he'd said in the road that day about smashing out Dixon's teeth. Didn't matter. Dixon came anyway, begging Marcus not to fuck him in order to get Marcus to fuck him, which Marcus did, happily. It was all previously arranged and agreed to, or the core of it at least, if not some of the grislier details.

Dixon would never have been able to tell Jaye about any of that. If Jaye knew, it would have changed his mind about being with Dixon. He'd see Dixon as Marcus saw him, for the fuck-up Dixon really was, when push came to shove.

"You injured anywhere?"

"I don't think it's safe for you to be around me," Dixon murmured, head bowed.

"Would you answer the fucking question?"

Dixon shot him a look, telling him wordlessly to back off.

"Do you need the hospital?" Jaye demanded, not put off at all.

"No," Dixon said, standing.

"Look at me, right fucking now."

Running his tongue over his teeth, Dixon tried to stay mad, to keep fighting, but Jaye's will was stronger. Dixon gave in and looked.

"We're going inside and having dinner. Then you're going to bed to rest. Got it?"

He realized then, that this kid, this sixteen-year-old-looking, wanna-be thug was telling Dixon, a grown man and a cop, what to do. And Dixon loved it. Jaye yanked on the leash and Dixon only wanted to follow. It was sick, and fucked-up, but Dixon knew it to be truth. He loved having Jaye tell him what to do.

"Okay," he agreed.

Dixon wasn't exactly an active participant in dinner. The chili smelled fantastic, waking up his senses enough to encourage him to eat, despite his restless stomach. With his bowl filled, a piece of bread and a glass filled to the top with wine, he sat at the table and dug in. Jaye stayed next to him, helping Brekken serve and fetch drinks, but then settling beside Dixon at the table.

Everyone had been served plenty of wine except Jaye. When Jaye declined a glass of his own, Dixon realized Jaye probably never had the stuff before, due to his age and circumstances. Dixon and Brekken drank like they wanted to get buzzed as fast as possible to ease the tension. Grant was staring at him. Dixon could feel it, and could feel the presence of a shotgun that wasn't really in Grant's hands at the moment, only figuratively so. Brekken pretended everything was normal. They talked but Dixon didn't really hear what was said. They didn't ask him any more questions about what had happened. That was good. Maybe the shell-shocked nature of Dixon's every reaction convinced them to collectively back off.

Or maybe it was Jaye. Dixon had admired the "don't fuck with me" air about him ever since they'd met. It didn't come from a badge or age or any of the usual routes. It came from within, and from dearly-tested experience with worst-case scenarios. Kill or be killed had been the story of Jaye's life for years. Meanwhile, Dixon's life had been more a case of constantly pleading for mercy. He had learned guns did no good. Weapons in general, in fact, did no good. Logic didn't matter, nor right and wrong. Physical strength didn't even play that big a part. It was simply, when you boiled it down, a matter of who wanted it more. Plain and simple.

When everything else was stripped away, what Dixon wanted

most was to survive, even if that meant acquiescing to terrible things in the process. If he was still alive and whole at the end of the day, that's all that counted.

The best way to ensure one's own safety around volatile people was to not fight back and not argue. You let them take the reins, or think they had them, anyway, before defusing the situation in the ways the law taught them to.

Part of him wanted to believe Jaye had experienced the same reactions, but that wasn't true. Jaye always fought back, in his mind if not with his body. Dixon had learned as much. If Jaye was going to be tortured, raped, and murdered, what did he do? How did he react? He slit that motherfucker's throat, then ran after the guy who'd been holding him down.

When Jaye was stabbed in jail, he couldn't avoid it, couldn't fight back. Not right away. He waited, got better, biding his time. Only then did he seek revenge.

It was beautiful, inspiring, and encouraging.

It all rolled over and over in Dixon's mind, going downhill like a snowball, collecting rationalizations and musings along the way. He got swept up as it gained speed, his reflections taking him with them.

Someone took his hand and gave it a gentle squeeze.

He blinked and looked at his right hand, jabbing a piece of his bread into the chili but unmoving, frozen in the act. He wondered how long he'd been holding it there. The juice had sucked up into it and made it soggy.

Jaye had his other hand. That much was clear thanks to his peripheral vision.

"You all right?" Jaye asked, his voice low and deep.

"No, not at all, really."

"What can we do?"

"Feed me to the wolves. Save yourselves."

"Dixon," Brekken said sharply, a hiss.

"He's just tired, right?" Jaye said. "It's been a hell of a day."

"Yeah. Sure." He prodded at some beans and pieces of meat in the chili. "I am dog food. I'm fuckin' Alpo."

"Would you knock it off?" Brekken scolded. "Stop talking like that!"

Dixon drank his wine, gulping rather than sipping. Jaye gave him a strange look.

"Your sister just asked me if I'd seen the prostitutes hanging out at work. Said they tend to slip the law when you all try to crack down."

"Lot lizards. Sleeper leapers. Spring up like weeds," Dixon murmured. "Easy money, I guess. They come in all shapes, sizes, and ages. It's the damnedest thing."

"Truckers need company too," Jaye said.

"Yeah. I suppose."

A short while later, Dixon excused himself. He and Brekken had finished off most of the bottle of wine between themselves. It was making him feel heavy and sleepy, but in a good way. He brought his bowl and empty wine glass to the sink, then went to brush his teeth so he could go collapse in bed.

It didn't turn out like he expected.

He just kept brushing and brushing, squeezing more paste on his brush when it ran out, scrubbing harder and harder at his teeth.

He was breathing roughly and crying again when Jaye pulled on Dixon's arm, telling him, "Stop!"

Dixon shook him off and rinsed his mouth, planting both hands on the sink's edge, doing everything he could to not look at his reflection in the mirror.

Finally, he undressed and got in bed, burrowing under layers and layers of blankets to stop the shivering. His head was swimming from all of the wine he'd had.

"I've never seen you like this, man," Jaye said, sitting beside Dixon on the bed. "This is all because of Marcus, isn't it? Because he came back and fucked with your head. He's just one guy, you know. If you don't give him power, he won't have it. You get to decide how much control he has over you, and you're giving him one hell of a lot of it right now. It's your job to protect your sister *and* me. Making that fucker think he's got you under his thumb doesn't help anybody. You really want to leave us and go be with that asshole instead?"

"Of course I don't," Dixon murmured. The vacant, worn-down feeling was overwhelming. All he wanted was sleep, and the ability to hope the morning might bring better things.

"You planning to kick his ass, tell him to fuck off?"

Dixon sighed, rubbing a hand over his face. "I'm really fucking tired, okay? Just let me sleep right now. I'll be able to think more clearly after I recharge. I really don't know what to do right now. There don't seem to be any good options."

Jaye gestured to Dixon's body, how he was curled up under the covers, feeling like a screw-up in every way that mattered. "You were different at the cabin, with me. You were intimidating. It impressed me, and I'm hard to impress, Dix. But as soon as you started talking about the ways Marcus hurt you, you became this. And now? After today?" Jaye shook his head. "You can do this, Dix. I know you can. You just have to believe in yourself a little."

Dixon had no response. It meant something that Jaye believed in him, and saw strength Dixon didn't feel. Maybe that could be the hope that would get them through. He just had to figure out how to see himself through Jaye's eyes instead of his own.

"You're not going anywhere, right?" Jaye asked severely. That gleaming edge was in his eyes again, like he was capable of anything, would do anything necessary to get by. It was what drove him to come on so hard to Dixon in order to ensure his own protection, what had gotten him out of jail in one piece, mentally and physically. Now it was directed at Dixon for other reasons, other motivations. "Or do I need to cuff you to the bed?"

"You think I'd go?" Dixon asked with honest curiosity, not knowing the answer, himself.

"I asked you a question."

"I don't know; I kind of want you to cuff me to the bed." The smile that had been coming so easily to his face since he was just a baby in his mother's arms was there now. That was something else Marcus took from him. It had been a few years since smiling had come easily, but there was something about the improbability of who Jaye was, at heart, that made Dixon want to smile again. That was another good thing to chase after and hold on to. It made him really grateful to have Jaye there, at his side. Dixon could feel the smile on his lips, but the gathering darkness in Jaye's expression told Dixon maybe something cruel was lingering in his smile that hadn't been before.

"Do I look like I'm fucking kidding around? One way or another, you aren't going anywhere."

"Hmm," Dixon grunted, nodding. "Well, okay then, boss."

He was asleep seconds after Jaye climbed in bed with him, and didn't wake until dawn was creeping in through the windows, slowly shedding light on the terrible thing that had happened during the night.

Chapter 18
Fighting Back

Part of Jaye knew he'd be tracking down Marcus even before Dixon showed up at the truck stop that day with the innate good-guy spirit that usually shined from him hacked brutally away. The trooper that had gone out of his way to buy a hungry stranger groceries with his own money, giving him a lift home, fighting hard against Jaye's come-on attempts just because it was the right thing to do, had vanished. The friendly inner light that had drawn Jaye to Dixon like a moth to a flame had vanished. After being surrounded by nothing but people constantly only looking out for their own interests for years, Jaye knew Dixon's giving, caring nature was rare and precious. There was something fragile about Dixon that Marcus knew how to shatter, and Jaye suspected Marcus was the only one who *could* break Dixon. If Marcus wasn't around, Dixon would flourish and become the man Jaye knew he could be. He'd be a better cop for Zus, a better protector for Jaye, a better brother for Brekken, and he could go through each day with absolute confidence.

After what had happened during that traffic stop, Dixon was convinced the only way to save the people he cared about was to let Marcus destroy him and his good heart. He was too mired in his history and learned behaviors to see the only thing that needed to be done, was for Marcus to be taken out.

As the night had went on, and Jaye learned more, it hadn't really affected what Jaye knew was going to happen, it just sharpened his goals.

He'd known people like Dixon, and he'd known people like Marcus, too. People like Dixon had a spark inside them, glistening so brightly with gladness and appreciation for the wonders of the world it drew human vermin out of the dark. The more Dixon gleamed with humble peace, the more the corrupted wanted to dull that shine. That was Marcus. Someone like him saw the faint, welcoming smile that was always dancing there, in the shape of Dixon's mouth, ready to glow from within, and their instinct was to beat it down. Maybe it was jealousy, knowing they could never take the kind of simple pleasure from living those like Dixon did. Maybe not. Maybe it was just evil in their veins, polluting everything they touched instead of shining on it.

It was good to know what needed to happen. It gave Jaye more focus than he'd had since being released. When he'd been set free into the world, he had floundered. It had been uncomfortable and frightening, to have so many possibilities.

Now, his path was clear. He had to fuck Marcus up.

It was nature, just as much as the dynamics between Dixon and Marcus were nature. Dixon couldn't fight for himself as hard as he should where Marcus was concerned. He was convinced Marcus would always find a way to beat him, even though that wasn't true. Marcus had taught Dixon to think that was the case. So, Dixon would be constantly drawn to surrender, in the hopes of saving others from harm, and that's just how Marcus liked it. Marcus was someone Jaye didn't yet know, personally, so he was judging merely by type. And there was no doubt Jaye knew that type. If there was anything more satisfying than beating the piss out of an abuser and brainwasher, Jaye didn't know it. That was something Cash had helped him see. It was good to own that taste for blood, when it was directed at people like that, who brought others down in order to pull themselves up. They had it coming. The law wouldn't give it. Society wouldn't give it. Only people on the edge, people like him and his crew, would give it. It was the law of the jungle.

Marcus thought he was leader of the pack, the hard-ass, the biggest and meanest. That might be true, but it was only because he was standing on top of Dixon, grinding his boot heels into Dixon's back to keep him low. Jaye was pretty sure that, compared to Marcus, he was smarter, faster, younger, and had more incentive to feed his bloodlust. All he had to do was the dirty work of knocking Marcus down in order for Dixon to find his feet again and take over. Jaye was willing and able to do the one thing Dixon couldn't. When Jaye tore out Marcus's throat, then *Dixon* would be leader. The pack would be his, be safe. Brekken and Grant wouldn't have to worry, and Jaye wouldn't either.

That was figuratively speaking, of course. Jaye didn't literally intend to rip out Marcus's jugular. It would be fun, but it would be too obvious. He had to go for subtle, because he wanted to do this himself, and he didn't intend to get caught.

The first thing he needed was an address. He acted once Dixon was passed out, hopefully out of reach of the nightmares, drawn too deep by the trauma inflicted upon his body. Jaye couldn't stop seeing the dead look to Dixon's eyes that had been there when he'd turned his own fingers, in the shape of a gun, on his own mouth and ate the barrel. It made Jaye so angry he could taste it. It was bitter, like acid, and he wanted to spit it in Marcus's face, hoping it would make the skin slough off, bubbling and oozing.

The sexual component, Jaye could only guess at, taking cues from Dixon's open mouth as he'd shifted the imaginary pistol to his temple, and to the way he'd brushed his teeth feverishly for ten minutes without stopping. Jaye suspected it was worse than he thought, that Dixon wasn't talking about it because of how bad it had been, which only urged Jaye on.

He slipped out of bed and found Dixon's wallet. It was sitting on the nightstand beside the bed with the other random items from his pockets. Jaye had noted the street name and house number as they'd pulled up earlier that night. The address on Dixon's license didn't match. It wasn't Brekken and Grant's home listed there. It was Marcus's.

Got you, motherfucker, Jaye thought, and smiled.

CLANG.

The sound seemed real, even though he knew it wasn't. It echoed down a long hallway as the metal door of his cell pulled shut, sealing him inside with the one guard who especially had it out for him. He scrambled back on the cot he'd been living on in administrative seg-regation—commonly known as solitary confinement—since they'd thrown him in there. They didn't know any details, only that he'd been involved in the attack on a rival gang. They didn't have any proof he was the one who had carried out the attack in its entirety, with his brothers holding the target down. No one ratted him out because no one wanted Jaye to do to them what he'd done to Tio.

The guard swung his baton, wearing a cocky, rapist's smile. It was just the two of them. No one was around. If he had the stamina, he might have hours to torture Jaye without threat of interruption.

You're gonna be really fucking sorry you landed in here, piggy. Not gonna be much of you left by the time Cash gets you back.

The talk wasn't as cocky as the smile, though, because the guard had seen Tio, with blood covering his face, when he'd been escorted to medical. Tio had been screaming.

Jaye's hand itched for a weapon.

"Those are real pretty eyes you have," Jaye said, soft and scary, while standing in Dixon's temporary bedroom. He said it just like he had before, in his cell.

The guard stopped advancing. Then he backed up a step, rethinking his plan.

"There's no one else here," Jaye whispered, and the ghost van-ished.

Jaye memorized the information, checked his phone for direc-tions, then snuck out of the bedroom. Holding his shoes, he gathered his coat, hat, and gloves and took Dixon's key with him as he crept out onto the front porch to finish getting dressed. He locked the door behind him.

The long walk was rather pleasant. The cold kept him hustling, jog-ging most of the way to keep his blood pumping. The night was clear and the stars bright. It was beautiful. The world was asleep. Everyone but him was unaware. When he was moving, the world stretching out in all directions around him, ripe with possibilities, he never felt bet-ter. The ghosts couldn't touch him. He was too quick for the lurking shadows, the landscape open around him, enabling a quick escape if needed. He wasn't trapped alone in the dark. He was free.

It took hours. Carefully, Jaye noted the street name as he headed down it. He needed only glance at the house number, because the truck he'd seen at the pump earlier that day was there, in the driveway.

It was Marcus. He was there.

As cold as he was, as he began to imagine everything Dixon had been through in that small home, over years and years, Jaye felt like he was breathing fire. Dixon—*his* Dixon—had been beaten, broken, raped, tortured, and brainwashed. He imagined Dixon's smiling, hopeful face, asking to go to his sister's party, being deliberately smashed against a wall. He imagined Marcus holding Dixon down, stripping him, hurting him, and violating him as Dixon pleaded for help that never came.

Jaye was moving before he knew it. There was a shed on the side of the property, near the emergency generator around the side of the house. It was where Jaye would find what he needed. He drew a pair of homemade tools from his pocket and set to work on picking the lock. About a minute later, he had access to multiple cans of gasoline.

Sometimes Jaye thought about how things could have gone if Cash hadn't been there for him. He wouldn't have made it. He would have been worm food. His life in prison would have been short, brutal, and painted red with his blood and screaming.

Dixon never had someone like Cash, willing to protect him at all costs. Jaye resolved to be that for him now, unasked, so Dixon could become the man Jaye, in turn, needed *him* to be.

He peeked in a window; saw the outline of a man lying in bed. Then, staying hidden in the shadows, he quietly splashed the house's outer wall with some of the gasoline probably intended for the generator. Jaye covered the outer bedroom wall pretty thoroughly, spreading the fuel. He emptied every can that was in the shed. It didn't take long.

The smell of it filled his nose, pungent and powerful. There was a small stove heater in the bedroom, located against the outer wall. Jaye concentrated the gas around that spot, knowing it would be his cover. The empty cans were stacked neatly back inside the shed, just like he found them. He locked it back up and checked the ground for footprints, scuffing out any he found as he backed his way out of the area.

When his work was done, he stood there, savoring his efforts, meditating on the monster housed within. The lighter was in his pocket, the same one Jaye regularly used to start the fireplace in his own home. He flicked the starter. The small flame wavered in the wind. Cupping a hand around it, he watched it burn—small, pure, and true.

"For Dixon," Jaye said quietly, reverently. "May you never fucking touch him again."

He lit the end of a stick and threw it.

The world erupted and Jaye ran.

He kept running until he was gasping and clutching his bad side. Collapsing to the earth, he sprawled there, wincing.

"You fuckers," he growled. "God damn it."

The pain was a spear, like the metal that had pierced him, clean through, twice. He pressed a hand against it, like he was still staunching the blood which had first flowed over his fingers that night, long ago. He didn't yet have all of the confidence he'd found in prison. There was no certainty he could fight his way out somehow, or outsmart his attackers like he learned he could, like with the rapist guard who quickly grew too scared of Jaye to fuck him over anymore. He was just a teenage kid who thought he was dying, that his intestines would begin to spill from his gut in long, slick ropes in which his feet would get tangled. Imaginary attackers yanked at the wet organ, tugging it inch by inch from his belly, wrapping it around their bloody hands as they laughed madly. He pressed harder to make them stop, to keep his insides inside.

Fingers wriggled in the wound, digging around, looking for something to pull out of him and he rolled onto his stomach, gagging. "You're not real. You're not here. Fucking stop it, you pussy. Get out of here. Get home!"

Gonna slice open your belly, piggy. Pull your insides out. Make you watch.

He slapped his palms against his ears, pressing hard to silence the voices, yelling, "Shut up!"

That piggy cop's gonna make you pay for what you did. He liked being raped, just like you did. Gonna make you pay. Gonna tie you down. Gonna slice you open.

"Shut UP! Shut up. Shut up," he grunted, willing them away, trying to breathe more normally, to slow his racing heart.

The fingers wriggled in his guts. They reached down his gullet. They fondled between his legs, parted his cheeks and poked around in his ass. He remembered a few of those times in the dark, when he didn't want it, when someone was pushing their flesh into his body, burrowing deeper, rutting and grunting like a pig, pumping and sweating, treating him like meat, something to carve up, ingest, and shit out.

They held him down; hurt him where it hurt the most.

And there wasn't anything clever or terrifying he could say to save himself or scare his pursuers more than they scared him, because they were in his head. He couldn't kill them, and he couldn't keep convincing himself they always lied.

"Did it for Dixon. I did it for Dixon. For Dixon," Jaye repeated, beating the phantoms and memories away with the power of his heart. He saw Marcus sticking a gun in Dixon's mouth, Dixon not even pleading for help, just giving up, thinking he was dog food, that he was better off there, getting hurt again. Moaning out some of his disgust and fury, Jaye curled up in a ball on his knees, holding his head. It was worse when it was true. He couldn't reason it away with pitiful assurances.

If they find out what you did, they'll send you back. You'll never get out. You'll be someone's piggy forever.

"It's worth it if he's safe. He'll be safe. Dixon will be safe."

You gonna sacrifice yourself just like him? Lie down at the altar of the monsters; let them use their cocks, knives, and guns to take you apart?

Jaye took a deep breath, blew it out. He did it again, feeling the frigid air filling his lungs, blowing it out as fog. He opened his eyes and got to his feet.

Then he started running again, putting the ghosts behind him, trying to outpace them.

When Jaye got back to the house, Grant was sitting on the front porch with a mug of steaming coffee in hand and a shotgun across his knees.

It was still night. The world was silent except for the two of them, two pairs of eyes in the dark.

Jaye's panic crawled up his throat and threatened to strangle him, but he tried to play it cool, to act as if everything was fine, though it was as far from fine as it could be.

"Couldn't sleep, either?" he asked.

"Not really," Grant said, looking him over. "Strange time to go for a walk."

"Yeah, well, I keep strange hours these days. I get claustrophobic," he lied. "Need to remind myself of where I am."

"Makes sense. It's because of Dixon, isn't it? Because of what he told you."

Jaye didn't want to talk about Dixon. He wanted to get inside, wash the gasoline smell off of his hands, get undressed and pretend he never got out of bed in the first place.

"Look," he started, "I can't talk about that. If Dixon isn't ready to tell you guys—"

"Marcus fucked with him, didn't he? The secrecy makes that much evident. And that jackass is out there, right now. Dixon didn't stop him, or call for backup. Sesi didn't know a thing about an assault when Brekken talked to her. That means that piece of human shit could show up, at *my* house, at *any* time to collect what he thinks is his, and to hell with anyone that stands in his way."

"That shotgun might convince him otherwise," Jaye said evenly.

"Go on inside and get warm. You look freezing," Grant told him, inclining his head toward the door.

Marcus isn't freezing. Marcus is burning.

Jaye hesitated only a moment longer. "You gonna kick Dixon out? I mean, he's the one bringing this down on you two, right?"

"I'm gonna keep him *safe*," Grant said, looking Jaye square in the eye. "He's family."

"Good. That's what I want, too."

"I see that," Grant agreed, nodding. "You being here helped last night. Sometimes Brekken doesn't know what to say to him to help. He puts up walls. If you, uh, plan to stick around, that's fine with us."

"Thanks. I'm gonna head in."

He tried to rush past Grant as fast as possible, but the voices of the ghosts told him Grant could smell the gasoline, he was damned and doomed, it was only a matter of time now before Hell reclaimed its chosen and the ghosts won at last.

Chapter 19

Begging For It

It was a tough night. The first thing Jaye did was dump his coat, hat, gloves, clothes—all of it except his underwear and his boots, which might smell like gas just due to where he worked—in the washing machine, which was located on the opposite side of the house than the bedrooms. He hoped it could run without anyone hearing the noise. In the shower, Jaye scrubbed and scrubbed at his skin, trying to wash the smell off. He couldn't tell if it was stuck in his nose or really still there. After the long shower, he put his wet gear in the dryer and quietly closed the laundry room door. With wrinkled fingers, shivering, exhausted, and triumphant, he crept to bed and slipped under the covers.

Dixon didn't stir.

It was very dark in the bedroom, and the shadows talked. For hours, Jaye tried to ignore them. Sleep eluded him. Every time he closed his eyes, he heard the whoosh of flames igniting. Behind that were gentle whispers filled with malice. Further back, deeper down, was the imagined sound of Dixon pleading for his life with his own pistol aimed at his head, Dixon being raped, Dixon terrified.

The old craving for a weapon was strong. He could taste it, how much better he would feel if only he had a sharpened edge in reach, just in case—but in case of what, he couldn't say.

The way he coped, at first at least, was to tuck his body up close to Dixon's, seeking warmth, comfort and someone blessedly tangible. When Dixon reacted to contact by rolling over and wrapping Jaye in an arm, drawing him closer, Jaye was glad. He liked being held by Dixon, knowing one less danger was out there, hunting those he cared about.

The closer Jaye got to dawn, the more time and exhaustion took its toll. There would be no sleep that night. He knew how he must look, still feared the smell of gasoline, too. In the end, he could only turn to something that used to serve him as an effective distraction to life's troubles. It was something he had forsaken, something utterly useless except for in situations like the one he was in, where his mind ran away with itself. It was a pursuit that utilized all of his senses, and all thought was channeled to one sole purpose. He was focused, concentrating so hard, nothing else could touch him. There were no worries, no fear, no doubt, no creeping dread or niggling uncertainty.

He hoped to be finished before Dixon woke, but it was not to be.

Blue eyes opened to stare right at the tablet of paper held in Jaye's left hand. The pencil in the right paused, twisted sideways and was rubbed against the paper at an angle as Jaye deepened the shadow under Dixon's jaw, covered with short, shining stubble.

"What're you doing?" Dixon asked groggily.

"Go back to sleep," Jaye replied, fixing the edge of Dixon's jaw and the slight curl of hair at his forehead. For an hour, he'd been fussing with the way that delicate strand lay adorning Dixon's forehead. He frowned and sighed when Dixon remained stubbornly awake. He drew the pad away, intending to drop it beside the bed, out of sight and reach.

Dixon grabbed for it before Jaye could get it completely out of the way.

They both had hold of the pad of paper and there was a brief struggle for control of it. Desperation drove Jaye while simple curiosity seemed to fuel his companion.

"It's not for you," Jaye growled. "Let go!"

The pad slipped from his fingers when Dixon gave one last hard yank. A moment later, he got it turned around to face him, gazing with wonder and surprise at the paper. Jaye tried to ignore the reactions. He didn't have any desire to be judged, by Dixon or anyone else. He rolled to his back from his side and exhaled heavily.

"You can draw?"

"No."

"You drew me. You drew me while I was sleeping. That's..."

"I know what it is. Give it back." He held out a hand, expectant and angry.

"This is really good," Dixon commented as he gazed down at the sketch, his voice softened. "I mean *really* good. It's kind of amazing actually. This is how you see me, huh?"

They gazed quietly at each other for a long moment without saying anything.

"You look better today," Jaye told him.

"You look like shit."

"Gee, thanks," Jaye sneered, making another grab for the tablet, but Dixon kept it out of his reach.

"What is this?" Dixon asked, lifting the pad. With his other hand, he reached out and caressed the side of Jaye's weary face. "What's *this*?"

"Nothing. It's nothing. Don't worry about it."

Jaye had been waiting for a phone to ring, but the house had been quiet. Not a single call had come through. He didn't know what that meant. Surely the fire had drawn attention. There was an obvious connection to Dixon. And yet, there was nothing. The drawing had been a way to distract from worry. As long as he was tracing the contours of Dixon's facial features, the creases in the blanket and pillow, measuring details and shading to catch the light, nothing else could invade his thoughts.

"Tell me. Did you not sleep? How long have you been awake?"

"I don't sleep well. It's an ongoing problem. And it's *my* problem, not yours."

"Now it's my problem," Dixon said stubbornly.

"I have trouble letting my guard down," Jaye reluctantly confessed. "Makes it hard to doze off."

"It really still bothers you, doesn't it? All of those fuckers that hurt you?"

Jaye didn't like the frown on Dixon's face, or the intensity of his stare. He had never seemed more like a cop, an authority figure, someone older and wiser than Jaye. Dixon scrutinized him, probably seeing bags under his eyes and emotional bruising behind them.

"No, Dix, I'm completely over it," he said sarcastically.

"No one is going to hurt you. *No one*, you hear me?"

It was more of that cop voice, that *guard* voice.

"Yes, sir," Jaye replied with less sarcasm than before, though Dixon probably couldn't detect the difference. It had always been the safer bet to respond to commands politely than to mouth off like he wanted to. That was now an ingrained way to respond in all similar situations, whether Dixon was actually speaking with a cop's authority or not.

Dixon rolled off the bed and stood next to it. After retrieving his watch from the nightstand, he started to fasten the strap. "You don't need to hide anything," he said, still using a stern tone.

A chill ran down Jaye's back.

CLANG.

"I'm not hiding anything," Jaye murmured hollowly, feeling very far away. He drew his legs up and held his head in his hands.

"You know you are," Dixon countered, finishing getting his watch strap tightened. "And you've had every reason to hide things before." He turned to face the dresser, sliding open the top drawer.

Turn and face the wall. Drop 'em. All the way, good. Now, hands up. On the wall. I wanna see those hands.

He didn't like that he was naked under the sheet. He drew it more tightly around him, shaking his head slowly back and forth.

"I'm just saying you don't need to do that anymore. I'll take care of you, no matter what it is you're afraid to show me. The more honest you can be, the better I'll understand what you need."

"...stop... *Stop...*"

CLANG.

Where're you hiding it, huh? Got a tip. Sounded legit. Only two places I figure it could be. Think I'll check up here first...

They were touching him. The door was shut. Locked. Another guard was standing watch outside.

Dixon pulled a shirt from the drawer and turned back toward the bed, saying with an affectionate chuckle, "I'm not gonna *stop*, J-bird."

The fingers twisted up into him. They were so long and clammy, the scream bubbled up, but if he screamed, things would only get worse, because the guard knew just what to do to shut him up, fast. "I don't want it. I don't have it! *I don't have it!*" He was naked, helpless, scared. The vision and reality suddenly matched. In both he was pinned, in both he was exposed and vulnerable. Someone was grabbing him, touching him, holding him still so they could hurt him some more. Curled up on Dixon's bed, fighting to free himself from Dixon's hold on his arms, Jaye screamed, "*Cash, help!*"

"Jaye, stop! Hey! Hey! Look at me! Look at where you are!" Dixon pulled him up, right up off the bed so he was kneeling, facing Dixon. His face was held in Dixon's hands. Jaye was clawing at Dixon's arms, gasping for air through gritted teeth, half of him still seeing the cell, half seeing the bedroom. They both existed in the same space, over-lapping. He heard a sickened moan and only a moment later realized he'd made it.

"I would never hurt you," Dixon swore, looking upset instead of angry.

"I can feel them," he hissed. "*I can still feel them.* I don't know how to make it stop."

"Christ. Jesus Christ," Dixon cursed, drawing Jaye into a hug, keeping him there. "Okay. You're okay. You're not alone."

Someone knocked loudly on the door. "You guys okay in there?!"

"Yeah, Grant!" Dixon called back. "Just a nightmare! We're good."

"Okay, just checking," Grant called back. Footsteps receded down the hall.

Dixon told Jaye, "You know where you are, right? Look." He gestured to the room, harmless and plain. "It's just you and me. None of those fuckers who laid hands on you are ever going to hurt you again, you hear me? I'm protecting you now. No one gets close. You're safe."

"That's bullshit," Jaye accused. "*You're* not even safe! The shit you went through yesterday? He's *out there*, right now!"

Blue-green eyes hardening, lip curling in a subtle sneer directed not at Jaye but somewhere else, Dixon said, "That ends. I'm not mak-ing any more mistakes. Nothing is more important than keeping you safe."

"How about you keep yourself safe first and I'll worry about me?" Jaye pushed him away, climbed off the bed.

"No, we made a deal. I did my part. You did yours. This is our arrangement." Jaye looked back over a shoulder at him. Sure, Dixon was furious at things he couldn't fight. It tensed his posture, twisted his friendly appearance into something colder and meaner. Beneath that, he was also gorgeous, tall, fit, strong, and intended to use Jaye's body in every dirty way, no matter what was happening in Jaye's head or with Marcus, the evil fuck.

"I spread, you keep me safe," Jaye said hollowly.

"Yeah." Dixon cleared his throat, averted his gaze as Jaye looked around for some clothes to put on. His were still in the laundry room. "I'll make good on my end. Trust me."

Since they were all he had, Jaye pulled on his underwear.

"I need clean clothes. Mine are dirty."

"I'll do some laundry." Dixon crossed the room, walking up to Jaye. He waited for Jaye to get the message but when Jaye didn't act, said, "Take 'em off."

"What if your sister comes in?"

"The door's locked."

Jaye slid the underwear back off, handed them over. There was only pride left and no fear at all for Jaye—not even an old echo—when he saw Dixon ogle his naked body. It was one of the things Jaye appreciated most about Dixon. When it came to sex, he always set duty, titles, and the badge aside first. There were a lot of men who couldn't or wouldn't do what seemed to come naturally to Trooper Rowe.

"How far would you go to protect me?" Jaye asked.

"As far as I had to," Dixon answered. It sounded honest.

"Cash went pretty fuckin' far."

"Don't underestimate me just because I'm a trooper. I know my way around the law."

"So do I."

"Is that why you called out his name? You think he's better than me at taking care of you?"

"Jealous?" Jaye asked with the merest hint of a grin.

"Just means I've gotta give you more reasons to call out my name instead."

"Yes, sir, Trooper Rowe."

Dixon took hold of Jaye's chin. Then his gaze slid down, down, down Jaye's nude body. The hand released him to brush down his chest, his abdomen, and along the length of his cock, gently.

Dixon's expression changed, then, distorting with some breed of regret. He turned his back.

"I want you to know that I'm going to get tested today. I don't want you to be afraid to be with me. That's part of how I intend to keep you safe."

The anger came back, strong, thinking of how careless Marcus had probably been with Dixon, fucking him bareback while fucking other people on the side, too. With anger came the whoosh of flames. Jaye wished, then, that he'd stayed longer. He wished he'd heard Marcus screaming. He wanted that memory to add to his others.

"I'm coming with you," Jaye told him.

"You're staying here," Dixon argued. His jaw clenched. Every muscle in his body went tight, like he was ready to pounce and grapple. "You're not going to work either. It's not safe for you to go out right now."

"You're going to keep me locked, naked, in your bedroom?"

"Yes," Dixon snarled, turning back to face him.

The heat of Dixon's gaze, the fire of his determination, the raw need to do the right thing and safeguard what he could, it turned Jaye on like a switch. He started to get hard, knew Dixon could see it. But Jaye couldn't argue properly if Dixon knew the way he was acting was intensely alluring.

He fought an inner battle for a long moment, part of him waiting for Dixon to claim his stake again, needing it, desiring the closeness and contact.

Then, with effort, he set pride aside.

"What if I get fired?"

"I'll explain for you. They'll understand."

"And if they don't?"

"Then I'll deal with that too. You don't need to worry about the job. You only worry about one thing, and I can see that you want it. You're not getting it until I get tested."

"You fucking had me yesterday! It doesn't matter!"

"It does to me. *I keep you safe.* You understand what that means, right?"

"Let me get tested with you," Jaye asked, softening his tone. He turned on the charm, wanting out of that bedroom, wanting Dixon all for himself, and Dixon safe. He palmed Dixon's cock through the boxers he was wearing, squeezing gently around his shaft. "You wanna fuck me bareback? We can lose the condoms. Any time, any place, I'll sit my ass down right on this and fuck you dizzy, because it's just you and me now, right?"

"We'll be losing the condoms anyway," Dixon said darkly, watching Jaye get harder.

Reading between Dixon's lines, Jaye understood for Dixon it was a given that he wasn't fucking other people anymore. He moved to slip his hand inside the boxers, instead.

"Hands off," Dixon commanded. "Just let me look at you a second."

Thinking maybe Dixon was in the mood for the shy act instead of the blatantly slutty one, Jaye changed tactics. Biting at the inside of his cheek, Jaye put his hands on his hips, his eyes averted. Dixon cupped Jaye's erection, then stroked it lightly.

"I like this, that I make you hard."

"Please let me go with you. We're *both* safer that way. What good are you to me if you get hurt or sick?"

Dixon dropped the pair of underwear Jaye had passed him, sat on the edge of the bed and pulled Jaye down onto his lap, his back to Dixon's chest.

He spread Jaye's legs by pulling his thighs apart with both hands, then cupped his balls with his left. Tugging on them, he caressed with his right over Jaye's pelvis, his ink, hooking the hand around his root.

"Say please again."

"*Please*," he breathed.

Dixon began stroking, light and slow, so Jaye began to thrust into the touch for more contact.

"No, stay still. Don't move."

Jaye growled, but obeyed.

His balls were gently squeezed, his shaft played with. Dixon teased his crown, then stroked some more, very lightly. Jaye's hips twitched. He cursed, grabbing Dixon's legs under him. It went on and on, until suddenly, he was about to shoot. He leaned back into Dixon's chest, breathing hard, flushed.

"Gonna come?"

He grunted.

"Ask for permission."

"*Fuck*. Please. Please let me come."

"You want to?"

"*Yes*."

"Okay."

His dick slid through Dixon's fingers, pumping up and down with hardly any friction. He thrust against them once, twice, a third time, and made a soft cry as he shot.

"Please," he begged hoarsely as his cock pulsed. "Let me come with you?" Dixon stroked him through it as he convulsed in his lap, still coming, lip bitten.

"Okay. But you owe me for the worry it'll cost me to have you out there."

"I can pay."

"I can be creative," Dixon warned, and Jaye could hear the grin in his voice. It made him smile, too.

"Good."

Chapter 20

Fire and Ice

They retreated to the bathroom to shave and take a shower. It was an oasis of peace in the chaos waiting beyond the door, due to arrive at any moment. Having Dixon there, watching from over Jaye's shoulder as the blade scraped dark stubble from his jaw, then sharing the hot spray as Dixon washed Jaye's back, being a strong, mostly silent presence, made him feel comfortable and cared for. It was always better when there was someone else to ground him.

The noise in Jaye's head was louder than ever — the whoosh of flames, concern about the new framework of rules Dixon was establishing, putting Jaye's new job in danger, and anticipation for the ringing of the telephones, on top of all of his usual trouble with surviving day-to-day issues. But at least he wasn't starving anymore. At least he was warm and had light in the dark. With those basic needs taken care of, it made it more possible to carry on with the rest. Sometimes all that was needed to get through that day, that hour, that minute, was to endure it, knowing time always moved on. When everything else was stripped away, that fact remained, and it was good.

Jaye got out of the shower and wrapped a towel around his waist. His hand went to the back of his neck. It was still strange to feel it bare, the air drying the dampened skin, the chill pebbling the flesh.

Though the heat was on in the small home, frigid Alaska surrounded them on all sides, pressing in. He could feel it in the gentle air currents that snuck through cracks and crevices. It bit at him with razor-sharp teeth, a beast willing and able to kill at leisure. The only things keeping them alive were the efforts of their modest propane heater and the semblance of society keeping the wild at bay.

Jaye thought of how much time may lay ahead of him, waiting out the hours in Dixon's room without anything to do, nor clothes to wear until the laundry was done and Dixon was ready to go to the clinic. Wilderness lay just beyond the walls, with beasts more terrible than the wind, and some even less tangible than it.

"I'm gonna go get some coffee on my way to the room," Jaye said, moving toward the door.

"Just go to the room. I'll get the coffee."

Jaye glanced at the shower curtain, drawn over to hide the man behind it. There were already so many secrets between them. Jaye was used to keeping secrets, so it didn't bother him. Lies were another good way to stay alive and happy.

"Okay," he said, and turned the knob.

In the hall, he peered down in the direction of the living area. A light was on in the kitchen. The beginnings of daylight crept through the windows in the living room. There were soft voices.

He sought them out.

With one hand on the edge of his towel, he discovered Brekken and Grant, huddled together in conversation by the sink. They were both dressed for work and they glanced his way, their gazes slipping down, then back up as he stood there inviting scrutiny, not letting it touch him. He had learned ways to keep the physical and the mental separate long ago.

"Morning," he murmured.

"Hey," Brekken replied, her gaze snapping back to the mug in her hand after lingering on his midsection. "You going to work?"

She sounded doubtful, probably due to living with her brother as long as she had.

"I wish. Looks like I'm not going anywhere for a while."

"You don't know Marcus," she told him, her expression darkened with experience. "And, I mean, no offense but you're just a kid. Things are really dangerous right now."

"You do know who I am, right?" he asked with a hint of a grin.

"Doesn't change anything," she insisted. "This has been going on for years. It's different."

"Different how?" he asked, walking up to the counter and taking an apple. He tossed it up in the air, caught it. Grant was looking at the black and grey blue jay wrapping his body. "And, just for the record, kids don't last long in prison. I haven't been a kid for a while. You sound like him, you know. You both argue the same way. It's funny."

He took a bite of the apple and said what he came out there to say.

"Look, do you have some books I can borrow? I can't just sit in that room all day. I'll go crazy."

"Yeah," Grant answered. "What are you looking for? Non-fiction? Mystery? Sci-fi?"

"Anything."

"I'll get some," Brekken said, hurrying away.

When she was gone, Grant said quietly, "It's dangerous for you to be with him. Very dangerous."

"So?"

"How old are you again? Twenty-three?"

"Twenty-one."

"God," Grant sighed, sipping his coffee. "Marcus could take you apart like it was nothing."

"I'd like to see him try. I'm not brainwashed like Dix is. I can take care of myself."

"What the fuck are you doing out here?"

Jaye glanced over his shoulder. Dixon stood there, wearing a pair of pants and nothing else. He looked angry again.

"I told you I'd get the coffee."

Jaye said nothing, didn't move or blink, just gave Dixon a cool stare.

"Get in the bedroom!"

"He wanted to borrow some books. Get off his back, asshole," Brekken scolded, reappearing with three paperbacks in her hands. She handed them over to Jaye, who murmured his thanks.

"I could have gotten him books," Dixon fumed.

"Dix doesn't like to share his things," Jaye explained with a taunting glare in Dixon's direction, rolling the apple over in his hand.

"I need to know where you are at all times. It's not safe—"

"In the kitchen?" Jaye chuckled, shifting his weight to his other foot, licking his lips wet. Water droplets continued to trickle down his chest and back. Drips fell from the ends of his hair onto his shoulders and neck. "What do you think's gonna happen to me, huh?"

That's when the phone on the counter started to ring. They collectively turned to stare at it as its shrill shriek filled the air.

It was Brekken's phone. Jaye lingered just long enough to see her reach for it before he hurried past Dixon to go to the bedroom as ordered. He wouldn't have gone unless Dixon threw him over a shoulder and made him go if not for Jaye's overwhelming desire to not be there as they heard the news about Marcus.

As he shut the door behind him, chewing on his lip, he thought about it being her phone that rang as opposed to Dixon's. Maybe it wasn't a call about Marcus at all, he told himself. He didn't believe that for a second, though. He could feel it in his bones that it was about the fire.

He didn't like that he was naked, with no access to clothes should he need to bolt out of there in a hurry.

They know you did it. You burned him up. They're gonna make you pay. Dixon will make you pay. He'll cuff you to that bed and set you on fire, see how you like it when your skin crisps, turns black and flakes off as the flames eat you alive.

You'll wish I'd pulled your insides out. You'd already be burning in the devil's fires in Hell. Could've saved you the trouble.

Jaye started to frantically search Dixon's drawers for a pair of pants he could wear and maybe cinch in at the waist. Something with a drawstring would be best.

When he found one, he tossed it on the bed and began to search for a sweatshirt to go with it. He needed something heavy so if he had to go out a window, he wouldn't freeze to death before he found shelter.

Fire and ice. Fire and ice.

That's how they'll punish you, whore. You filthy whore. You perverted homosexual, begging old men to bugger you and make you their kept boy.

Gonna jab an icicle up in there, let you wriggle on it while that sharp edge slices through your guts. Then they'll warm you back up with a hot poker. How'd you like that, piggy? Piggy piggy piggy...

172

"Shut up. Shut up!"

If Dixon doesn't do it, they'll just throw you back in prison. They'll throw away the key. Cash won't be there this time, neither. No one will save you. No one will help. It'll just be you, and us, and the dark...

With a panicked whimper, knowing the truth in those whispers of his damnation, Jaye found a sweatshirt in the closet. He dropped the towel and started to step into the too-big pants. His hands shook. He waited for screaming, for pain and suffering.

The door burst open.

Dixon's eyes were wide and glassy, his mouth a tight line. He seemed wound-tight and wild. Jay yanked up the pants and gathered the excess in a hand at his waist. When Dixon made for him, Jaye recoiled, stumbling back a few steps as the instinct to get away overtook rational thought.

"Don't," he begged pitifully as Dixon crossed to him, fast.

Jaye was backed in a corner. The instinct of self-preservation took over, battling the terror. It made him clumsy, his reactions slowed. He tried to push Dixon back, but Dixon was too big. Worse than that, Dixon wasn't even there. Jaye searched his face and saw it was blank, empty.

But Jaye knew empty things were never truly empty. They were merely filled with the dark. And the dark *moved*.

"Don't hurt me," he heard himself say, pleading softly.

Dixon didn't seem to hear him.

He caught Jaye's arms, which pushed at Dixon's shoulders, prying them off. Dixon held both arms together between their bare chests. Jaye had his arms held like that before, just before the wrists were tied together, just before it got *bad*.

His fight notched up, fueled by adrenaline. It began to wash out his awareness and ability to think. But the harder he fought Dixon, the calmer and emptier Dixon looked, and Dixon wasn't budging. Jaye wasn't going anywhere.

His wrists ached where Dixon held them in a bruising grip. The overlarge sweatpants fell, exposing him, and that was worse. He could hear himself crying, pleading, and couldn't stop.

Then, from far away, he heard Dixon say, "There was a fire. The whole place burned down. My house—"

"Please let me go. Just let me *go*," Jaye beseeched shamelessly. "I didn't mean it. I had no choice. *I had to.*"

"Stop! Listen to me!" Dixon yelled, desperate. Jaye sobbed, his knees giving out. Dixon held him up, braced against the wall. "Look at where you are. You're here. You're fine. Get out of your damn head and listen to me for a second! I'm trying to tell you something!"

Jaye couldn't breathe. It felt like his chest was wrapped with thick, constricting rubber bands. His lungs wouldn't fill. His heart pounded. Fingers twisted around inside of him like worms.

Dixon's voice was heavy and flat as he looked back into Jaye's eyes and said to him, "There was a fire. My house—Marcus's house. It started in the bedroom. The whole place burnt down. Do you hear me?"

Jaye squeezed his eyes shut, grunting thickly, pulling at his trapped arms, and sucking oxygen in thin trickles through his nose.

"Look at me, J-bird. That stupid fuck almost burnt someone to death. He'd picked up a guy at the truck stop, one of the lot lizards. Whoever it was, he was sleeping it off in Marcus's bed and now he has third degree burns all over his body."

The world stopped.

Jaye's eyes sprang open.

He stopped fighting Dixon as confusion and a dull panic weakened his ability to respond. As soon as he went lax, Dixon gathered him to his chest, holding him there.

"What?" Jaye blurted.

"Why are you wearing these?"

Dixon had finally noticed the overlarge pair of pants pooled around Jaye's ankles. An icy dread froze Jaye to the spot. It hadn't been Marcus in the bed. It was just a random hooker.

You fried an innocent man, piggy. Dixon's never gonna forgive you for that, no matter what your intentions were. Dixon's going to hate you. You think you're hot now? Dixon's going to tie you up, set you on fire, and see how you like the heat then.

"*No.* No, I... I don't know," he said. "Didn't feel safe, I guess. If I had to run, I'd need clothes."

Dixon frowned, but not with anger, only shades of worry and sadness. He crouched, took hold of the fabric, drew it up to cover Jaye and began to tie the strings, pulling them as tight as they'd go to keep them up on his slim hips.

"No one's gonna hurt you. That's what I'm trying to tell you," he said urgently.

"What about Marcus? Was he even there?"

"Oh, yeah, he was in the shower when he smelled the smoke. He got out through the hall door. The bedroom was already engulfed." As he fought harder to concentrate on what Dixon was saying, Jaye could begin to hear the relief in Dixon's words, behind the shock. "He's in the hospital with minor burns and issues from smoke inhalation, but he'll be okay. He's got the cops to deal with, though, and the house is gone. Anyway, Marcus can't hurt you now. That's what I wanted to tell you. Seems this all happened hours ago, in the middle of the night. They didn't call me earlier because I'm not his next of kin. Marcus was passed out. He's still out. Sesi found out what happened, overheard the chatter. She's been over there helping to investigate the scene, but didn't call because she knew about how fucked-up everything has been with me and him. She wanted to have some facts about the fire, the guy they pulled out of the bed, and Marcus's condition before telling me anything. You know he didn't even try to save that poor guy? He just ran out of the house and left him in there. It's amazing the guy's still alive. I think he jumped out a window or something."

Jaye shook his head, grunting and trying to deny it. He closed his eyes and Dixon just held him tighter, stroking Jaye's hair.

"*Fuck.* Fuck, okay. So, Marcus is alive?" Jaye asked, needing to make sure it was real, that he'd really heard what he'd heard.

"Yeah. But he's not conscious yet. Sesi said he collapsed in front of the house after getting outside. I can't believe it," Dixon said with wonder. "I feel so bad for the John Doe, but for Marcus it's like cosmic payback for hurting me yesterday. He's in a world of trouble now and his whole life is fucked up. Maybe this is a terrible thing to say, but I really feel like things are going to be okay now. I know it was just a stupid accident, but it's... it's like a sign that people like him don't always get everything to go their way. Like karma. Like after everything, he finally gets something coming back at *him*."

He wore a triumphant expression, his face lighting up from within. His blue eyes shone. His rosy lips pulled back in a tentative but gorgeous smile, showing white teeth as he leaned in to kiss Jaye once. Dixon smelled of soap and skin, warmth and life.

"It's just crazy, you know? He'd gotten me to agree to come home yesterday, yet he goes out to pick up someone for sex anyway, like it didn't matter if he thought we were together, he was still going to fuck around anyway. *And this is what he gets.*"

"Yeah," Jaye murmured, still fighting to process it all and shaken to the core with guilt. But the guilt was all for that random bastard, not Marcus. Jaye knew he had to react normally for Dixon, so he wouldn't suspect the truth, but it was tough to do. Jaye was certain if Dixon found out he was responsible, he'd see Jaye as nothing but a murderer, a pyro, and a seriously fucked-up person not worthy of his care. "I'm sorry, I just can't believe this. I can't even process it. It's so fucking twisted."

"I know," Dixon agreed wholeheartedly. "But, look, we don't need to be afraid. Neither of us. Okay? I know it's been tough, that after everything you've been through, having to deal with my shit too... I get it. I know how difficult it's been for you since yesterday. I don't want you to be afraid anymore. This is all pinned on Marcus. There's no way he could ever expect me to go back to him now, with the whole town knowing he'd picked up a hooker, then nearly killed the guy. *This is real*, J-bird."

"Okay. It's real," he said. He realized he was still breathing hard, on edge and wary. More than anything, he needed to watch his words and actions, *very* closely.

"And Marcus is going to see now, because of this, that he's not invincible. He's lost everything. He'll have to find somewhere else to live. Maybe he'll move closer to the coast now that our place was destroyed. It was keeping him here, but now it's gone, and it's not like he has a ton of friends eager to take him in. He's got an older brother with an apartment near the docks, though. That's probably where he'll need to stay, and that's hours from here." Dixon was becoming gradually more and more happy, the more he thought it through. Revelations buoyed him, one after the other.

"They called Brekken," Jaye said, trying to piece together the puzzle of what he knew compared to what Dixon knew.

"Yeah. Sesi called her so Brekken could break it to me. They don't want me on the case or to have anything to do with it. Are you okay? You were really freaking out there."

He held Jaye's face in his hands, looking him over. Jaye couldn't think of a good way to answer, so he let his tense, rattled silence speak for itself. Dixon kissed Jaye's temple and caressed his jaw.

"No one's coming after you," Dixon promised. "You're safe."

"*You're* safe," Jaye countered.

"Yeah. But that means you are, too. I'm going to be able to do this, now. He doesn't have the upper hand anymore." Confidence visibly strengthened Dixon, making him seem to grow even larger before Jaye's eyes. "I'm gonna get my shit together and focus on keeping you safe. It's gonna all work out. You'll see. Come on and have some breakfast."

He stepped away to get a t-shirt from one of the dresser drawers and handed it to Jaye.

"Here, this shouldn't be too big on you. Relax, check out the books from Brekken. I'll cook you something before we go out. We'll stop by your place to get some clothes. Later on, you're gonna take a nap. I can see how exhausted you are."

Jaye pulled on the shirt. "I thought you wanted me to stay in here?"

"Because I was scared," Dixon explained, slightly abashed. "I'm not scared anymore."

"Just like that, huh? Must be nice."

He tugged the shirt down, head bowed and avoiding Dixon's gaze. Suddenly, dressed in the too-big clothes, he felt like the kid they all kept telling him he was more than he would have thought possible.

Dixon held out a hand for Jaye to take. After hesitating slightly, Jaye took it.

"I'm with you now," Dixon told him. "Anything you need, I'll take care of, no matter what it is. You've got someone to fight for you, to make sure that nothing bad ever happens to you again. You're mine and I promise to take good care of you. After we eat, I'm taking you with me to the clinic."

Jaye raised his eyes, felt the intensity of Dixon's stare. It gave him a heady rush. For all that Cash cared about Jaye's wellbeing, it was always more of a cool interest. Jaye was an investment that needed safeguarding for his value. It was business. But with Dixon, it was way more than business.

It was personal.

He remembered then, what had been said between them at the cabin. Jaye remembered the feel of Dixon making love to him, telling him he was cared for, as more than something to fuck.

The nature of Jaye's fear shifted on him, then. Outside forces weren't the primary danger any longer. Now, the only danger he had to worry about was the man holding his hand and telling Jaye he belonged to him, body and soul. If Dixon ever knew who he was protecting, and what kind of person Jaye really was, it would only ruin more of Dixon's ability to trust people. He'd hate Jaye and be just as happy to witness his downfall as he was to witness Marcus's.

"No one else touches either of us, from here on out. We'll make sure we're both clean; then we can be together without any worry."

"What about work?" Jaye asked warily.

"No work today," Dixon said, without leaving any room for argument. Jaye would have argued. Being employed was part of their deal. If he didn't have a job, that made him nothing but Dixon's whore. "After the clinic, we're coming back here. Sesi warned Brekken that some troopers were coming by. They'll need to take our statements about last night, since there was an incident yesterday that I'll need to officially report which ties me to Marcus. Luckily we were all here all night, so there's nothing to worry about. Then you can get that nap, get some rest. You need it."

"I need my *job*," Jaye insisted, but the prospect of giving formal statements to the law was making it hard to be calm. He could feel the nightmare scenarios congealing in his brain, just waiting to play out so the ghosts could mock and threaten some more. And there was also Grant to consider. Grant, who knew they weren't all there all night, and who might have smelled gasoline on Jaye when he'd returned from his 'walk'.

But all Dixon said was, "We've already talked about this. Come on."

He pulled Jaye along behind him by their linked hands, and Jaye was helpless to do anything but follow and toe the line.

Chapter 21

Making It Official

"I understand you used to live at the residence."

"Yeah. We were romantically involved. Not anymore. Not for a while."

"When was the last time you were in contact with Marcus Slater?"

They were all looking at him—Brekken, Grant, and the officials who had come to ask their questions. Jaye was hovering nearby, unwilling to sit down and the only one not looking at Dixon. Jaye's skittishness over the past day or so Dixon chalked up to being entirely his fault. It was Dixon's fault Jaye was in danger, that bad memories had been stirred. He knew he had to make it right, somehow.

The deputy fire marshal waited for Dixon's answer. Dixon looked right at him. He was an older man named Brant Paxton. They'd crossed paths once or twice before in more casual circumstances, and once had a chat about their favorite hobbies. Paxton was nearing a retirement filled with his favorite pastimes of hunting and fishing. If there was ever a man of the earth, born of it, and itching to return to it, it was Deputy Paxton. He'd told Dixon how nature always made more sense to him than people did. Dixon could understand that. Most of the time, he didn't understand people either. They tended to do the damnedest things, without the faintest idea why. The biggest part of Dixon's job was to save them from themselves and their misguided ideas.

The night had worn on the deputy. Dixon saw it in the man's face. He supposed Deputy Paxton had seen the unfortunate man who'd been burnt up in Marcus's bed—previously *Dixon's* bed. Dixon kept imagining crisp, blackened skin and patches of raw red flesh, though what he couldn't imagine was how one dealt with that kind of agony. That could have been him. He could have returned to Marcus and been the victim of a faulty fireplace or something or other.

There were a couple of troopers there with Paxton—a man and a woman who Dixon hadn't ever worked with directly before, and whose names he was having trouble remembering. They were strangers. There were too many people in the room for Dixon's liking. He almost wished they had simply taken him in for questioning rather than handling it here.

"Come on, son," Paxton urged with the wisdom and kindness of a grandfather. "Answer the question."

Dixon's tongue was thick and heavy in his mouth. It wouldn't form words. His jaw was locked tight.

He was seated in a chair. Brekken and Grant were on the couch. The deputy was on a kitchen chair that had been pulled up in front of Dixon. Brekken had gotten up and returned with a glass of water, which she passed to Dixon.

"Thanks," he murmured, taking it. He took a sip. To Paxton, he said, "Yesterday. Saw him yesterday."

The older man's gaze kept going to the circular bruise on Dixon's temple where the gun's barrel had been grinding against him.

Dixon pretended to ignore it.

"What circumstances?"

There was a pad open in Paxton's hands. A pen was poised, taking notes.

In his mind's eye, Dixon saw Marcus striding up to him, cocky and calm. He tasted the Glock, the tang of metal and oil. He remembered how that felt, to be so close to having the back of his head blown out across the desolate roadway.

"I, uh," he stammered. "I can't. I..."

"Take it easy," the deputy said, soothingly, his words coming slow, his tone pleasant. "One thing at a time. Where were you?"

"He followed me," Dixon blurted, glancing up briefly, then down again.

"Mr. Slater did?"

"Yes, sir. I was on the south end of town, on a routine traffic stop. We were finishing up. I turned to return to my vehicle. Marcus was already walking up to me."

Silence drew out. It was a loud kind of silence, as if everyone's thoughts were amplified, hammering his ears on a strange frequency. They were all looking at him, all of them but Jaye. The female trooper was by the door. Dixon glanced her way, measuring the sour look on her face.

"What happened then?" Paxton urged.

Dixon swallowed around a lump in his throat, hating the shame he felt.

Rotating the glass of water, running his thumb through some of the condensation, he said, "I froze. He makes me nervous. Our relationship was... violent. I was too shocked to respond like I should have."

Just say it. Spit it out. Tell them what they need to hear and get it done.

"I hate this," he sighed. Brekken reached out and squeezed his knee. He gave her a grateful smile that quickly died on his lips. "He got my Glock away from me. Turned it on me. G-got me down on my knees. He, uh, threatened me. Said if I didn't come home, he'd hurt me or the people I care about. I'd moved out while he was at sea, fishing, without warning, so, you know. He was angry about it. The barrel of the gun was digging into the side of my head." He gestured to the bruise. "But I was able to talk him down. He backed off and left."

"That's it?"

Dixon felt Jaye staring. After so many minutes of being deliberately ignored, the weight of his attention was keenly felt. Dixon did everything in his power to not meet that stare.

"Yeah," he replied. "That's it."

"Were there any witnesses?"

Thinking of that wide open, empty landscape, and the overloaded pickup driving away, Dixon shook his head. "No."

"That's felony assault on a law enforcement officer, and assault with a deadly weapon," Deputy Paxton said softly, tipping the end of his pen at the bruise.

"I know. I'll come in and report it. File a restraining order and all of that."

"See that you do," Paxton said, as he made some more notes.

"Okay, so where were you last night between midnight and three a.m.?"

"Here. Asleep. With, uh..." he felt his face coloring. "With him."

The deputy followed where Dixon nodded to. "Mr. Larson?"

"Yes, sir."

"You were with him all night?"

"Yes, sir. My sister and her husband were down the hall, asleep also."

"Um, actually, that's not true," Grant said, speaking up. Dixon caught a strange, frowning expression on Jaye's face in response, but was too distracted by Grant's words to figure it out. "I couldn't sleep. I was worried Marcus would show up with another gun to come after Dixon, so I sat on the porch for a few hours with my shotgun, watching out for him. That was probably between that time frame. Maybe two a.m. to four. Didn't see anyone. It was quiet."

"So no one came or went?" Paxton asked, taking more notes.

"No, sir."

"The house... it's all gone?" Dixon asked quietly.

"Yep. The whole thing. Nothing but ashes. It's a miracle they both made it out of there alive." Paxton shook his head solemnly. "Did you have many possessions kept there?"

"No, like I said, I cleared out a few months back. Took everything that was mine with me."

"Okay then. You'll need to come in today to a file the report about the assault charges and take care of that restraining order."

Dixon sighed again, twisting the glass in his hands. Paxton gave him a hard, stubborn glare, waiting.

"Yeah, okay," Dixon relented.

"If you remember anything else, you give me a call."

"Yep."

A few minutes later, Deputy Fire Marshal Paxton and the troopers cleared out. Brekken and Grant stayed seated and said nothing but kept watching him, concern darkening their expressions.

"Jaye needs some rest," Dixon said to them, taking him by the arm, guiding him toward the hall.

"We're going to head in to work," Brekken replied. "Better late than never. You'll be okay?"

"Yep. Go on ahead."

Brekken and Grant gathered their things to go. Dixon took Jaye back to the bedroom and shut the door. They had already made the trip to the clinic. It was done quickly, and without any problems, but the stress only compounded with everything else going on. The first thing Jaye said when they finally had their privacy was, "Why didn't you tell them about the rest of it? They should be charging him with a hell of a lot more than fucking *assault.*"

"Can we not? Please?" Dixon asked, sitting heavily on the bed.

"You're not protecting him, are you?"

"Of course not! I don't have *proof* of anything else. I barely have proof of the assault. I don't want everyone talking about it. It's a small fuckin' town, you know. It wouldn't do any good; it'd just piss Marcus off and get everyone up in my personal business. I'll follow through with the assault charges and the restraining order. It's enough. And we're not talking about it anymore. It's done. I'm clean. I just want to forget about it."

"I won't forget," Jaye said under his breath. Dixon heard him clearly enough, though.

"What does that mean?" he asked defensively. "I'm damaged goods?"

"Am *I?*" Jaye retorted. That's when Dixon saw how angry Jaye was. At first, Dixon didn't get it. He initially chalked it up to being sensitive and defensive about the traumas he'd survived. "Why the hell would I think you were damaged goods just because an evil fuck abused you? You do remember what I did, right? To those fuckers who impaled me on a butcher knife?"

Finally, Dixon got it, that Jaye was angry at Marcus, and about what had happened to Dixon. He'd probably be angry, too, if Jaye was the one who'd been so recently hurt, and the attacker so nearby.

"You don't go near him, you hear me?"

Jaye just smiled. Dixon didn't like that smile at all.

"I mean it," Dixon warned. "I can't protect you from him like I need to. Don't you see that?! Everyone else, I can handle, but... him?" He shook his head. "Part of the way I intend to protect you is by keeping you away from dangerous people."

"Maybe sometimes you should let me protect you, too."

"That's not part of our deal."

"Oh, so this is all still just business to you, Trooper Rowe? Fine then. Look at it this way—I'll help protect you from Marcus so you can fulfill your end of the bargain."

Lying back on the bed, Dixon closed his eyes, covering his face with his hands. In memory, he saw Jaye's concentration as he sketched Dixon's sleeping face, the way he bit his lip, his eyes tracking the movements of the pencil and visually tracing Dixon's features. He saw the vulnerability in him when the drawing was taken away, his fear of harsh critique of something so private. He saw, too, the way Jaye's lower lip tended to quiver as he came, his eyes closed, brow furrowed, hands grasping as he submitted completely. In those moments, there was no more fight in him, just surrender to someone he trusted.

Dixon wanted to be worthy of Jaye's trust.

Jaye climbed on the bed, on top of Dixon. He was a warm, welcome weight perched on Dixon's thighs. A hand caressed up Dixon's stomach, under his shirt.

"When you're done with me," Jaye asked in a whisper, "you gonna throw me away like trash? Is that what I am to you, Dixon? Am I your trash? Something to come into and walk away from once you're spent?"

Eyes burning, fighting what was stirring in his heart, fighting it hard, Dixon let Jaye peel his hands away from his face, disclosing the tears slipping down. He wove his fingers through those soft brown curls like silk, brought Jaye's forehead down to press against his, and felt his breaths.

"You're worth more than that," Jaye whispered.

Dixon kissed him.

"I am too."

"I love you," Dixon told him, on a wavering exhale, thick with tears and heartache.

Jaye pressed into the kiss, taking more. He moaned and Dixon chased his mouth, wanting all of it, all of him.

After a long time, they broke apart. Jaye pulled back a few inches and searched Dixon's eyes, drying them with his fingertips, then briefly kissed each eyelid.

"Me too," Jaye murmured, sounding uncharacteristically shy. "I love you too."

Dixon smiled all the way down to his toes, chuckling a little. He smiled so much his cheeks hurt. Jaye lay down on his chest and Dixon wrapped him in his arms, leaning in closely, smelling his hair, and his skin.

He was the flower that grew in shadows, the bird with a broken wing, learning to fly again. Dixon knew the darkness Jaye sprung from, and himself too. It was all around them, trying to pull them both down. But, for the first time, he felt that if maybe they held on to the good tightly enough, and each other, then they really could break free.

"You're not trash," Dixon admonished, his voice still choked with tears, clutching Jaye to him. Jaye's legs straddled his hips. One of Dixon's hands wrapped one of Jaye's thighs, the other slipped under his shirt to feel the heat of his skin, vibrantly young and alive, radiantly beautiful.

"*You're* not damaged." Jaye's thighs pressed against Dixon's hips. His lips brushed softly against Dixon's arm.

"Can we just stay like this awhile?"

"Yeah," Jaye said on a sigh. "Fine by me."

Love was a funny, foreign thing for Dixon. It was never really a part of his relationship with Marcus. If he'd ever said it, it wasn't truly felt. There was commitment and passion apart from any of the more tender sorts of feelings.

Because of living so long without enduring or expressing deeper emotions for a partner, Dixon felt even more responsible for getting his shit together after telling Jaye he loved him. It changed things between them, and affected Dixon's mindset. It wasn't a game anymore, or a random, passing flirtation. What they had with each other meant something to both of them. It was worth fighting for. The love he had for Jaye grew moment-to-moment. As soon as it was unleashed, that love fed and gained in size until it was the constant elephant in the room with them.

Because of the initial awkwardness, they spent a few quiet days just going through their normal routines without discussing Marcus, the attack on Dixon, or the fire.

Jaye returned to work the next day, and Dixon did too, though they kept him behind a desk rather than behind the wheel. A warrant had been issued for Marcus's arrest, due to the assault charges. Late in the day, Marcus was brought in, and locked up. It was something Dixon heard about, but didn't witness. He stayed away from the whole thing. Marcus was never one to keep much of a nest egg, and now he didn't even have property to borrow against, so Dixon wondered if Marcus would be able to make bail, or be stuck in jail pending trial or an influx of cash from his home insurance. It was hard to say how it would play out, so it left Dixon feeling a little on edge. It was a relief to have Marcus locked up for the time being at least. Dixon asked Sesi to notify him should there be any change in Marcus's status.

The reality of the situation slowly sank in. The weight of worry was gradually lifted, leaving Dixon free to focus on Jaye. They were apart more than together, but Jaye filled Dixon's every waking moment. The feel of his curls against Dixon's cheek, the touch of his lips, the way his lips drew up crookedly when he smiled, as if he saw the secret joke behind every happiness—it all haunted Dixon. It constantly distracted him from what he should have been doing and made him hard at inappropriate times. He'd be sitting at work monitoring the phones, but thinking about scraping his teeth over Jaye's tattooed flesh, getting him naked, spreading him wide, doing things to make him gasp, moan, and smile that crooked smile. But it was more than that. Dixon was used to fantasizing about sex. With Jaye, it was so much more than that. Things simply felt better when they were together. The tension and guardedness he'd endured while living with Marcus and anticipating his needs and moods, that was gone. Dixon was lighter, free to experience pure joy.

That was an entirely new phenomenon. Marcus never made Dixon feel relaxed or content when they were close. He kept Dixon on edge instead of helping him feel comfortable and cherished.

The joy Dixon found in being close to Jaye, or talking to him on the phone, or knowing they would be together in a few hours' time—it snuck up on him, opening up unexplored worlds where fear and dread had no place.

They'd both been through so much. Jaye's troubles were over, if Dixon had anything to say about it. Ahead was only possibility and hope. Dixon wanted that. He wanted to put everything with Marcus behind him.

There was only one way it would feel unquestionably real to him, though, and that was to take a firm, confident step forward, farther away from where he'd been. However, he suspected no one was going to approve or agree with him about the way he wanted to do that.

Chapter 22

Screwed Up

Dixon spent most of his days fantasizing about having sex with Jaye. The imagined sounds of his moans, the taste of his kiss, the feel of him undulating on the end of Dixon's cock or giving it to Dixon hard—it was everything. He breathed it, kept the daydreams wrapped around him like a fog, concealing him from whatever else life might want to throw his way.

When he got home with Jaye, though, it wasn't like he imagined it to be, at least not for that first week. They'd gotten tested, found out they were clean. Marcus was charged with assault and being kept behind bars. The restraining order was initiated. They had confessed their love and more dark secrets.

A lot had changed in a short amount of time.

Dixon could see in the way Jaye looked at him, all of the confessions they had each made. They were written in his expression, told through his quietness.

They had exposed too much, too fast, and were left raw and bleeding. Jaye was becoming guarded the way Dixon used to be guarded. There were accusations in his eyes for Dixon's cruel admission of love and for his unwillingness to share more details about what Marcus had done to him on the side of that road. Part of Dixon was, subsequently, nonsensically, moved to apologize for things he had no rational cause to apologize for.

Marcus had trained him to appease a displeased lover by submitting, but Dixon was healing, too. Another reason why he allowed his fantasizing about Jaye to run wild was to block out the memories. As it was, they slipped through now and then. When they did, he'd go and lock himself in the bathroom until it passed. At work when this happened, people left him alone. At home, though, Jaye was always there, on the other side of the locked door, waiting with that hard-edged, anguished look in his eyes once Dixon emerged again.

They didn't speak about it. Jaye's presence was enough. He witnessed all of Dixon's pain silently, diligently, and without casting judgment.

On the first day they both were off from work again, Dixon could feel it coming to a head.

They were at the cabin. It was where they'd been sleeping, and Dixon's presence there during the nights seemed to help Jaye find more sleep. He would give Jaye a massage before bed to relax him and make it easier for him to drift off. Then, if Dixon awoke to find Jaye awake again, drew his attention and talked to him to let the memories and phantoms ease back. He made Jaye promise to wake him if he couldn't sleep, or if there was something on his mind. Jaye was reluctant to do that, though, but Dixon kept insisting. Sometimes Jaye would argue that Dixon was expecting him to open up when Dixon was keeping his own secrets.

The night before, they had passed the evening with Dixon lost in thought, watching Jaye sit cross-legged by the fire, his back to it, pad of paper in hand. He kept glancing Dixon's way like he was drawing Dixon's form, lying in bed, but Dixon couldn't be sure. Jaye never showed him his drawings if he could help it. He hid the pads, stayed carefully out of reach, or drew when Dixon wasn't there.

When Dixon woke the next morning, the sun was already up. Jaye was still in bed, reading one of Brekken's books.

Dixon glanced at his Glock, set aside with his duty belt in the corner on a table. Just like that, he could taste the barrel. Then it was grinding into his skull, and he remembered how hard he gagged when Marcus forced himself down Dixon's throat. Worst of all was after, crawling to the Expedition, stripping down and sitting there without a fight. He hadn't protested or even said no. He'd just let it happen like nothing had changed, allowing Marcus to believe he was still in charge. Maybe he'd always be in charge. Maybe he would always be able to manipulate Dixon and make him doubt himself, no matter how much Dixon tried to resist and make a better choice. Maybe

Marcus would seek Dixon out again and take him away for good, out of reach of everyone that cared about him. It was possible. If pushed, Dixon knew he still, after everything, would sacrifice himself before anything could happen to anyone else, if there was no other choice.

He would protect Jaye at all costs, even if that meant putting himself between Jaye and harm's way.

He got out of bed, went to the bathroom and shut the door. Sitting with his back to the edge of the tub, Dixon held his head in his hands, trying to figure out what the hell to do next. There was a small window behind him that let in a shaft of golden light. The walls, the floor, the ceiling, and the cabinet above the sink were all dark wood. It was like being in a cocoon.

Sniffling, angrily wiping his leaking eyes on his arm, he sat there for who knows how long before the door opened. Maybe he should have been surprised, but he wasn't.

It was cold in there, so Dixon was shivering constantly, low tremors working through his body to keep it alive as Jaye unwound Dixon's arms and sank into his lap, facing him, straddling him. Dixon turned his head away, trying to cover it with a hand to hide his pitiable state. Jaye just peeled the hand away, kissed Dixon's cheek and wrapped him in a hug.

"I'm sorry I've been such a frigid bitch," Jaye told him. "I guess I'm used to people being more direct about what they want from me, and you haven't seemed to want anything from me. Or maybe I'm just an idiot. If it was me, I'd want everyone to leave me alone, so I tried that. But you don't do better when left alone."

Dixon smiled at Jaye's insight, though feeling filled to the brim with regret. "Yeah, you're right about that. God, I'm just so stupid! I keep doing the wrong things. I'm just trying to get past this shit with Marcus so I can be there for you, but even that is fucking me up enough to disappoint you."

Jaye was wound around him, warm, vital, and beautiful. He was gently, constantly drying Dixon's tears, wearing that same clench-jawed expression he'd been stuck with all week long.

"You look so mad," Dixon commented, tired of wondering if it was because of him, if he'd screwed something else up. "Are you mad at me?" The shivering was subsiding; he held on to Jaye to draw heat from his body and waited for a reprimand.

"Come back to bed," Jaye urged. "You're freezing."

But Dixon's body was too heavy to move. He was weighted to the floor, and not because of Jaye. It was the intangible things holding him down.

His right hand caressed up Jaye's thigh, along his side. His left hooked under Jaye's ear, the thumb brushing over the inked tear under his eye.

"You feel good," Dixon murmured.

Why can't I be strong like him? He's smaller than me, younger than me, and probably more of a man than I'll ever be.

"You feel *cold*," Jaye persisted stubbornly. "Come on."

"Then warm me up."

He grabbed a handful of Jaye's crotch through his soft sleep pants, fondling gently, rolling the flesh. Jaye rocked instinctively into the touch, undulating on Dixon's lap, biting his lip. It was the hottest thing Dixon had ever seen. Some of the fight was still there in him, but Jaye reacted to the stimulation instantly, so abrupt it was nearly unbelievable. As Dixon manipulated him, he got hard, fast.

He's still mad, though. Look at his eyes. There's something he's not telling you. It's there. Right there. He's chewing on it. Has been all week long.

He looks like he's ready to punch someone. Maybe he'll punch me. It'll be like old times.

Dixon wasn't hard, but he didn't need to be. Not for this.

He stopped touching Jaye and dropped his gaze to the floor.

"Get up. Go on."

Jaye got to his feet but stood his ground, giving Dixon that look he'd been so unable to puzzle out. With the way Jaye was able to hold on to anger, Dixon could see how he'd been able to lash out at his attackers, killing at least one of them. He was hard as nails under that pretty veneer.

He's waiting for direction, Dixon realized when Jaye didn't move.

Well, I can give him a hint.

Dixon strode past him to the main room, crossing to the bed. As he passed the fire, the heat wafting from it was glorious after the cold of the bathroom. His belt was piled on top of his clothes. He took it, folded it over and brought it to bed.

"What the fuck are you doing?" Jaye asked, sounding as angry as he looked.

Dixon kept his back turned, standing up against the side of the bed. He dropped his pants and bent over. The belt he set down, beside him.

"Use it."

"No. Fuck you."

"I said use it!" Dixon yelled.

"And I said, *fuck you*! I'm not going to hurt you like he did!"

"You know, I bet you didn't give Cash shit like you're giving it to me. No, I bet you were *real* nice and obedient with him."

His voice wavered on the words. When it came right down to it, he just wasn't as tough as Jaye. He never would be. But it worked anyway. Jaye was on him in a flash, taking out his stiffened cock, spitting thickly in a palm, smearing it on his shaft. As he pressed into Dixon, Dixon gasped and bore the ache. He growled curses through gritted teeth as Jaye first breached him, then furiously burrowed deeper.

"Oh fuck. Fuck. Ahh, fuck," he moaned. Jaye wasn't letting up or going slow. His cock pushed farther inside with the help of some more saliva. Jaye fed it to him with harsh little grunts. When he was most of the way in, Jaye intentionally knocked the belt off of the bed with the back of his hand. He grabbed Dixon's ass, spread him wider, ground into his passage, and kneaded the muscle. It hurt in the best way.

As he started to move, building to a rapid pace once he was sliding easily enough, Jaye reached around Dixon's hips to find him more than half-hard from the rough treatment. Jaye jacked him ruthlessly with the hand he'd been spitting into. Dixon yelled and braced his knees against the bed's side, hands planted on the mattress.

He thought he could hold out longer than Jaye, but he was wrong. Coming with a whined, "Motherfucker," he unloaded over Jaye's fist, clenched up with the force of his orgasm, and wrung the climax from Jaye, too.

Jaye swallowed his cry with effort, rocking slower into Dixon's ass as he came down, moving easier with the lube of his own come.

Then he pulled out. Dixon glanced over a shoulder as Jaye tucked himself away. Jabbing a finger in Dixon's face, he growled, "I will never *hit* you! No fucking way! You wanna get fucked? Fine. That's what I'm here for, right? But I will *not* be that guy for you, Dixon."

The anger was so close to the surface now, Dixon was sort of in awe of it. He'd never seen Jaye this furious—breathing hard, face flushed, ready to fight. It was the sexiest fucking thing Dixon had ever witnessed.

"Why not? I'm asking you to. I want you to."

"Why not?! 'Why not?' he asks," Jaye laughed maliciously with that crooked grin that drove Dixon crazy. He was pacing, restless as a caged tiger. "Marcus isn't even here, but he's *still* beating you down. You're better than him and you're better than the person he wants you to believe you are. You're not his bitch. *He deserved to die!* He should have fucking *died* for what he did to you! No one deserves to be treated like that! No one! But fucking especially you, you aggravating fucking son of a bitch."

Dixon watched Jaye's chest heaving, his fists balled up tight.

"Why not?" he asked calmly.

Jaye surprised him then by stalking over to the front door, opening it and going through, slamming it behind him. It was well below freezing outside. He was wearing only the thin pair of sleep pants. No shoes, no shirt, and no jacket.

"Fucking idiot," Dixon hissed, chasing after him.

Tugging his pants up as he went, feeling the come dripping down his legs as he did, he yanked open the door. Jaye was standing on the stoop, staring out at the horizon line, hugging himself and breathing hard.

"Get the hell back inside, you crazy shit," Dixon scolded.

"I'm cooling off!" Jaye snapped.

"Okay, but less literally, please," he said, grabbing Jaye by the arm and hauling him back inside.

"Let me go!" Jaye frowned, wriggling as Dixon shut the door again. Dixon released him and rubbed Jaye's arms to warm them back up, ignoring his own renewed shivering.

They stood there like that for a long while, calming down. Jaye refused to look at him. Dixon tried to repress his smile.

"You hate that you love me, don't you?" he asked softly.

"Fuck you!" Jaye snapped.

"It's not my fault, you know," Dixon said. "It's not like I put a gun to your head."

Jaye turned on him then, shoving hard at Dixon's chest. *"That's not funny! That is not fucking funny, Dixon!"* Dixon giggled despite himself. The shove was all he got. After that, Jaye raged in a more solitary way, safely a few feet away. "God, I hate you," Jaye said with passionate wonder. "I really do. You make me crazier than anyone else ever has. Why would you say something like that? It's not *funny!* It's not a *joke!* It *matters!*"

All of Dixon's humor drained away at the sight of Jaye's tears and the intensity of his sincerity.

"It matters!" Jaye yelled at him, his voice breaking.

"Okay," Dixon hushed to him, gathering his strung-tight body in an embrace, kissing the top of his head. "Okay."

Jaye held on to him, breaths hitching. Infusing Jaye completely with all of Dixon's love for him, Dixon smoothed his lover's hair, caressed the remaining chill from his skin, and fell even deeper at the display of Jaye's devotion.

"Can you just admit to it, please? I can see the way you look at that gun since you've been on the wrong end of it with him. He's the one that scares you. You're only scared of the gun because of the way he used it."

"You're projecting," Dixon sighed. "I'm not scared of the gun and I'm not even scared of Marcus. It's just the circumstances that make me nervous. Marcus is not like those guys who served time with you, or like the guys that hurt you and landed you there. The reason why I'm all screwed up about him is because I *like* what he does to me. I *invited* most of it. When it went too far, I'd hit back, start an argument, and hold a grudge until he made it feel so good I didn't care anymore. The reason I'm scared is because he brings out the worst in me. I don't like who I am when I'm with him."

"Bullshit. There's something you're not telling me about that day when he surprised you on the road and he took your gun." Jaye frantically searched Dixon's eyes, looking for the truth in there. "Why can't you tell me what it is? I already told you I've seen worse, lived through worse. You're not going to shock me. All you're doing is making me assume things. If you want me to be ready for that fucker once he's out and about again, I need to know the whole story."

They were sitting by the fireplace, wrapped in a blanket big enough to enfold both of them as they huddled together.

Dixon knew Jaye had a point, but he was still reluctant to be so honest.

"How about we make another deal?"

Jaye snorted. "I don't have anything else to give you. You have everything already. What could you possibly want now? My cabin?"

When Dixon didn't respond, and only chewed his lip, Jaye's mouth fell open with amazement.

"That was a joke, you know!"

"If I tell you the rest," Dixon started. "Will you consider letting me move in with you? That's the deal. If you're not interested, I understand. I'm just tired of freeloading off of my sister and Grant and thrusting all of my drama on them. If we're together, and you're involved in all of this anyway, I'd rather it be just you and me. We can handle it. I could stay here with you and protect you more effectively. Plus, you know, I kind of love you and all."

It wasn't said bravely, or confidently. In fact, Dixon bowed his head and lowered his voice the farther he got into the little speech, so by the time he finished, Jaye was leaning in to catch it all. His mouth was still agape with shock, which Dixon didn't think was a good sign.

"Well," Dixon prodded, frowning uncomfortably as Jaye stared at him. "Say something already. It can just be 'geez, you're stupid and lame', but give me something here."

It turned out that his answer came in the form of a passionate kiss, with Jaye's lips moving over Dixon's, coaxing them apart, slipping his tongue inside and wearing his own mysterious frown. By the time Dixon pulled back, his eyes mostly closed, his lips tingling, he was still confused, though less worried.

"Um, okay. Thank you? That's not an answer, though."

"How do you function as a trooper when you're this unsure of yourself," Jaye wondered. "Yes, okay? I accept. I don't like the idea of you being out there on your own either, and, as cool as your sister and Grant are, I don't intend to move in with them."

"So you're really okay with it?" Dixon asked, feeling so much lighter, his smile coming so much easier. It got bigger and bigger until his cheeks ached.

"I said yes, didn't I?"

"God, it's like you're too good to be true," Dixon grinned.

But Jaye wasn't smiling. "Does that help you trust me more?"

"Of course I trust you," Dixon admonished.

"Then trust me," Jaye dared. "Trust me with all of it."

Still, Dixon hesitated. "It's just that I know how it's going to sound. It'll sound worse than it was and you'll get the wrong idea."

"Try me."

"Shit," Dixon grimaced, rolling his head on his shoulders. "Okay. So when he had me out there, he fed me the gun's barrel, told me to get on my knees. He threatened to break all of my teeth if I didn't blow him gently enough. But you know...." Dixon searched for the words, trying to resist the urge to glance up at Jaye's expression. "It wasn't the first time he's said shit like that to me. It's just the first time I really heard how fucked-up it was. He forced his dick down my throat and kept at it, kept choking me with it until I puked. The whole time he had the gun to my head. Then he, uh, told me to crawl to the Expedition, had me get rid of the rest of my gear and take my pants down. I was unarmed, and he had his finger on the trigger, so I had no choice. He put me behind the wheel, got in the car with me, then sucked me off. He didn't have the gun for that part, and he threw it back at me, how I'd changed. That it was my fault. A while back, I'd asked him to try out a rape fantasy. I *asked him* to do it. I wanted to feel scared, feel overpowered, but in a way that was somewhat controlled. Sure, Marcus could be ruthless, but he wouldn't do anything to permanently hurt me, even if he might threaten to."

"Dixon," Jaye hissed. "*How could you?* How could you do that to yourself?! Didn't you see how unstable he is?! Oh my god. *Oh my god!* Rape isn't sexy. It's not *fun.*"

"I know!" Dixon argued, feeling small and disgusting. "I know that! But we'd been together for so long, and it really just boiled down to rough sex with Marcus again. Or that's what I told myself. He jumped me one night after work. He had a gun. *His* gun. He used it to scare me. Told me to get naked, put the barrel against my head as he had me kneel in the kitchen and handcuffed me to a pipe down under the sink, so I was forced low to the ground. He was threatening me, telling me all of this sick shit he was going to do to me. I thought it was lies, a way to get in my head. But then he got my belt, and whipped me across the middle of my back until there was blood running down from the wounds. He just didn't stop. I screamed. I begged him to stop. But I didn't use the safe word. Then he stuck the gun against me, but not against my head. He put the end of the barrel against my asshole like he was going to stick it inside me."

"Dixon," Jaye moaned, gripping Dixon's hands, searching his face. "*Holy fuck.*"

"He didn't force it very deep," he said, feeling empty, the words dulled, not letting himself go back there and relive it. He just said the words like he was reciting instructions or a recipe. "But he kept it in there while he brought me off with a hand, laughing at how I liked it. It, uh... it really hurt when he had sex with me, after he forced me to come. There was blood. I didn't realize it was from *there* until after I showered.

"It was the same thing on the side of that road. I was terrified, but he got me to come, right? That means I wanted it."

He looked up at Jaye, not understanding, not at all. "Why did I let him? Why did I do that? Why didn't I get out of it when I could have? Why did I *enjoy it*? I don't want to be that person anymore. I want to be someone better. A *lot* better. I want to respect myself enough to say no to things that will hurt me. It was good to pull the gun on Marcus, even if he wound up taking it from me. It was the first time I really tried to stand up for myself when it mattered. It was like a cycle, you know? Marcus tempted me to do things no one else would have let me try. When I tried them, I liked them and wanted more, even if it was bad for me and made me feel shitty about myself. Then I just always felt so bad about myself it was like I had it coming. All of the things he did to me, it was earned because I'd chosen it. Here I was, trying to uphold the law, every day, and I couldn't even take the first step toward a safe life in my own home."

Jaye's expression was all twisted and horrible. Caressing the side of his face to soften some of that, Dixon ached all the way through.

"I am better than that, right? I'm worth you loving me? I want to be. God, how I want that," Dixon murmured, wiping his tears with the heel of a hand.

"Yes," Jaye answered, holding Dixon's stare. "You're a good man and a good cop and fuck anyone that tries to make you question that. Fight for this," Jaye urged, laying his other hand over Dixon's heart. "Fight for it as hard as you can."

"You're so good at that," Dixon sighed. "Fighting for yourself. I admire that."

"Whatever you've done, all of it, any of it—it's over. I forgive you of anything and everything, okay? Clean slate," Jaye promised. "Just don't hurt yourself like that anymore. That's *my* deal. *My* condition. I want to find other ways to turn you on. Think I can do it?"

"Mmm," Dixon hummed, smiling just a little, bravely. "Something tells me you can."

Chapter 23

Eye of the Storm

Jaye suspected there might have been less chaos inflicted upon his cabin, his refuge, if a bear had gotten in and torn through the place. Once Dixon moved in, everything started to change, scattered by the whirlwind.

The kitchen was suddenly always stocked with food; the fridge packed with offerings the likes of which Jaye had never seen. There were new plates, bowls, glasses and utensils in the cupboards. New appliances were delivered and installed. A new couch arrived, and a larger table. A cleaning service did an overhaul of the place, scrubbing every nook and cranny, clearing out every cobweb. A wine rack was installed, though Jaye was barely legal and had never before tasted any sort of alcohol.

Most shocking of all, Dixon began to frame and hang Jaye's drawings. In all of the cleaning and reorganizing, his stowed tablets had been found. Dixon selected his favorites and used them in his decorating schemes, much to Jaye's annoyance.

It was hard to stay upset about it though, once he saw how Dixon loved to stare at them and pine for hours over sketches which Jaye had thought nothing of. Drawing was a comfort and a distraction, nothing more. To Dixon, though, they were really something.

Sitting on their bed, on new, unbelievably soft sheets and with a recently purchased, fluffy down comforter spread over his lap, sipping a glass of Riesling and grimacing fiercely at the sweet and bitter taste, Jaye watched Dixon fuss with the latest addition—a drawing of a view of Dixon's back while seated in front of the fireplace, backlit by the flames. He kept checking it with a level and frowning at the angle, swearing it was off.

"Maybe the cabin's crooked?" Jaye suggested.

Sparing a glance over his shoulder, Dixon repressed a smile and said, "You hate that stuff, don't you? No one's forcing you to have some."

"No, maybe the god-awful taste will wear off if I get a little drunk," Jaye insisted. "Ugh, the beer was worse. How can people drink that piss? Boggles the mind."

"You're so cute," Dixon grinned, chuckling a little. "Keep making that face. Once I fix this you can pretend to be my underage conquest again. It'll be our first experiment with intoxicated sex."

"Yeah, because you really need to get me liquored up in order to get in my pants," Jaye laughed.

The cabin's main living space was ringed with his work. The most elaborate frame contained a self portrait, done by looking in a hand mirror, which Dixon had bought for that purpose. Dixon had mounted Jaye's likeness over the fireplace. Some sketches were attempts to capture the view from the windows, but most were of Dixon, Jaye's favorite subject. Every time Jaye tried to draw him, he was looking to capture a glimmer of what Jaye knew was there, inside, needing to hint with the crude tools of graphite and paper the biggest miracle of his life. There were so many layers to him—the delicacy of his blond eyelashes, the maturity in his eyes, which were neither blue, nor green, but a shade between them. There was his physical strength and emotional vulnerability. Each sketch was a glimpse of those facets of Dixon's identity.

Taking another deep sip of wine, he followed it with a groan of disgust, sticking his tongue out like the air might cleanse it.

"Fucking *awful*, man. Really," he said.

"Stop drinking it then, kiddo."

"Yeah, you come over here and call me kiddo to my face, one more time, and see what it gets you."

"Hmm. Blowjob?" Dixon guessed. Setting the ruler down, he seemed to decide to try testing his luck. Weaving around the furniture, Dixon approached the bed. Crawling up the bed, toward Jaye, Dixon said, "How about I take you shopping?"

"Again," Jaye marveled. "For what? We have everything. You got us *everything*. There's shit in the fridge I can't *pronounce*. We have a *maid*. It's *insane*."

"Doesn't matter. Only thing that matters is you," Dixon grinned, looking love struck.

"Wow," Jaye said softly, swirling his stinky Riesling. Dixon leaned in and kissed Jaye's lips like he was sucking the taste of the wine from them. The more he got, the more he seemed to want, taking the kiss deeper, licking Jaye's lips and sucking the flavor from his tongue.

They broke, gasping, but Dixon wasn't through. Trailing a line of kisses down Jaye's throat, he said, "You need warmer clothes. Better boots. A new coat."

"And kinky underwear?"

"*Definitely* kinky underwear," Dixon agreed wholeheartedly. The kissing stopped abruptly. Dixon asked, "Did you make that appointment with the dentist?"

"You're insane," Jaye whispered.

"I'm taking care of you," Dixon whispered back.

"There's nothing wrong with my teeth," he replied, still whispering.

"When's the last time you had a checkup? It's important. Your health is important. You need to get back in the habit of doing this kind of stuff."

"You're insane."

"Drink your wine."

"*You* drink my wine."

"I'll make you a deal," Dixon proposed. "If you can finish that, I'll make you feel so good, you'll be sure you're dreaming."

"I'm already dreaming," Jaye smiled. "You're amazing. *This* is amazing."

He gestured at their modest home, filled with both their things now, and possessions not belonging to one or the other at all, but both of them.

"You deserve it. You deserve more. Do you still hate that you love me?"

Tracing the shape of Dixon's lips, Jaye found himself mapping the curves, measuring the shadows and highlights.

"No," Jaye murmured. "You don't have to be perfect, Dix. You know that, right? I'd love you for nothing. I'll love you forever."

Dixon's smiled changed. His eyes got too bright.

"No, don't do that. Don't cry. Please," Jaye pleaded softly.

Taking a deep breath, exhaling heavily, Dixon smiled with glistening eyes and said, "God, I'm lucky."

All of the trying, going out of his way to please, to tend and transform Jaye's modest existence—it spoke loudly of Dixon's fear. Though it came from a sincere place, every gesture just reminded Jaye that Dixon felt he needed to compensate for the shortcomings he saw in himself. Sure, part of it was Dixon trying to come through on his promise to be Jaye's protector, but it was Jaye's greatest hope that Dixon would soon be able to stop trying. Jaye just wanted Dixon to be the way Jaye knew he could be, without glossing over the darkness that would always be there anyway. Jaye was ready and able to take the good with the bad. He didn't want a false lover. Honesty, even if harsh, was better.

"Relax, okay?" Jaye urged. "Sit with me. Have some smelly wine with me. I'll take you up on that deal, by the way. Something tells me I'll be glad I had the drink once I find out what you've got planned."

"Wow, okay, this is kind of intense," Jaye chuckled breathlessly. On his back, with his ankles hooked inside straps tied to the headboard, pulling his legs apart and back, he closed his eyes and palmed the back of Dixon's head. He'd been sucking on Jaye's balls for a few minutes now, with no sign of getting bored soon.

Glancing up, Dixon let Jaye's sac fall from his lips to say, "Remember, you can slip your legs out if you want. You're not tied down. This is just to keep my hands free and you comfortable."

"Oh, I'm pretty comfortable, thanks," Jaye snickered. "Well, the ring kind of sucks, but not as much as you."

"Cute," Dixon grinned. Checking the metal cock ring constricting Jaye's balls and the base of his shaft, Dixon asked, "It's not too tight, is it?"

"Of course it's too tight! Look at how red I am down there and it's really... you know. Squeezing me."

"That's the idea, smartass. It'll keep you hard, keep you from coming. Probably. I'm sure if you try hard enough, you could still come."

"So, now what?"

"Now you relax," Dixon told him.

"Relax with my legs in the air and my business all up in your face?"

"Yes. Try."

"Can't we just fuck?" Jaye sighed, letting his head fall back as Dixon began trailing kisses and little licks down the underside of Jaye's left leg, from the back of his ankle to the inside of his knee, then across his thigh, moving lower and closer to Jaye's ass. "This seems complicated. And unnecessary."

"Some things are more fun than fucking, young'un."

"Don't call me that, old man. And I don't believe you. At all."

"Yeah?"

Jaye had finished off the wine with one last gulp. It took him a while to recover from the nasty taste, but once he had, he discovered that the room had mysteriously started to spin. Or maybe it was just the bed. Maybe Dixon installed wheels underneath it somehow when Jaye wasn't paying attention.

"Whoa! Fuck!" Jaye hollered, clenching and sitting up a little, getting up on his elbows as Dixon sucked a kiss right to Jaye's asshole. Staring, he watched Dixon take a slow lick over the wrinkled knot, then trace around it in little circles. With a hand, he began to fondle Jaye's balls, rolling them as he kept licking.

Breathing hard, quaking subtly from the feel of Dixon's soft, wet, wriggling tongue teasing his opening, Jaye tried to keep his voice from breaking, and failed, as he let out a moan, which turned into a whimper.

"Something tells me Cash never did this with you," Dixon grinned.

"Nope," Jaye muttered tightly, staring up at the ceiling, every single muscle in his body tensed with anxiousness, his hands clawing at his own thighs.

"How about the sweet little boyfriend?"

"Nope."

"How about this?"

"Mother*fucker*," Jaye gasped as Dixon pressed his pointed tongue through the clenched ring of muscle, riding it with a few pumps of his head, making Jaye tremble and grunt.

Hands cupped and caressed Jaye's cheeks. Dixon withdrew his tongue in order to kiss the spot again, blowing on it gently before licking once more. It felt better than Jaye could have ever dreamed. He gave in to need and let his hand fall between his strung-up legs to tug his cock, relieving some of the pressure built up there.

When the tongue slipped back into him, stretching even farther, Jaye whimpered again. A flash of Dixon's vibrant eyes told him Dixon was getting off on the whimpering, and in a big way. He watched Jaye masturbate while worshiping his ass with his mouth, taking his time, drawing it out.

Soon Jaye was a wreck, sweating, breathing unevenly, the wine making his head buzz and the stimulation charging his body. His nerves crackled. His rim was engorged with blood from all of the gentle, focused attention. Dixon propped himself up on an arm and began rubbing repeatedly over Jaye's rim, drawing even more blood there, making Jaye beg with guttural, gasping sounds.

"The hell is that," he asked on a heavy exhale as Dixon grabbed a toy from the bed, sliding it closer and opened the lube. "It looks alien."

Dixon just smiled, biting his lower lip as he slid his middle finger through Jaye's opening, burying it to the hilt, making Jaye gasp loudly, then moan. Head fallen back to the pillow again, he began hissing, "Oh fuck. Oh fuck. *Oh fuck*," over and over again, under his breath. The position made him feel powerless and not in control at all. Maybe that was the point. It changed things drastically, though. It made it much more of a head trip than a brief, primal, physical act.

The toy was oblong and had weird curving arms that didn't make any sense.

"God, you're not gonna tell me, are you?" Jaye realized, face scrunched up as he prepared himself for anything.

The finger slid out, replaced right away by the toy, which Dixon fed up Jaye's ass. Pulling on one of the arms, Dixon rocked the toy forward. The second arm pressed at the patch of skin between Jaye's hole and his balls. The oblong part inside him pushed firmly at the inside of the passage. Then Dixon rocked it the other way, setting a rhythm.

A hard, broken whimper ripped from Jaye as he shuddered, gritting his teeth, feeling an even rawer yell bubble up in his throat. Grabbing at his legs, blowing air through his lips, sweating and barraged with jolts of sensation from whatever Dixon was doing to him, he was frantic, growing desperate.

"Dix," he moaned, reaching out a hand.

Dixon folded their hands together, brushing a thumb over the back of Jaye's hand.

"That's your prostate gland," Dixon told him. "This is designed to massage it. See? The insertable part is curved like that to target your gland and the handle presses on your perineum to stimulate the internal root of your penis. All of that pressure is just going to milk your gland really slowly."

Clear fluid began to pulse from Jaye's slit, dripping over his swollen erection.

The combined sensations were overwhelming, especially given the cock ring which made relief much harder to get. The nudging of the toy felt strange, too, provoking a reaction like he had to go to the bathroom. Grunting and whining, Jaye threw his head back, not wanting to watch anymore. Feeling it was enough to try to handle.

"It's too much," he growled, convulsing subtly as Dixon rocked a little faster and Jaye's body twitched in response.

"Close your eyes, relax your muscles. Deep even breaths, okay?" Dixon let go of Jaye's hand in order to stroke Jaye's cock, slicking pre-come along his shaft as the other hand kept triggering him internally.

Trembling helplessly on the bed, little cries continuously startling from him, Jaye was swept away in the overload of agonizing pleasure. Nothing had ever felt like that. It was indescribable. He wanted to come, needed to come, but the metal ring binding him staved it off, keeping it just out of reach, prolonging the build-up more and more.

Endless minutes passed, until Jaye was almost worn out. Pre-come was everywhere, coating his cock in a slick slide as Dixon tugged it ceaselessly, keeping Jaye torturously close to an orgasm that never materialized. The toy was taking him apart, loosening his ties on the world. Eyes rolled up in his head, hair stuck to his forehead with sweat, gulping air, shuddering against the unending jolts of pleasure, part of him wasn't there at all. There were no worries, no cares. It was just his body and the ways Dixon was triggering it.

When the toy was removed and Dixon shifted between Jaye's legs, lining his cock up with Jaye's tender hole, Jaye sobbed softly as it breached him. Dixon had him by the ankles, pushing them back even farther, bottoming out in one rough push. Dixon's hips pumped, taking him deeply. The position let him go far enough to make Jaye shout. Soon Jaye was growling, writhing against each inward thrust, his head thrown back and his mouth working to find air.

The ring binding him was released with a flick of Dixon's finger before Jaye came hard enough to black out.

It all fell away.

He woke up hours later. The sun was in a completely different place in the sky. The recently acquired silky sheets and new comforter covered him. Dixon lay beside him, watching with a content expression. The back of Dixon's finger brushed down the side of Jaye's face once he had opened his eyes.

"You let me sleep," Jaye complained, frowning.

"You needed it. You were exhausted. Plus you're kind of gorgeous when you sleep. No nightmares either."

Jaye's hand moved on its own, instinctively, searching down the side of the bed. Dixon glanced at it, then gave Jaye a complicated sort of smile—both sad and accepting. "I know about the knife. Found it under the mattress when I was making the bed."

"It's not—" Jaye fumbled. "I wasn't—"

"It helps you feel safe. Able to protect yourself," Dixon guessed.

"Yeah, something like that. Having it nearby makes it easier. I wouldn't use it. I just need to hold it sometimes. I used to keep it under my pillow, until you moved in. Look, I'm sorry," he apologized. "I don't want you to be scared of me."

Dixon caressed Jaye's cheek, smiling more. "Oh, I think I can handle you. Besides, trust is a process. I get it. Plus, those guys took you right out of your bed. It makes complete sense that you'd want a way to defend yourself if you were surprised like that again."

Jaye glanced over at the closet, where he used to sleep. Now, it was filled with Dixon's things—clothes, boxes, and shoes. The entirety of Jaye's things fit inside two drawers of the single dresser. If Dixon intended to buy him lots of new things, though, that might change in a hurry. But, he figured, everything else had changed. Why not that too?

"Where are your parents?" Dixon asked gently. "A while back you said you didn't have any family left."

"Yeah, well," Jaye sighed. "Dad ran out when I was little. I hardly remember him. Mom was... well, she was a dancer."

He gave Dixon an awkward, heavy look.

"Oh," Dixon said after a pause. His eyebrows rose. "That kind of dancer."

"Yeah, she worked at this creepy club. We had a shitty little apartment. I was an only child. She had me when she was *really* young. People always said I look just like her. Some people thought we were siblings. Whatever. I moved out before I was out of high school and went to live with my boyfriend. Part of it was about getting out of her hair, but she was never around anyway. It was just... bad. A bad situation all around. Then she disappeared. Never showed up when I got hurt, or during the trial, or when I was locked up. I figure she died a few years back. She, um... she had a really hard life."

He was looking down at his hands. When Dixon didn't say anything, Jaye glanced up.

Dixon was searching Jaye's face like he could see her there if he tried, frowning. Reaching out, he took Jaye's hand and held it.

"I'm sorry you lost her," he said quietly. "She must have been really beautiful."

"She was," Jaye agreed. "How about you? Where are your folks?"

"Georgia," Dixon said simply. "There's extended family down there. When Mom started to develop severe arthritis, they took off for warmer weather and haven't been back since. And Bri and I don't ever get to Georgia, so it's been a few years since we've seen them. There's pretty constant phone and email contact, so it's something."

"Huh. Do you miss them?"

Dixon shrugged, then nodded. "Sure. But we have our own lives.

It's just the way things turned out."

"You should visit sometime, while you still have them," Jaye urged somewhat bashfully, given the starkness of his longing for his own mother.

"Yeah, I probably should," Dixon agreed, leaning in to give him a brief, tender kiss.

After, he pulled back with a regretful sort of sigh.

"Look," Dixon started, his tone of voice sounding strange, like he was segueing to a touchy subject. "The knife isn't all I know about. Grant talked to me a week or two ago, after we all realized Marcus wasn't going to be able to make bail. He told me he was there when you came back to the house that night, right about the time when the fire happened. He said you told him you'd gone for a walk, but he smelled gasoline, and noticed how frazzled you looked. It was you, wasn't it? You started the fire?"

Maybe Jaye should have felt angry, or defensive, or terrified. Before Dixon had shaken up Jaye's life, probably he would have been. He might have fled the bed, then the cabin entirely, running as fast as he could before he could be dragged back for vengeance. But he was wrapped in the soft comforter Dixon had bought just for them, after sharing as much as they had. He'd just given Dixon complete control over his body before falling asleep and dropping his guard completely. His body was weary, his emotions supercharged like they'd never been in all of his life, and all Jaye could do was cry.

Once he'd started, the weeping grew stronger. He hid his face with both hands until Dixon peeled them away, exposing his tears.

That innocent guy in Marcus's bed, now barely alive and scarred for life. I did that.

And Dixon knows.

"Please don't turn me in," Jaye begged shamelessly, his breath hitching on the words. "I can't go back there. They'll *kill me*, or worse. Please. Please, I'll do *anything*. I don't want to die! I don't want you to hate me! Please don't hurt me. I was just trying to help. That's *all*. I swear I'm not a bad person. I was just trying to protect you from him."

Choking on the words, each one was a struggle fraught with emotion—sincere love, wholehearted devotion—things he'd never had and which now stood in his way, preventing him from even pleading his case.

"Please, Dixon," Jaye whispered, desperate. "I'm *so sorry*. *Please* believe me."

Though Dixon still wore that tormented look, seeming much more a cop than a lover, he leaned down and enfolded Jaye in an embrace, smoothing his hair, hushing to him as Jaye clung on quickly and tried to calm down.

"I've known for *weeks*, Jaye," Dixon was telling him. "I didn't just find out. Grant told me before I moved in with you, to warn me. Brekken doesn't know. Grant won't tell the police. He's sticking to his story. So am I."

Crying too hard to speak, Jaye held on to Dixon, letting it out—all of the fear, collected over all of the time spanning between the whoosh of flames and the current moment, enclosed in Dixon's arms, bathed in cooling forgiveness.

After a long time, he was able to breathe more normally. Dixon passed him some tissues.

"I'm sorry," he moaned. "I didn't mean for that guy to get hurt. The guy in the bed. I thought it was just Marcus in there. Don't hate me. *Please* don't."

"Hey, I love you, Jaye Larson," Dixon swore, frowning at him. "It doesn't change anything. I wasn't just *acting* like I love you all this time, to trick you or something. It doesn't matter to me if you did it. I *know* why you did it. It's your nature to fight back, because you're built differently than me. It wasn't your fault that Marcus wasn't alone. And I love you just the way you are."

"I—I had nightmares. You would t-tie me down. S-set me on fire. Punishment," Jaye hiccupped, tripping on the words.

Dixon gathered him up again, pulling him upright, guiding Jaye onto his lap and hissing, "Shit. Ah, *shit*. I will never hurt you, J-bird. Protecting you is my job, right? I meant that. I meant it all the way through. Cross my heart."

He kissed Jaye's forehead, sighing.

"I'm sorry," Jaye whimpered. "I'm sorry. I'm so sorry."

Chapter 24

Inescapable Darkness

Winter and summer in Alaska always had a strange effect on those trying to survive extremes of light and dark. Too much sunlight made people crazy as much as not enough of it. As they sank into the heart of winter, with the sun only rarely making its appearance, the calls Dixon went out on shifted in tone as well.

There was a lot of drunk and disorderliness. There were quite a few domestic disputes, too.

Those were hard. It was usually a woman, beaten up, pushed hard enough at last to get the police involved. Sometimes it was neighbors that made the call, and the couple in question tried to talk around it, claiming it was just a disagreement that got too loud, covering up the bruises with hands, clothing, or makeup.

Each time Dixon was put in those situations, filling the role of mediator, he couldn't help but personalize it a bit.

Grateful to be out from under Marcus's thumb at last, he got to come home with Jaye instead, their shifts finished. Dixon would say silent prayers of thanks, swearing to keep on the straight and narrow, to do better than he'd done.

Those calls always made him quiet. Jaye became good at picking up on it. He would try to offer himself, his body, up as comfort, stripping or falling to his knees as soon as they were through the door. Dixon told himself to resist, to talk it through instead of fucking out the pain. He'd always been physically driven, though, and Jaye was difficult to say no to when he was so plainly eager to let Dixon have his mouth, hand, or ass as a way of forgetting.

A few times it happened before they'd even gotten out of the Ex-

211

pedition. Knowing it was wrong to let Jaye blow him in there, while he was in uniform, barely off duty, the wrongness was what made it appealing. At least it wasn't hurting anyone.

The transition their relationship made in those days was bizarre. It had started out as a business arrangement—sex for safety. Then their hearts got involved. But those little deals they both liked to make kept slipping in there. *'Do this and I'll give you that,'* they'd say. As much as Dixon tried to tell himself it wasn't serious, they always fulfilled their ends of the deal, no matter what the deal was.

Then there were the times when Dixon would spend money on Jaye, buying things for the cabin, or just for him. Afterward, Jaye would offer sex, using himself as collateral. They never spoke about it, or made it official. Dixon always noticed, though. Jaye would initiate intimacy, submitting to whatever Dixon might be in the mood for, right after the monetary transaction was concluded.

So, Dixon started to insist he be the one receiving, almost all of the time.

But Jaye would simply set his ass on Dixon's lap, open his pants and take what he wanted anyway. As Dixon's cock inched into Jaye's slim, snug body, he couldn't protest. He gave in without fail.

On an icy, overcast, starless black afternoon in November, Dixon picked Jaye up from work. There were shopping bags in the backseat, filled with more warm clothes for Jaye since the temperature outside kept dropping. He peeked into the bags as they drove from the truck stop to the cabin. No sooner had they pulled up in front than Jaye was loosening Dixon's buckle, slipping a hand inside to stroke him hard while undoing the rest. Then his mouth was on Dixon's erection, tonguing it, suckling the head.

"You don't need to do this," Dixon grunted. "I don't buy you things to get favors!"

Jaye pushed his hand farther into Dixon's pants to cup his balls while he sucked him off.

"It's not a favor," he hummed.

"It feels like it is! You're not my *whore*! And I love you too much to let you act like one."

"Tell me to stop, then. Make me stop," Jaye dared.

Marcus and the fire were always there with them in those days, hovering at the edge of everything. Maybe it was the way darkness had closed up around the daylight, crowding it out. Dixon had always known how much Jaye didn't like the dark. It was setting him on edge, his worries inescapable. Jaye acted like he needed to prove himself, his self-confidence ravaged. He was turning back into the tense kid Dixon had picked up from the Stop and Shop, seducing Trooper Rowe again and again in order to curry favors.

Jaye's silky soft lips ran over Dixon's shaft. He mouthed Dixon's balls, trailing heat, moaning softly.

"Fuck," Dixon grimaced, hating how good it felt. "Stop! Stop it. Now."

Disbelieving, Jaye did stop, staring up at Dixon with wonder. Then he laughed, shaking his head.

"Wow," he said. "Didn't think you could do it. Proved me wrong, I guess."

But Dixon was already acting, reacting, and unstoppable. He grabbed Jaye, manhandling him, turning him around in the seat. Yanking Jaye's pants down, tugging his legs closer, Dixon got Jaye free of his pants and swallowed his cock without ceremony.

Laughing again, more breathlessly, Jaye thrust into Dixon's throat, palming the back of Dixon's head. Given Dixon's frustration-fueled enthusiasm, it didn't take long. Soon Jaye was unloading; spurting hot as Dixon wrung him dry, swallowing every drop, licking him clean.

"Guess you showed me, Trooper Rowe," Jaye chuckled.

"I'm not Cash!" Dixon shouted, sounding hurt, sitting up and wiping his mouth. "Our arrangement is over. I don't want your favors. Take it or leave it. If you want to take it, I'll be inside our home, waiting for my partner."

He got out of the vehicle, slamming the door behind him.

It took Jaye a long time to settle down and cool off. When he finally did walk into the cabin, closing the door quickly as the arctic chill rushed to devour the warmth of their modest home, it was a huge relief. Dixon had started to think maybe Jaye wouldn't be coming in at all.

Shivering violently, despite the coat and layers, Jaye hung his head, teeth clacking.

"I told you, I don't know how to do this," Jaye argued.

"Stop trying to fix everything by getting me off. That's all I want. I want you to respect yourself as much as I respect you."

"I'm just trying to contribute! Am I not supposed to touch you? I can't buy you things, Dix. This is all I have," he shouts, gesturing at his body. "You know that."

"Then what are these?" Dixon challenged, indicating the framed drawings. "Huh? These aren't *nothing*! These are amazing gifts you've given me, which have *nothing* at all to do with sex. Or when you made chili at Brekken's place, to cheer me up when everything felt awful? Or how great you are at making me laugh? Being with you makes me happier than I've been in years, Jaye, and not because you know how to get me off. Stop selling yourself short. You're not that kid you used to be. You're the man I love. So, act like it already."

It ended sounding less confident than Dixon would have liked. The stricken look to Jaye's face made it hard to keep the iron in his voice.

"Fuckin' c'mere," Dixon grumbled, standing and going to Jaye. He shivered in Dixon's arms, silently.

"I'm sorry," Jaye murmured eventually. "Old habits die hard, I guess."

"I know they do," Dixon sighed. "Believe me."

Of course it upset Dixon to hear how Jaye had deliberately caused the fire, but he'd never had any delusions about who Jaye was. Dixon didn't expect him to be any different than his true self. Marcus had been an impatient, arrogant hard-ass, but Dixon always found things about his personality to appreciate rather than focus on the negative. How important he was to Marcus, how good he could make Dixon feel, those were what Dixon pushed to the forefront of his mind. With Jaye, breaking the law was something seen as a viable option in order to solve near-impossible situations. Starvation drove him to steal food. A physical attack caused him to fight back with a vengeance.

So when Dixon was disarmed, raped, and his life threatened on that road, Jaye's solution was to try taking Marcus out before something worse could happen.

Maybe Dixon would have been more disturbed if the police had found evidence of Jaye's involvement, or if the cause of the fire was still in question in an official sense. By the time Grant had his private conversation with Dixon, the matter was as good as settled with the law in Zus. Jaye wasn't a suspect. Both Marcus and his overnight guest had received treatment for their injuries. They were both alive. If they were careful, no one would ever have to know Jaye did it. Just like Dixon had always been careful so his fellow troopers wouldn't suspect his bruises came from Marcus.

In addition to that, he knew Jaye was smart and the last thing he wanted was to go back to jail. He had no delusions about what Dixon's job was, and the people who were more likely to interact with them on a daily basis from then on. The temptation to break the law was lessened when you had the law surrounding you all of the time. And Jaye's apology had been sincere. Dixon felt that. The nightmares he suffered, the fear and the guilt—it combined to be a better lesson than Dixon could have ever come up with for him, and more effective than any preachy speech.

If it made him a bad cop to hide evidence about the fire, then Dixon would live with that. His loyalty to Jaye outweighed his loyalty to Marcus, and, in that case at least, also outweighed his duty as an Alaska State Trooper. Jaye wasn't a menace or a threat to the public or himself. He was just a scared kid trying to survive.

Maybe it was selfish.

Maybe it was wrong.

Certainly, it was dangerous. But they lived in a dangerous world, and sometimes you needed to defend yourself from monsters.

The previous day, Dixon had driven Jaye to meet with his parole officer. Dixon had waited outside, letting Jaye have his privacy. While Dixon was sitting there, Sesi called.

"Marcus is still trying to get his brother to bail him out," Sesi told him with heavy implication. "So far, it's a no go. I'm guessing the insurance money from the fire is his best bet. It's been almost a month, Dix. That money's going to be coming in soon. If Marcus posts bail, he can't go far, but that's part of the problem. He knows he can't go near you because of the restraining order. That doesn't mean he won't try."

"Got it. Thanks for keeping me in the loop. Let me know if there's any change."

Afterward, with worries about Marcus in his head and Jaye reminded of his ongoing predicament with the remainder of his parole, both of them were unusually quiet for the rest of the day. At one point, Dixon asked, "Is everything okay?"

In response, Jaye just gave a forced smile and answered, "Yeah, it's all cool," without disclosing specifics.

That evening, Jaye huddled on the floor in a corner with his drawing pad, with no interest in dinner or conversation. They went to bed early. Dixon had to fight to stay awake long enough to make sure Jaye was going to sleep instead of lying there, worrying about things he shouldn't.

The next morning was fairly routine. Dixon had work, Jaye didn't. Dixon got ready for work, ate breakfast, and they shared a chaste kiss goodbye at the door before he drove away.

It was full dark when he left, and full dark when he got home. He was still in uniform when he walked through the front door, but ready to get undressed quickly, since it always felt awkward to be in uniform around Jaye, given the way they'd met and everything that had happened since.

As soon as Dixon was inside, expecting to see Jaye tucked in a corner somewhere, reading or sketching, instead he was thrown off by getting a heated kiss before the door had even shut behind him.

Dixon's fingers went to his duty belt instantly, wanting to get it off and remove his holster.

"Leave 'em, okay?" Jaye murmured. "I want the handcuffs. Just this one time."

"No," Dixon protested. "No way. You know my rule."

"Fuck your rule, Trooper Rowe. *I need this*. Give me this. Show me I can trust you like *this*."

Jaye's hand was fisted in Dixon's shirt and there was a hard shine to his eyes that made queasy tickles wriggle in Dixon's gut.

"Look," Jaye said, "There's this one thing I can't get out of my head. I need you to do some role play with me, and I need for you to keep going with it until the end, no matter what. Afterward, I'll explain. Promise. But for now, trust me."

Looking like a pissed-off kid, a delinquent in need of a firm hand, Jaye pulled his shirt off and went to the table where they ate their meals, laying his hands upon it, bent over slightly like he was waiting to be patted down.

There would be no discussion, no options. It was either go through with it or walk out, and it was way too late to walk out.

Dixon tried to get a read on Jaye as he took the cuffs out and brought Jaye's arms around to his back in order to snap them on. A muscle in Jaye's jaw twitched as he ground his teeth together. His eyes were focused on one of the front windows, not on Dixon in head-to-toe uniform behind him. Jaye's body tensed as soon as the metal was fastened around his wrists. With shallow, quick little breaths through his nose, Jaye leaned forward over the table, laying the side of his face upon it, his ass bent over in front of Dixon.

I don't want to do this. I can't do this to him.

Even as that thought rang through Dixon's mind, his hand reached out, defiant, to touch his captive. It felt like all of the parts of Dixon that wanted to flout the rules, be a bad guy instead of a good guy for a while, were all channeled into those fingers as he unfastened Jaye's pants and pushed them down to Jaye's upper thighs. Ass bared, buttocks clenched in nervousness or self-consciousness, Jaye shivered slightly, lips parted and eyes momentarily closed.

"Please don't hurt me, Trooper Rowe," Jaye begged in such a wanton way that made it instantly clear to Dixon he was asking for the opposite, role playing like he sometimes did when he acted like he was underage and Dixon was taking advantage of his innocence. "Not the baton, *please.*"

"Fuck," Dixon groaned in protest, gazing up at the ceiling instead of at Jaye's tight little ass. "Are you kidding me?"

"Don't touch me there with it," Jaye asked, glancing back over his shoulder and giving Dixon a look that asked for something else.

No. No way. I can't do this. He's just a kid. This is wrong. This is...

The baton was in his hand and extended before he realized he'd taken it out. He took a few steps away to get the lube, because even if he played along, he didn't want to hurt Jaye. He quickly smeared the slick over the baton, then extended it. The narrow tip teased between Jaye's cheeks, tickling at his knot. Jaye's lips parted on a sigh, his eyes closing with pleasure. Spreading Jaye with his left hand, Dixon gripped the baton with his right, then pulled him apart to expose his hole. He ran the tip of the baton over the clenched opening, then applied some pressure.

He could hear Jaye's breathing get heavier, his body flushing. Dixon was getting hard.

Another push and the tip slid through Jaye's rim. Only an inch was inside him, but he made a low noise and tilted his hips slightly to stick his ass out farther, like he wanted more. Dixon fed another inch inside, watching Jaye's asshole take the black stick.

"You like that?"

He let go with his left hand and reached around to feel Jaye's cock. It was fully erect. Cradling it as he fed another inch through, Dixon squeezed the shaft when it pulsed, twitching.

"That's it. Nice and easy. It doesn't have to hurt. Just stay nice and still for me, now."

Still pushing, slowly but steadily, he made Jaye take more and more of the stick, wondering how much he could fit. Leaving it embedded, Dixon slid his hand up the baton to grip it near where it vanished up Jaye's passage. Then he began to pump Jaye's cock with long, complete strokes.

Jaye's hands twisted in the cuffs and he moaned. When Dixon started to tug the baton back out, just as slowly, Jaye shuddered hard and shot a jet of come. Working Jaye's shaft until he was spent, Dixon watched avidly. A deep blush covered Jaye's skin and he was unusually quiet, lost in his own head somewhere.

Taking his time, Dixon finally got the baton free, sliding his index finger in to the hilt in its place.

"There, how's that?"

Jaye grunted thickly in response, turning his face away.

When Dixon added a second, working them slowly, steadily in

and out, Jaye whimpered.

Trying to stay in character for Jaye, Dixon asked, "You're not hiding anything up here, are you, kid?"

Jaye gasped. It shifted quickly into a scared-sounding whine. Dixon reached deeper, twisting the fingers around and Jaye writhed, making soft pleading noises. Getting his cock out with one hand, Dixon spat onto his hand to spread some saliva over his shaft. When the fingers pulled out, he replaced them with the head of his cock. The plum-shaped, reddish-purple head pressed at the opening, much larger than what had just been inside. He spread Jaye's cheeks with a hand, pressing at him, but not hard enough to breach him yet. Waiting there, letting him feel it, Dixon took hold of the handcuffs, tugging on them to force Jaye to arch his back, coming up off the table a little. He pushed his ass back onto Dixon and Dixon added his own forward pressure, too. Gradually, enough to make Jaye's cry break off, Dixon began to enter him, parting the muscle. Impatiently, Jaye pressed back harder, taking the head and gasping roughly.

Caressing the side of Jaye's ass with the hand not holding the cuffs, Dixon eventually reached around to fondle Jaye's balls, feeling him quiver and tighten around Dixon's cockhead.

"You feel nice," Dixon told him in a whisper.

Grunting and panting, hanging his head, arms straining in the pose, wedged between Dixon and the table's edge, Jaye slowly became a wreck. Keeping things at the same, unhurried pace, Dixon gradually worked his way into Jaye with little pushes that soon had him sweating, cursing and crying out.

"How's that cock feel, kid?" Dixon asked.

"Good, sir," Jaye answered gruffly, not like himself at all. A chill raced down Dixon's spine.

"You like getting fucked like this?"

"Yes, sir. Thank you, sir."

"Jesus," Dixon hissed, horrified. That was training talking. That was *experience*. Dixon had been party to a lot of fucked-up sex with Marcus, but this was different. The last place Dixon wanted to be in was that of Jaye's abusers. Letting Jaye hear how shaken he was, Dixon said, "Okay, enough. I won't do this to you if it's reminding you of — "

"*Do it!*" Jaye yelled, his voice breaking. "You want me to trust you?! Prove I can! I need to *face this* instead of hiding from it! You're a cop. Fuck me as a cop for once."

Dixon had stopped moving and was holding Jaye more tenderly. He took a deep breath and decided to follow Jaye's lead a little longer. That didn't mean he couldn't speed things up.

After caressing along Jaye's body for a moment to let things settle down before going back at it, he began to fuck Jaye in earnest. The change in pace made Jaye shout. Dixon held him down and gave it to him good and hard, driving his whole length inside, going as fast as he thought Jaye could comfortably stand.

"You like getting fucked like this?" Dixon asked again.

"Yes, sir," Jaye gasped, hiding his face.

Coming with a guilty but no less spectacular explosion of white fire as his balls unloaded deeply inside Jaye's body, Dixon wondered what he'd just been a part of. He needed to know.

The cuffs were unfastened before he had even pulled out. Guiding Jaye's arms around and up to extend by his head, Dixon folded his larger body over Jaye's smaller one and kissed in a line up his neck, nuzzling tenderly there with a sigh. Arms overlaying Jaye's arms, Dixon held him, weaving their fingers together, claiming Jaye's heart as well as his body.

"Thank you," Jaye murmured. "I know you didn't want to, but it helped. Real things are always less scary than the ghosts and nightmares."

"Who was it?" Dixon asked softly.

"One of the guards. He'd had it out for Cash. The guy was sick of the gang causing trouble, picking fights, going after other gangs, stirring shit up. He took it out on me, since he knew I was valuable to Cash. He'd come into my cell or find me when I was in the showers, and get me alone. There were always other guards there watching out, watching me."

"What did he do to you?"

The answer was a drawn-out sigh, coupled with a child-like frown Dixon tried to kiss away.

"Scared the hell out me, that's what," Jaye told him, then fell quiet again.

Chapter 25
Preyed Upon

We know you have it. We've got it on good authority, so where'd you hide it, Johnny?

"They'd trash my cell, pretending to search for some smuggled thing they knew I didn't have. A weapon. Drugs. Who knows. When they didn't find it in there, they decided they would need to search me."

They were seated on the bed. Dixon had removed most of his uniform, but still had on his pants and his white undershirt. Jaye was still shirtless and flushed from the sex. Dixon passed Jaye some water, which he stared at rather than drank.

"Maybe if it had just happened once, it wouldn't have been so bad. But it happened a lot. Regularly. There was nothing Cash could do. The guy didn't have any family to go after in order to make him stop, and it was too difficult to take him out at the time. Cash promised, though, that someday, he'd get it all back—everything he did to me—and I believe that. Sometimes you've just gotta be patient."

Strip!

"He'd tell me to get undressed. He'd put me over by the toilet in my cell, or take me to one of the stalls in the bathrooms, and tell me to grab behind my knees," Jaye said, looking down at his hands. "He was big, the guard, like NBA big. Tall and skinny with these really huge hands, unnaturally long fingers."

Where'd you put it? There's only two places it could be, I figure...

"He'd stick one of those big, long fingers up my ass while I was bent over like that, rooting around with it, prodding, being rough. Then he'd add a second, stick it way in to the hilt. I never knew fingers could reach that far. But then, he would..." Jaye's sighed, trembling. He glanced up at Dixon. There was fury and anguish in his expression.

"Keep going," Dixon said firmly. "I've got you."

"He would tell me to open my mouth wide, stick my tongue out as far as I could. Then, with his fingers still inside me, he'd reach down my throat with the other hand, reaching as deep as he could, and he could reach *far*. He'd make me gag, keep reaching deeper, forcing my mouth wider until I puked, finger-fucked me while everything was coming back up, my body forcing it out, my eyes watering, making these awful sounds 'cause I could still feel him in me—down my throat, up my ass."

Nope, still can't find it. Let's try again!

"It wouldn't be once. He'd do it a couple times. Sticking his fingers down my throat with one hand while digging in my ass with the other. By the time he gave up, I was shaking from all the puking. I was a mess."

Smell that, piggy? How's that smell? How about this?

"He'd force my head down near the toilet so I could get a good whiff of the stink. Then he'd take his fingers out and force them up my nostrils, hooking them in there. It was just... I mean, I still have all of these waking nightmares where I feel people touching me, reaching into my body. It's because of the knife attack and because of that guard." Glancing right at Dixon, Jaye confessed, "Sometimes you sound like him, like that guard. It fucks with my head, which is why I needed this. I need to see if I could feel safe with you, even when you're doing things he used to do. I mean, I'm saying I feel like it helped. It helped a lot. Because you are different. Completely. Of course you're different. I just needed to experience the difference, I guess."

"God, Jaye, after everything else you had to deal with, to think you had someone like me trying to make your life hell, too? I'm so sorry. I'm sorry for what you went through *and* for reminding you of all of that. Thank you for trusting me with this part of your life, though. I can imagine how hard it is for you to talk about."

"Actually, it's good to talk," Jaye said, looking down at his hands. "Gives the ghosts less ammunition, makes them easier to beat."

"Good. I'm glad." Dixon paused, then asked, sounding skeptical, "Is that all he did? Because the way you responded just now...."

"When I was getting closer to my release date, it got worse. He made me call him sir. He would take me places with less chance of being observed, even by other guards. He'd fuck me with his baton. Then just fuck me. It was kind of pathetic. His dick was small. I mean, with those weird spindly fingers, you'd think...." Jaye sighed again, shaking the memories loose. "He was just trying to scare me, Dix. And he did, don't get me wrong. But it wasn't the worst thing that's ever happened to me. I just wanted you to know why I sometimes get weird with you about the authoritative voice and the uniform and all. That's part of why I can't go back there, though. I can't go back to people like that scumbag. I'd die first. I know I'm not a saint, and won't ever be, but I promise you I'm done screwing up. No more breaking the law. No more recklessness. You have my word on that. Okay?"

The fire crackled in the fireplace. Dixon softened, letting the anger go, leaving only sadness behind in his expression. "C'mere," he beckoned, pulling Jaye onto his lap, wrapping him up in a tender embrace, kissing his shoulder and the side of his jaw, clasping the back of his head. "I trust you. I love you. You're safe."

Jaye let go of the rest of the tension in his body, savoring the feel of Dixon's lips moving so softly over his skin, and the reverent, careful slide of his hands.

"I love you, too," Jaye murmured, liking the feel of Dixon's powerful body wrapped around him, and the possessiveness in his every touch.

"You're never going back there," Dixon promised. "Not if I have anything to say about it."

"Okay," Jaye smiled.

Pulling back a little, Dixon looked hard into Jaye's eyes, holding his face in both hands, then kissing the tip of his nose.

"Okay."

The next day was more normal. Jaye still slipped his pocketknife into one of the side pockets of his cargos when he got dressed, just in case the panic started to gnaw on him again. He didn't have to be at work until later on in the day and Dixon wasn't on duty either until after lunch, so to fill the time, Jaye decided to cut more wood.

He liked the exertion required to swing the ax and hit just the right spot with enough force to split the log in one try. It focused the mind in an even more primal way than drawing. The weather was awful, though, with a frigid, biting wind that made your skin hurt as soon as it whipped you, like it was crisping the flesh. His eyes watered and he had to keep blinking them clear in order to see what he was doing.

Telling Dixon about the reason for his issue with the cop voice helped as much as he'd said it did. The handcuffs hadn't been painful or scary, and Dixon had been tender with him, even with playing along with Jaye's game of being the poor, scared victim of Dixon's feigned cruelty with the baton and the force fucking. They both had gotten off, and Jaye was left with one less burden after, so he counted it a success all around.

He found a good log segment and brought it over to the stump where he chopped his firewood. The wind blew steadily, forcing him to keep his head down and out of the way of the gusts. He thought he heard, faintly, the sound of Dixon's cell phone ringing inside the cabin.

The wind was louder, though, and it whistled in his ears. Blinking his eyes against fresh tears, Jaye glanced up to find he wasn't alone.

It was a ghost, materialized.

He blinked his eyes again, vaguely remembering the ax was still over by the woodpile, a good ten feet away. The ghost came closer.

He's not real. You're imagining things. Get it together.

"Well, shit, I never figured Dixie for a kiddie fucker, but I guess we all have our secrets, don't we?"

The words wouldn't even come. Jaye just grunted with horror and fright, backing off, tripping over a ridge of icy snow on the ground. It sent him stumbling to his ass and he struggled to get up. Marcus was on him before he could move, with a hand locked around Jaye's throat, cutting off any attempt to cry out for help.

Dixon was inside, but the last place Jaye wanted Dixon was near Marcus.

The knife was in Jaye's pocket. It was right there. If he could get it out, he could do Marcus just like he'd done to the other, the one he'd given the red smile.

"Now, I'm no kiddie fucker," Marcus was saying coolly, not ruffled, not exerting himself very much, just calmly closing Jaye's windpipe with a brutal grip. The complete inability to breathe was agonizing and terrifying. "But I can't really pass up a chance to fuck with Dixie's new toy, so I'll make an exception, just this one time."

He yanked Jaye up onto his knees.

Marcus's free hand slipped behind his back. He drew out a huge hunting knife with a solid grip, a well-sharpened edge on one side and a serrated edge on the other. Bringing the blade around, he let go of Jaye's throat and slipped the knife's smooth edge under Jaye's chin, tucking it up against his throat. Violently inhaling air through his nose, Jaye fought to be perfectly still. One small movement of Marcus's wrist was all it would take to give Jaye a taste of the same death he'd dealt his attacker.

"Been thinking about this for weeks, you know. Not much else to do to keep busy, and if I'm gonna be locked up anyway, like my lovely, court-appointed lawyer tells me I am, then that really narrows my options. I figure I might as well cut the shit and do what needs doing. Now, see, after everything I gave Dixie, and all the ways I've provided for him, I figure he owes me. I'm here to collect. Since you, little boy, are the unfortunate shit he's taken up with, you get to pay."

Marcus had opened his fly with his left hand, since he didn't need to work very hard to keep Jaye still. Pulling out his cock, Marcus held it in hand and seemed to wait for Jaye to take a good look at it.

But Jaye wouldn't look. Maybe he could still get his pocket knife out, but any movement might provoke Marcus to split Jaye's throat wide open. Marcus had all of the power and nothing to lose. Still, Jaye made the effort to move beyond blind terror to rational thought. He detached from what was happening to try to see around it from all angles. Patience had won him his life once. He could do it again. He'd been impaled on a similar knife, had someone reach into his opened gut and still lived to tell the tale. Jaye would try to play it safe again until he saw a way out.

The flat of the blade shifted against Jaye's neck, lowering a little, and Jaye knew why.

"That's it, open wide," Marcus grinned as Jaye didn't hesitate to open his mouth. "Guess this is why Dixie's fucking you, huh? You know your place. You *love* sucking cock, don't you?"

"Yes, sir," Jaye murmured tensely before opening his mouth again, doing it slowly to avoid a fatal injury. He didn't see Marcus slide his long, thick cock between his lips, but he felt it. The flesh was warm, the musky smell distinct as he tasted the wide column sliding back over his tongue.

His focus spanned outward, away from what was being done to him and around the yard instead. It was better not to think about how it felt, but to look for any advantage, no matter how slight.

Memories of Dixon's story of what Marcus had done to him during that missing hour replayed as Jaye lived the reenactment. Marcus's cock slid right back into Jaye's throat. A strong hand clamped behind Jaye's head to hold him still, letting him choke on it. Right away, Jaye's throat seized up. It tried to expel the obstruction and couldn't. He tried to puke and couldn't, tried to breathe and couldn't.

This is what he did to Dixon. This is how it felt.

Panic tried to cut his resolve to ribbons. Mentally screaming at himself, Jaye stopped trying to find an out and instead just forced himself not to move. Not moving was more critical than not suffocating, because if *he* moved, the blade would move and he'd be dead. His blood would be a hot, red spray over the snow and Marcus's legs. He imagined it there, soaking into the ice, spreading outward through the crystals in pretty blood roses as he convulsed with death spasms.

Throat seizing, making awful sounds so similar to the ones he'd always made with the guard, Jaye was blinded by his tears and the looming figure blocking his view and his hope.

"Let him go. Now."

The words came from far away, but only because of the roaring in his ears from the pounding of his heart and the constant retching.

The goddamned cock eased out of Jaye's throat, but stayed filling his mouth. At least he could breathe, but Dixon was there. It was his voice. Jaye was certain. It wasn't just his overactive imagination. Dixon was right there and Jaye faltered in his desperate attempts to inhale. He blinked his eyes, but still didn't move — wouldn't move.

Though Jaye couldn't see him because his view was full of Marcus, Jaye knew Dixon was standing directly behind Marcus. It didn't make any sense. How had he gotten there? The front door was to Jaye's left and slightly behind him. If Dixon had come out that way, Marcus would have seen. He'd have threatened Jaye before Dixon could get so close.

Even though it was impossible, Dixon was there. Did he have his gun drawn? Aimed at Marcus? He had to. There was a distinct note of threat in the command. It was the cop voice.

"I said let him go," Dixon repeated, his voice wavering only a little.

Jaye could still feel the knife. It tugged upward and he whimpered, trying to raise his chin to avoid it, but unable to because of the flesh filling his mouth.

"Come on, Dixie, we all know you're way too much of a pussy to pull," Marcus said in a hushed, mocking, verbal jab. "Got my knife right where I need it. One flick and this cocksucker's carotid unloads all over our shoes. Drop the fucking gun. Go get in my truck. Once I'm finished here, we'll leave. Your whore will live. That's the only way this goes."

"I don't want to kill you," Dixon hissed. "Why couldn't you just let me go?"

"You've never fired that gun at a real person. I know that for a fact," Marcus said, still sounding way too calm and composed. Did he know something Jaye didn't? "You and me aren't done. I just lost my house and everything in it that ever belonged to me. Now it seems, thanks to you, I'm even going to be losing my freedom. Maybe not, though. Lots of places to get lost around here, aren't there? We'll find someplace together, just you and me. Make a fresh start. I'm not losing you too. Not to some underage cocksucking whore like this. *Go get in the truck, Dixie.*"

The blade tugged upward again and Jaye was certain it was parting skin. With a horrified wordless plea for his life, voiced around Marcus's girth, Jaye began to tremble.

Stop moving!

He tried to stretch his neck. Marcus's hand was still holding the back of Jaye's head, preventing him from escaping the knife's razor-sharp edge.

I'm done. I'm dead. I'm sorry, Dix. I should have stayed that night to make sure it was him in the bed. I should have done better for you.

Still not moving, Jaye sobbed, not ready to die, not like this. Another rapist. Another knife. Another red smile, but this time for him.

Maybe it was owed. Maybe this was what he had coming all along.

On his knees, tasting Marcus's pre-come, Jaye felt a sharp pain along the front of his neck. He voiced a choked scream.

"Okay! Stop! If I get in the truck, will you drop the knife?!" Dixon shouted frantically.

The blade eased off. Jaye panted with shallow breaths through his stuffed mouth and his running nose as his fear shifted abruptly. Dixon was giving up.

"I'm not getting in the truck if you kill him!" Dixon yelled.

"Okay," Marcus soothed. "Look, see? I'm putting it away. I—"

BANG.

The shot echoed.

Jaye screamed over and over, nearly flattened against the icy ground as Marcus fell on top of him. There was red, wetness, and weight and he scrambled out from under, pushing Marcus off. He crawled through red-splattered snow, still screaming hoarsely, wordlessly, as loud as he could.

The bang rang in his ears.

His hands went to his throat, ready to hold in his blood again, or die trying.

Someone was touching him, pulling at him, and Jaye fought. He skittered back a few feet over the frozen ground, feeling like a hunted animal, not a person at all.

There was a dark spot in the upper center of Marcus's back. Marcus's body lay were it landed. A creeping redness unfolded in a circle from beneath his chest.

"Let me see! Jaye, let me see!" Dixon was yelling. He yanked Jaye's hands down and out of the way, even though Jaye was too shocked to cooperate.

Dixon's hand ran over Jaye's throat.

Jaye wondered why he hadn't felt the bullet pierce him. He felt over his chest for a hole, blood, gore, or spilling guts. His eyes were

full of tears. The sounds he was making were rough, primal, and guttural. Was he dying? Was he bleeding out?

"Jaye! Babe, it's all right! Hey!"

Arms gathered him up, hugging, trying to soothe away his fight.
Lips pressed against his temple. Breath warmed the skin and Jaye felt
their shaking, *their* fear.

"You're okay," Dixon told him. "You're going to be okay."

"Dix," he rasped, still unseeing, still not understanding. "What's
happened? Am I...? Did he...?"

"I've got you. You're okay." There was a pause, then Dixon's
voice changed, became instantly, eerily, that cop voice again. Jaye
tried to focus, to look, but he didn't want to look. It was better to keep
his eyes closed and hold on to Dixon. "Yes, this is Trooper Rowe. I've
got a man down here at my home address. He needs an ambulance
right away."

There was more. A badge number, the street address, but it was
lost in the rush of blood in Jaye's ears and the screaming in his brain.
The adrenaline was still exploding within him. The fight instinct was
slow to fade. But Dixon held him with one arm, kissing him between
instructions given into the cell in his hand.

Chapter 26
Flowers on Snow

There were paramedics surrounding Marcus, who had been rolled over onto his back. The dark crimson spot in the pristine white snow grew bigger by the moment in the center of his chest, the blood soaking through layers and layers of clothing. His eyes were open, but he wasn't blinking. His expression was slack.

Troopers were there, people Dixon worked with every day, who knew the rumors about Dixon's boyfriend. They had heard the reasons for Dixon's quietness and the marks that sometimes remained as evidence on his skin, drawing speculation, no matter what excuses were made. They knew, too, about the fire. They knew about the attack, the restraining order, and how, until just an hour or two ago, when the insurance money had finally come through, Marcus had been held pending trial on assault charges.

Dixon wouldn't let go of Jaye's hand. There was a bandage over the shallow nick on Jaye's throat. They were both wrapped in coats and hats, in addition to blankets provided by the men and women who had arrived to make sense of the chaos outside of the cabin.

He could still hear Sesi's frantic warnings and apologies from when she'd called. She hadn't been on duty and sleeping off a night shift when Marcus had posted bail. She had found out too late that Marcus was free, to warn Dixon before something could happen.

He'd told them about the knife, about what he'd seen happening through the window before hanging up on Sesi and going for his gun. He wondered if the window he'd crawled out of was still open, freezing their home, leaving them no warmth to retreat into.

He'd told them about coming up behind Marcus while he was

raping Jaye, that knife ready to cut Jaye's throat. He'd told them how he'd tried to talk Marcus down, and had shot only when he realized he had no choice if he wanted any chance of saving Jaye's life.

What he hadn't told them about was how he'd gotten Marcus to begin putting the knife away before pulling the trigger. All they knew was the shallow cut on Jaye's throat, his shell-shocked demeanor filling in the blanks nicely. But Dixon had known he wouldn't shoot until he was more certain Marcus wouldn't kill Jaye intentionally *or* accidentally.

"He wouldn't have stopped," Dixon heard himself saying. "He would have kept raping Jaye and he would have killed Jaye to spite me. He admitted he was going to take off and try to run instead of going to prison willingly. He would have done anything to get what he wanted. I had to. Jaye had no chance, and he was crying out in pain, like the knife was already cutting his throat, so I aimed dead center and fired. Is he dead? Did I kill him?"

Brekken pulled up then, with Grant in the passenger seat. They came running over, skirting around the crime scene and the gurney on which Marcus was loaded. Lights flashed in bright blues and reds. It was dark again, already, and it only amplified the glare, made it seem more garish, more real.

Dixon was hugging his sister, hearing her ask him questions he couldn't respond to. They didn't reach him through the shock. He'd done his part. He'd fired the gun and called it in. The rest felt like it was happening far away, through a film of numbing black. Then Grant was hugging him. Brekken was hugging Jaye, looking him over, and asking him his own questions.

Part of him still didn't believe Jaye was all right, that he'd acted in time. Part of him was still waiting for that knife to pull sideways, killing the man he loved. There had been no doubt in Dixon's mind that Jaye was going to be ripped out of his life forever in an awful echo of previous crimes. It was one of those rare moments too horrifying to be instantly believable. It was a mishmash of the hell Dixon had known on the side of that road and what Jaye had miraculously lived through already. Sex, violence, and helplessness. He wished he could convince himself it wasn't real, just a tangled bad dream he would wake from soon. But that bandage on Jaye's throat mocked him. He couldn't stop seeing the knife pressed there, ready to slice. It was real, and it was a parting gift from the determined sadist who could never let Dixon have something Marcus hadn't approved of personally.

Dixon understood, then, why Jaye liked to hold a weapon for comfort. Dixon wanted to hold his gun again, just in case Marcus sat up on the gurney and tried to come back at them to inflict more pain.

"I had a knife, in my pocket," Jaye was saying. "It was right there. But... I didn't go for it. Why didn't I go for it when he first came at me? It was like I forgot it was even there. Then it was too late and I knew if I moved, that'd be it. I'd be bleeding out with no way to hold it in this time. All I wanted was to do the right thing, to get him to stop."

"Come inside," Grant told them as Brekken began speaking to one of the troopers. "Get warm. You've been out here long enough."

"But—" Dixon wanted to argue, to keep waiting to see if Marcus would finally blink, to keep watching for that abrupt twitch of Marcus's arm holding the knife to Jaye's throat.

"Come on," Grant said, not taking no for an answer. With a hand hooked under Dixon's arm, he drew him up to his feet and ushered them both back into the cabin.

Hours passed in a blur. Sesi stopped by to apologize again and left to give Dixon space to recover. Grant and Brekken stayed, making some food, building a roaring fire, then kept it going and fielded phone calls. When Jaye said he wanted a shower, Dixon went with him, unwilling to let him out of his sight for as long as the shower would take.

They washed off, lingering in the spray, staring at one another. Jaye held Dixon's hand. He laid his forehead against Dixon's shoulder, saying, "I think it's over. Let it be over."

Dixon kept waiting for the knife, for Jaye's blood to gush. He couldn't stop shaking.

"Don't leave me. Please don't leave," he begged Jaye, deliriously. "Please don't go."

"I'm not going. I'm fine. Dix, look at me. I'm *fine*," Jaye assured him, or trying to at least. Touching, kissing, holding, hugging—it was all Dixon could do to convince himself that Jaye was there, was still whole and not covered in his own blood.

They got out of the shower, got dried off. Grant was waiting right outside the door when they emerged. Brekken was behind him; hand over her mouth, eyes wide.

"What?" Dixon asked, feeling dread enfold him, wrapping its arms around his ribcage and squeezing the air out. He pulled Jaye to him, heart in his throat.

"He's dead, Dix. Marcus is gone. We just got the call."

Dixon had never cried so hard in his life. They guided him to the couch. Jaye held him. Brekken held him. Grant stood watch, like he was still waiting for the knife, too, pacing, fetching glasses of water and boxes of tissues.

It all was wrung out of Dixon, from way down deep. He had cared for Marcus, once. And he was gone. He was gone because Dixon had killed him. He'd killed him like Jaye had killed the man in that alley. A person who had been so big, so much a part of Dixon's head and existence for years upon years, had been snuffed out like a candle flame just because of Dixon's fear of a knife. It seemed like such a stupid, small thing when the price paid was an entire life.

Marcus was *gone*.

Feeling broken into pieces, like he was drowning, he saw Jaye and Brekken hug, but Grant was there, crouched at Dixon's feet.

"You did good," Grant told him severely. "You stopped him from causing any more harm. You stood up for yourself and you protected Jaye. Let him go, Dix. I know it's a lot, but let him go."

No charges were pressed. There was just a hell of a lot of paperwork. Dixon took a leave of absence though he wanted to stay useful, stay busy so he could stop watching for that knife to open Jaye's throat for a little while. It seemed they could see it in his face, the strain, that waiting.

When it came right down to it, it was just too hard to leave Jaye's side. Jaye wasn't safe unless Dixon was there with him, and ready.

Jaye went back to work on a part-time basis. Whenever he was on shift, Dixon stayed at the truck stop, sipping coffee and acting as

Jaye's steadfast bodyguard against a threat that was no longer actually there.

Four days after Marcus died, Dixon and Jaye drove home in silence following Jaye's five-hour shift at the truck stop. It was mid-afternoon. Too much of the day was still left unused, waiting to be filled up with inescapable memories, the unthinkable what-ifs, and jarring wonder. The aftermath had caused them both to draw quietly inward as they tried to recover, somehow.

Dixon pulled up to the cabin, not wanting to look at it and see things that weren't there, but not wanting to be anywhere else, either. This was their place. Nothing would change that. But being there intensified the way the truth of things tumbled around and around in his head, ceaselessly, without sticking or sinking in. It made Dixon want to duck and cover.

He cut the engine, got out, and jogged around to the passenger side of the Expedition to walk beside Jaye from the vehicle up to the cabin's front door, just in case the shadows decided to lunge. When Dixon had first insisted on staying at the truck stop during Jaye's shifts, Jaye hadn't argued or joked about it, and he didn't then either, even about something as silly as being escorted up a walkway. Instead, he only reached up to gently touch Dixon's arm as he dug out his keys. There was no motive behind it. No message. He was simply letting Dixon feel him there, knowing how hard Dixon was fighting every second to believe Jaye really was alive and whole.

Dixon unlocked the door and let Jaye through, but took his hand to keep him near until the door was closed and locked. The cabin was dark, but the heat had been left on to welcome them back to a cozy space. Cozy was sometimes deceiving, though.

"Wait," Dixon said, before going to check the bathroom, the closet, and every other little place that could hide someone, perched and waiting. Jaye remained by the door, patiently, unzipping his coat.

It wasn't anything as clear as a voice, whispering in Dixon's ear of the dangers in ordinary situations, but merely instinct. Chopping firewood had once seemed a fairly harmless chore, especially for someone used to doing it. Dixon didn't plan on making that sort of mistake again, or taking chances with someone who meant so very much. Maybe it was paranoia, and maybe it would fade after a little more time, but for now, it's what allowed Dixon to keep it together.

When he was satisfied they were, indeed, alone, Dixon returned to Jaye. He intended to take off his coat, set down his keys, and remove the gun holster he wished he was comfortable leaving at home, but wasn't. But, when he reached Jaye, and was standing toe to toe with him, all Dixon could do was wrap his hand around the side of Jaye's sweet face. Jaye's expression could only be called trustful as he leaned slightly into the touch. Leaning down slightly, Dixon inhaled the scent of Jaye's dark hair and closed his eyes. Jaye slowly took the keys out of Dixon's hand. He hung them on the hook by the door and unzipped Dixon's coat for him before pulling him into a hug.

Letting out a heavy exhale, Dixon felt the tense, lingering fear finally loosen its grip on his chest. To have Jaye held so completely in his arms after hours without that luxury was exactly what Dixon needed.

The urge to voice apologies, promises, and everything else he wanted Jaye to know, just in case, was strong, but too tangled up to make any sense. It all lodged in Dixon's throat. But Jaye's smaller body was pressed against Dixon, allowing him to feel the faint beating of Jaye's heart and the swell of each breath, and that was enough. Almost.

Jaye tugged at Dixon's coat. "Take this off. It's in the way."

Dixon let go long enough to do what he'd meant to before, and removed the coat, then his holster.

Pressing a hand to the center of Dixon's chest, Jaye guided him backward, step by step, until they were nearer to the bed.

Tugging next on Dixon's shirt, Jaye said, "Still in the way."

It would have—should have—made Dixon smile, but on that day, it just made him feel like he was falling apart. These were the small moments he almost never had. He needed to get rid of the fear. He knew it. It was eating him up inside. He just didn't know how, other than with time and effort to just keep going on.

Jaye looked up at Dixon, and his eyes were so beautiful. They were light, strong, steady, and full of that vibrant spirit which had kept him going against all odds and circumstances. They held everything that mattered.

Jaye was shaken, too. Dixon could see it and feel it. It wasn't just

Dixon who hurt, but Jaye carried it more easily. One corner of his mouth rose in a faint hint of a grin, saying we'll be okay.

He set to work on unbuttoning Dixon's shirt. Numb and oversensitive at the same time, in equal measure, Dixon could barely react other than to steal kisses now and then, lightly dragging the back of his bent finger over Jaye's cheek, covered in dark, rough stubble. It didn't take Jaye long at all to completely undress Dixon before quickly shedding his own clothes.

Pushing through the fog, Dixon guided Jaye down to the bed and pulled the covers over them. Dixon climbed on top. He liked being the barrier between Jaye and anything out there that could harm him.

First, Dixon kissed the healing knick on Jaye's throat. That small spot was the center of everything. It deserved all of the care Dixon could give. After his lips brushed the wound, an aching moan of horror shook him, taking him by surprise before he could bite it back.

"I've got you," Jaye said softly in his low rasp of a voice. "Just hold me." He wound his arms around Dixon's neck, spread his legs and hooked them behind Dixon's back, using them to draw Dixon in and bring their bodies flush together. The contact felt so good, Dixon tightened his grip, pulling Jaye against him even more, needing to feel all of him at once—head to toe.

Jaye shivered and Dixon sighed, breathing across the thin scab that was almost the end of everything.

He reached out with his right hand toward the nightstand, but paused to rest it on the bed, hesitating and second-guessing. His left hand cupped the side of Jaye's ass and his dick was getting hard, riding Jaye's crease. There was no hiding the battle between his desire and all of the conflicting noise of guilt raging in his head.

Understanding, Jaye told him, "Go on."

Still fighting it, not wanting to push for intimacy if there was any part of Jaye that wasn't ready, Dixon kissed Jaye's neck again. When he felt Jaye undulate a little, thrusting against Dixon's abdomen, it freed him, having proof that Jaye did want the same thing. It was okay.

Dixon finished reaching for the lube. Jaye started breathing harder as soon as Dixon had it in his hand, before he'd even gotten his fingers wet. Giving Dixon those little pushes, rubbing off on him, Jaye let

Dixon feel how hard he was. He vibrated with impatience until Dixon reached down and fed Jaye's ass two fingers on a slow push. Groaning long and low, Jaye gripped Dixon's back and added an extra little roll to his rocking movements, pushing down on the fingers before thrusting forward again.

There was nothing between them other than heat, breath, and everything they had no words to say. Jaye pulled Dixon in for a kiss and licked into his mouth. Jaye was frowning heavily, finally letting Dixon see all of his ache. A few moments later, when Dixon freed his hand and lined up to enter Jaye, only then did the frown ease. Dixon barely saw it happen, though. He was too busy kissing Jaye, gasping at the hot grip of him, enfolding and claiming.

Jaye pushed down to take and Dixon pushed upward to give until they were as close as they could get. Then they paused, and just held each other. More tension was blessedly released. Dixon caressed up and down Jaye's side while Jaye stayed wound tightly around him, refusing to ease his grip.

Neither of them moved to do more for a while. Sex wasn't the point, anyway.

Jaye's lips tenderly brushed Dixon's forehead on a slow sigh. Dixon's caress kept moving, wanting everything, all of him.

Then, with a soft whimper, like he'd edged past a point of tolerance, Jaye nudged Dixon into motion. Chasing that sound, drinking it in to make it his, too, Dixon kissed Jaye and took him with slow, complete thrusts that soon made Jaye restless and greedy. He countered every kiss and thrust with soft, wordless pleas for more.

The rest fell away. The inner storm eased.

Dixon climaxed before he wanted to, and came down slowly, shivering.

Jaye waited and picked up the discarded bottle of lube. When he was steadier, Dixon rolled them. Jaye's wet palm twisted up his shaft as Dixon pulled out and drew up his legs, letting Jaye settle between them. Cock in hand, Jaye pushed, parting the muscle to breach Dixon. His parted lips hovered over Dixon's mouth, catching each gasp, and Jaye smiled as he sank in deeply.

There was so much peace there, in that smile, it made Dixon tear up, his exhale catching on a sob Jaye quickly kissed away.

"Look at me," Jaye urged in a whisper, catching Dixon's gaze. *I'm here*, it said. *You're here.* The worry eased, then lifted entirely, temporarily. Dixon had him. Jaye was all right.

Jaye kept moving, building to a steady, rhythmic push and pull while Dixon kissed both of Jaye's closed eyelids, then the tip of his nose, his lips, and his chin. It was dark enough that Dixon couldn't see the tattoos, or any specifics other than the perfect shape of the one he loved so fiercely and who'd so nearly been stolen from him.

Every touch was a thank you, full of gratitude and promises to do better, to never take for granted and to never forget how lucky he was.

After Jaye was spent, Dixon left the bed just long enough to build a fire to warm them up even more. Then, he climbed under the covers to cuddle close. Jaye opened his arms, pulled him in, and there they stayed for a long time.

Dixon's father, Walter Rowe, appeared at the funeral. Dixon's mother couldn't attend for health reasons, but it was a great enough shock to have one of them there, in person, after so long. There were only a handful of people in attendance. Dixon and Jaye hung back, determined to see it through but unable to fully engage with what was happening.

His father looked at Dixon's hand, clasped in Jaye's. He didn't look at the tattoos or seem to scrutinize Jaye's features. It was that link between them that fascinated him most.

"This must be Jaye," he said with a small smile. "Nice to meet you."

"You too, sir. I'm glad you could be here," Jaye replied.

"You okay, son?" Walter Rowe asked his boy quietly. It was an indoor service, due to the weather, which wailed and blew fiercely beyond the walls.

"Getting there," Dixon answered.

"You should come visit your mother sometime, enjoy the warmer weather and get away from all of this for a bit."

Thinking of Jaye's parole, which forbade him from leaving the state, Dixon nodded, promising, "Someday soon. We will."

Of Jaye, Walter asked, "You're taking good care of him, right? Seems like he needs it."

"Yes, sir," Jaye answered, gazing up at Dixon. "I love him more than I've ever loved anyone. I'll keep him safe."

"Good," Walter smiled. "I'm glad to hear it."

Tearing up, Dixon drew Jaye into a quick kiss, bowing his head until he wiped his eyes dry.

Once it was over and they were outside, in a car driven by Brekken, with Grant riding in a rental car with Walter, Jaye said, "I should have used my knife. It would have spared you this burden, of having to carry this. You were with him for so long—"

"No," Dixon disagreed. "It had to be this way. We can't always protect ourselves like we need to, no matter how strong we think we are. Sometimes we need to let fate and instinct take over. Marcus was always my problem. I got myself into it with him, and I always knew I'd be the one to have to get myself out."

Brekken caught Dixon's eye in the rearview mirror.

"I wish it would have gone differently," Dixon said more quietly, gazing out through the windows. "I wish it had ended with him living by the sea, happy. I would have really liked that."

The tears surprised him, but grief was grief. The only way forward was to go through it; there was no getting around it.

"I refuse to believe he came to the cabin with the intention of hurting us," he said. "I want to believe he was just scared, lonely, and frustrated, and the moment got away from him. He just made a bad choice."

"He had the knife, Dix," Brekken countered. "He went after Jaye first."

"He wasn't a murderer," Dixon argued.

"We've each killed someone, and neither of us has the cruel streak Marcus had," Jaye told him. "I know how the guilt feels. Marcus wasn't like the guy that went after me. It was personal with Marcus. Everyone is capable of taking drastic measures if pushed enough when it comes to someone they care about. You were his obsession. I think he would have done anything to get you back."

Back at the cabin, alone again, Dixon felt Jaye studying him like he was working on a drawing. There was no paper in his hands, though.

They sat on their bed, side by side.

"When you said you were going to the truck," Jaye confessed. "I believed you for a second. That was the panic, I think. But when you waited until he pulled the knife away from me, and shot... I didn't see it coming and I'm sorry about that. For doubting you."

"There was nothing more important than getting that knife away from you," Dixon replied. "I would have told him anything to make him stop. I'm just sorry you had to wait so long before I could take him down. I was so afraid I'd fire and he'd kill you anyway."

"You didn't want to shoot him."

It wasn't a question, but it wasn't quite a statement either.

"No, I really didn't. He didn't give me a choice. He never did. It was my fault for not seeing there were other choices even if Marcus wasn't giving them to me himself."

Jaye reached out and folded his hand into Dixon's.

"You came through for me, Dix," Jaye murmured. "You stood up to him, and you protected me from him. Now there's nothing you can't do."

Dixon made the effort to bury his conflicted feelings along with Marcus. He reminded himself moment to moment what he was lucky to have in his life—the support of family and friends, a new home, and the love of someone who had risked his life for Dixon's sake.

Some days, Dixon liked to visit the burnt, snow-covered ground where his old life had been lived. It was so quiet there. He would leave flowers when he went, not for Marcus, really, but for missed chances and the ghosts of what could have been. After the first couple of trips, Jaye began going with him, leaving his own flowers for the dreams unfulfilled and the restless spirits of the past, hoping to put them to rest at last. From the way he carried himself when they left, Dixon felt maybe it was working, and saying goodbye was helping form the ending.

Spring crept up on them, a slow change felt most in the increasing spans of daylight more than any physical change. The snow remained, but the air grew less cold. Hope blossomed with the longer appearances of the sun, banishing shadows. Jaye started taking an art class. Dixon was back at work and feeding Jaye leads on new jobs with better pay and more opportunity.

Remembering back to the day when Jaye bolted into Dixon's life, his pockets stuffed with canned peas and potato chips, Dixon could only laugh at the change time had wrought as he picked Jaye up from work on one especially warm, sunny day.

Smiling hugely, chuckling with delight, Jaye sprinted across the empty parking lot to Dixon's awaiting Expedition.

"Whoa," Dixon said, holding his hands out, "Whoa..."

But, still laughing, glowing from within with joy, Jaye only sped up, charging at him.

"Mr. Larson," Dixon warned. "I'm going to have to ask you — *Oof!*"

Jaye jumped on him, wrapping his legs around Dixon's waist; arms slung around his neck, and kissed the words away.

"To love you for the rest of my life? Deal," Jaye grinned, chuckling again and brushing his parted lips over Dixon's mouth as Dixon groaned softly. "And I *thought* I told you to call me Jaye. Unless this is *Trooper* Rowe talking. Have I been bad, sir? Please don't handcuff and spank me. That would be *awful*, given how pure and innocent I am."

Snorting with laughter, Dixon tried to form a less amused expression, because it was difficult to be stern with a writhing, devious, gorgeous, horny Jaye wrapped around him. "Yes, that's exactly what I've heard about you — how you're the picture of innocence. Makes me want to *defile* it."

"Mmm, that sounds *horrible*," Jaye moaned as Dixon scraped his teeth over his throat. "Please don't defile me, Trooper Rowe. I'm quivering with fear of your huge cock."

"Yeah, I'm sure you are," Dixon snickered.

"Tell me more about how you're going to defile me."

"How about we move this back home, huh?" Dixon asked, giving Jaye's ass a little slap. "Rather than humping in full view of your customers. There are some peeking through the windows, you know."

"Ooh, cuff me and make me ride in the back!" Jaye said eagerly, his eyes lighting up. "And take my pants off! You can watch my cock get hard while we head home. You could even play with it at red lights."

"You are *unbelievable*," Dixon said, shaking his head.

Jaye grinned, "Yeah, I love you too, old man."

If you enjoyed this story, you can sign up for a free membership at ForbiddenFiction and discuss it with other readers and the author at the *Arctic Absolution* story page at http://forbiddenfiction.com/library/story/LK1-1.000188.

We do our best to proof all our work, but if you spot a text error we missed, please let us know via our website Contact Form at http://forbiddenfiction.com/contact.

Author's Notes

This novel was born because of a short, unpublished story I wrote few years back, titled Encounters at the End of the World, about two research scientists living and working in remote Antarctica, at an outpost a short distance from McMurdo. It was presented in the form of a diary kept by the main character and explored the effects of intense isolation in one of the most inhospitable environments on the planet. Everything you encountered or thought about either helped you survive or worked to break you down. A fairly rational man slowly lost his mind, listening to the creaking, cracking of the steadily shifting iceberg beneath him as he tried to sleep.

They were themes I knew I had to revisit. Instead of scientists, I chose a cop and an ex-con—men more used to physically grueling lives where other people present the real danger, rather than their wild surroundings. The isolation of Zus, Alaska (a fictional town created for the purposes of this story) I knew would play a more subtle role in undermining every choice or challenge these two faced. It can be freeing to be left alone to live in peace, until demons either imaginary or actual come knocking. If the possibility of calling for a bystander's help is stripped away, there is no choice but to fight or die.

It's been a fantasy of mine for years to leave it all behind, and go live out in the middle of nowhere. The idea of walking out the front door and being able to turn in a complete circle, seeing no other sign of humanity, seems peaceful... until you factor in things like bears, storms, earthquakes, or injury. There's a big price to be paid for sacrificing the convenience and comfort of society.

Dixon and Jaye are my wilderness warriors, who come from opposite ends of the social spectrum. They tackle the practical concerns of survival in different ways. They're both armed with various mental and physical weapons, but they each have their own weaknesses, and enemies. These guys have been living simultaneously in heaven and hell for years. The world around them is pretty enough for a postcard. They both know how lucky they are to have their desperately craved, long-sought freedom, escaping an abusive partner and imprisonment, respectively. But, daily life tortures them because of choices they can't unmake and the consequences they can't escape, no matter how far they run. So, they fight. They survive. They grab a gun, or a knife, knowing they'll use it if they have to. Because of this, they're two of the most capable and brave characters I've gotten to explore, and I love them for it. I wrote that initial short story because the setting seduced me, but this book was written because of the ferocious, flawed beauty of Dixon and Jaye. Like those scientists listening to the ice groaning beneath them, Dixon and Jaye lay alone, in the dark, waiting to see if their worlds will split open and eat them alive. But, Dixon's gun is raised. Jaye's knife is held in hand. Whatever comes, they're ready.

Many thanks to everyone who assisted me with research for this story. There was a lot to do, and every little bit helped. My heartfelt gratitude must be expressed, as well, to my invaluable editor, Rylan, and my fearless publisher, Dany, for convincing me not to be afraid of going dark and showing the beautiful brutality of a dire situation.

—Lynn Kelling

About the Author

Website: www.lynnkelling.com

Lynn Kelling began writing in order to tell stories that weren't afraid of the dark, didn't hold anything back and always strived to be memorable, forging lasting attachments between character and reader. Her inspiration comes from taking a closer look at behaviors and ideas lurking at the fringes of life—basically anything that people may hesitate to speak of in mixed company, but everyone wonders about anyway. Her work is driven by the taboo in order to expose the humanity within it. Lynn is an artist, designer and lover of any form of creative self-expression that comes from a place of honesty and emotion, whether it's body art or opera. She has had multiple novels published, has written over fifty works of erotic fiction of varying lengths, and always has several novels in progress.

Works by Lynn Kelling:

Deliver Us Series:
Deliver Us
From Temptation
Forgive Us

Twin Ties Series:
My Brother's Lover
Dual Affairs
Double Heat

Manse Series:
Loving the Master
Learning from the Master
Bound by Lies

Arctic Absolution Series:
Caged Jaye
Arctic Absolution

Other Works:
Whatever the Cost
Song of the Lonesome Cowboy
Threshold (Anthology)
Cursed Blessings (short story)

ARCTIC ABSOLUTION

Jaye Larson is an ex-con with a troubled, terrifying past. Dixon Rowe is a good man in a hard world, a cop with a soft spot for saving bad boys. Things change for both of them the night Dixon nearly arrests Jaye for petty theft and decides to help him go... Well, not straight, exactly. As it turns out Jaye is just Dixon's type, and Dixon's interest quickly rises beyond the professional.

As if their growing romance wasn't complicated enough, Jaye's history won't stay behind him, and it turns out that Dixon has a skeleton or two in his own closet. In order to build a future together, the two men have to put the past to rest.

Lynn Kelling draws intense emotion and raw, kinky sex from these characters and their lives, creating a multi-layered romance with deep history and real warmth. She makes Jay and Dixon work hard to earn their happy ending.

Works in this series:

1. Caged Jaye
2. Arctic Absolution

About the Publisher

ForbiddenFiction.com is a publisher devoted to writing that breaks the boundaries of original erotic fiction. Our stories combine intense sexuality with quality writing. Stories at ForbiddenFiction.com not only arouse readers through sensations, but also engage them emotionally and mentally through storytelling as well-crafted as the sex is hot.

ForbiddenFiction.com is also designed to be a social reading environment. You'll have fun even if just reading the latest post each day, yet you will have the chance for so much more. Readers and authors can be part of ongoing discussions of specific works and individual authors as well as more general topics.

Sign up for a FREE Membership today at ForbiddenFiction.com.